BEST OF DRAGONS

MAGGIE HOOPIS

ISBN 979-8-9923469-3-0 (hardback)

ISBN 979-8-9923469-4-7 (paperback)

ISBN 979-8-9923469-5-4 (e-book)

Library of Congress Cataloging-in-Publication data is available upon request

Book Cover and Map by Anastasia Campo

Chapter Header Art by @foxlore_art

Edited by Jessica Flannery, Allyson Wilkins, and Laura Ernst

Proofread by Laura Ernst

First edition: 2025

Content Warnings

Every woman has many stories. And every story sits in her heart in a different way. While I believe that good triumphs over evil, sometimes that win can be prolonged and scarring.

Please take care of yourself when reading and don't break your heart unintentionally. Note the following appear in this novel:

Abandonment/neglect

Abuse - physical (off page) and emotional by parent

Abortion – implied

Alcohol

Death

Divorce

Grief

Guns & shooting - it's the Wild West

Infertility

Masturbation

Misogyny & chauvinism

Pandemic - Covid was hard, I get it.

Post-Traumatic Stress Disorder

Prostitution

Sex

Suicidal thoughts

Swearing

Toxic masculinity

For the strong thunder of women that raised me, the thunder I currently fly with, and the thunder that my daughter will one day call her own.

Playlist

"Best of Dragons" playlist available on Spotify

Prologue: *The Weight* by Aretha Franklin

Ch. 1: *Know Your Enemy* by Burn the Breeze

Ch. 2: *Fix You* by Kelly Clarkson

Ch. 3: *Don't It Make My Brown Eyes Blue* by Crystal Gale

Ch. 4: *Send My Love (To Your New Lover)* by Adele

Ch. 5: *Gypsies, Tramps & Thieves* by Cher

Ch. 6: *Mr. Big Stuff* by Jean Knight

Ch. 7: *I Am Woman* by Helen Reddy

Ch. 8: *Me and Bobby McGee* by Janis Joplin

Ch. 9: *Wide Open Spaces* by The Chicks

Ch. 10: *Talking in Your Sleep* by Crystal Gale

Ch. 11: *Angeleyes* by ABBA

Ch. 12: *Cactus Tree* by Joni Mitchell

Ch. 13: *Blue Bayou* by Linda Ronstadt

Ch. 14: *these fruits* by Paris Paloma

Ch. 15: *These Boots are Made for Walkin'* by Nancy Sinatra

Ch. 16: *Time in a Bottle* by Lykke Li

Ch. 17: *abcdefu (angrier)* by Gayle

Ch. 18: *Gunpowder and Lead* by Miranda Lambert

Ch. 19: *Love Grows (Where My Rosemary Goes)* by Edison Lighthouse

Ch. 20: *Lady Marmalade* by Christina Aguilera, Lil' Kim, Mya, Pink

Ch. 21: *Wildflowers* by Miley Cyrus

Ch. 22: *House Tour* by Sabrina Carpenter

Contents

Part One

Prologue

*T*HUD. THUD. THUD.

Tara had no way of knowing what was behind the resolute knocking on the door. Jarred from her peaceful sleep, she flung her eyelids apart, adrenaline surging through her veins. Early morning sunlight kissed the floor through the window, greeting Tara's feet with warmth. Throwing a dressing gown from the base of her bed over her nightgown, she looped the ties around each other, securing them tightly to keep the cozy, dozing warmth wrapped around her. Bounding down the steps, she prayed that she would be able to go back to sleep after dealing with the echoing raps.

Poundings on the front door never preceded the entry of friends. One always knew to expect house guests from the arrival of letters the day before. Found family burst through the entrance like water through a crack in a dam. Even acquaintances were met on the porch before they reached the door to knock. But hammerings on the door needed to be let in.

Were the dragons alright? Was anyone hurt? She noted her healing bag hanging on the hook next to where her family's belongings were typically stored when they were not away from the dragon ranch. The running of Titan's Creek Manor fell to her with everyone away. Worry etched deep into her forehead, giving her a headache. She hoped she would be able to deal with the early morning disturbance. Footsteps behind Tara alerted her to the presence of the housekeeper behind her.

"Do you want me to answer it?" the housekeeper asked.

"No." Tara heaved a steadying breath, wiggling her fingers to use some of the adrenaline and calm herself. "I have a feeling that if you answered, you would need to call me to deal with the situation anyway."

THUD. THUD. THUD.

She silently prayed for the safety of her family, who currently traipsed around the continent. Whatever stood behind that door would change not only her plans for the day but the trajectory of her life.

THUD. THUD. THUD.

The knocking sped up her heart rate.

"Healer Fuentes!" The heavy door muffled the raspy, tenor voice on the other side. No more surmising about what it could be; she would need to answer it.

Her hand did not shake as it reached out for the doorknob. Not surprising, given her medgical ("magical-medical") training. She knew how to deal in emergencies, had been trained to. She much preferred to deal in the mundane, though. Well, not the mundane—the magic of everyday life. But most people would prefer to work with dragons every day rather than deal in life-and-death scenarios.

As she opened the door, the fiery colors from the sunrise poured in. She could barely make out the man's face with the light streaming behind him. No matter. She knew by the Association's seal, glinting in the light on the folded paper, that he bore an unwanted summons.

The Association of Healers had not called upon her since the cholera outbreak last June. She was able to push that off, citing that she could not afford to contract the disease or carry it upon her return to the dragons. As the largest dragon ranch on Cosimo, a disease in the Fuentes herd would have had major economic repercussions for their family and the continent that relied on dragons. She hoped this had nothing to do with the disappearing cities that she had been reading about in the newspapers, though she was not feeling lucky this morning.

The messenger turned and walked away silently as soon as the letter was in her hands. Tara stood motionless, eyes flipping between the mail and the person's departing body, wondering if she could possibly hit him in the back with the paper if she were to throw it hard enough.

Her toes tingled in the crisp morning air, a physical reminder of her Oath. She was required to open the seal and accept whatever the Association of Healers had in store for her.

Healer Fuentes,

As you may have heard, an unknown cold plague has befallen the land of Cosimo. Our brethren are in crisis. Your medgical skills are required in Grogtown. We are unaware as to the disease's effects on dragons, but this excuse will not be accepted at this time. It is a dire situation for our human race, and every healer is required to fulfill their Oath. You will be expected to report via message upon the state of the town in one month's time.

She did not want to venture out into Granny's Great Travesty, as her pa would call the land. She had no desire to see evil or the effects of man's lunatic power.

She was perfectly content to continue day to day as she completed the chores, like washing and healing common dragon ailments, such as Flaky Scales.

Tara tilted her head to the sky and closed her amber eyes. The dust from the dirt path that led up to the house swirled around her as she slammed the door shut.

"Fffffffuck."

One

Tara

The world was icy. Not that it had ever been less so toward a woman. But physically it had turned its back upon her. As she flew on the back of the gentle beast into the desolate space, her lungs filled with despair. A voice inside her beckoned her to turn around. Leave. Go back to her lap of luxury.

If only it were that easy.

But she was called upon to do better than her interior voice whined. She had made a promise to those who could not call out with their own voices across the chasm. And so, the healer and dragon traversed the dusty rocks and gritty soil east from their lush home to this deserted place, where Tara's map pointed they should be; this nondescript, barren region, full of dead dreams and the commands of foolish men. The dusty frontier town stood in snowy silence; only vestiges of the magical thrum that must have choked the life out of it remained.

The snow clung to the divots made by the claw marks from a dragon that would sit on the rooftops and wait for his friend, not so long ago. The divots remained, though the beings had moved on.

When the wind had stopped howling, a silence hung between the edges of catastrophe and salvation. That moment when the anticipation of what comes next and the realization of what just happened coexisted in perfect dissonance.

Her dragon's claws clutched at the frozen earth as she bounded into the drab clearing. A bigger dragon would have had trouble landing there in that narrow street. Luckily, her icy-blue dragon, Camelia, was a petite thing, though her will was huge.

Tara looked around at the surroundings. Not much to offer in the bare desert. A dilapidated ghost town. Well, not so much dilapidated as just unused. She breathed in the energy of the earth. Frost covered the wildflowers in the clearing that was generally set aside for the dragons, but currently abandoned. Her hands brushed over her long cotton skirt. Grimacing at the sweat that wet the fabric, she hoped that it would dry soon. She had seriously underestimated the condition of the town when she had packed and lamented not bringing wool clothing.

The flight out had occupied her headspace with different ways of approaching whatever she may find. She had studied plague mentality in medgical school. "Ghost town" had not been in the required research. She mentally noted that she would be submitting a paper to the Association detailing her experiences. She would start it with a joke. "So a healer walks into a ghost town ..."

Her leather boots, embroidered with tiny flowers and the mark of Mother Maker, clunked to the ground as her hands grasped Camelia's reins. The proud female dragon also laid claim to healing powers and did not shirk in the face of the danger of helping others.

Hopelessly lost wherever she traveled, Tara was not sure if she had landed in Grogtown at first. She had not done her best at guiding the dragon on a clear flying route. Plus, her map had flown away somewhere over a burned-down town just west of the river that led south to Lackluster Lake. Her niece, with the magical wayfinding skills, would have had a better chance of helping her find this less-than-monumental town. The only way she could describe its position was halfway between the mountains and a lake, between the high point of the Four Staircases and the deepest point of Below.

A small wooden sign in black paint announced "Grogtown, Population 238." The slight breeze echoed as it wound through the barren town, bouncing between the two rows of storefronts and homes. Where were the 238 people, then? Did all of them live in houses further from this main area?

The dust that should have whiplashed her eyes painted her boots a mucky reddish brown as the wet snow mixed with the clay. Using the toe of her right boot, she attempted to scrape the mixture off her left heel, then front foot, then vice versa. Consumed by the current task, she released the reins of the dragon. The animal took two steps away before halting to watch. Tara brushed the debris off her green and white leaf-patterned cotton skirt. Flying would never be a clean form of transportation.

Looking around her, the whole scene was held in some sort of not-quite-solid-ice-not-quite-melting stasis. Like a snow globe waiting to be shaken. Now, finally at this spot where bits of green peeked out from below death, Tara pulled her bandana off her face and breathed in the air, feeling as the energy that emanated from the soil traversed her spine to her heart and throughout her body in one quick movement. The lack of oxygen smothered her. Faint traces remained in the air of a more active energy that had gone stagnant.

Evil had been here.

In front of her, lines of wooden structures rose on the right and left, stretching into a deep fog and daring arrivals to its exploration. The buildings looked not much older than her own thirty-four years, yet they had collected enough dust to warrant a solid spring cleaning. The cobwebs, decorated with tiny droplets of ice, painted a few doorways with pretty impressions of a time gone by.

As Camelia's tongue approached the frozen grass, Tara cried out, "No, Camelia! I'll need to sanitize the water. We don't know what sort of evil or disease lurks within it. For now, we can use the water bag that I packed. We'll just have to ration it for a bit." Water droplets appeared on the frozen ground where it had been kissed by Camelia's warm breath

"Well, at least we know that your heat will melt some of the water, and it has typical physical properties." She pulled a small metal bowl off the side of the saddle. After filling it with an inch of water, she held it out to Camelia. The dragon sat back on her haunches, taking the bowl in her claws and dumping it into her mouth. Tara's growing up with the dragons told her that the dragon would have preferred to lap it lazily with its tongue.

"Beggars can't be choosers, pretty one," she told Camelia in a sing-song voice. "And while we have never been beggars, we are at the mercy of this environment.

Her uncertain steps crunched along the ground. First, though, she and Camelia would need water. She had packed enough preserved food for a month. But some would need to be warmed. And her water was due to give out in a week.

She looked around for a source of water. Though really, all the town residents would need water if they came out of this sickness. She had no idea how long they had been out. No concept of what to do to save them. The task was a mystery.

She knew nothing of this particular disease. She had experience with many major medgical problems. The most she could deduce from cookie crumbs that Grace, one of her closest friends, had supplied in her own firsthand experiences with Dimin and the cold sickness, were the basic effects and where it came from, and that this magic required magic to heal it. And Fuentes magic, which derived from the dragons, was the most powerful of them all.

"Camelia, you stay here and work on thawing a spot for us with that breath of yours. We'll reconvene and find out if this place can even support our presence here to help." Tara had always learned to put her own bandana on her face first when helping others in a dust storm. So, she pulled a blanket off her packs and wrapped it around her shoulders, needing to get the two of them situated first. She fixed her hat on her head and set off walking down the middle of what must have been the main street of the town in search of a water supply.

A small stone well that reached her hip stood at the end of the row of houses on her left. (She was sure her niece would know if it was north or south.) Pulling her blanket around her shoulders, she steeled herself against the chatty breeze and focused her attention on examining the well. At first sight, it looked maintained. The hand crank had not rusted, and a bucket was cleanly stored under the pointed roof that housed the crank's axle. A lid, constructed of wooden boards and branded with a worn "NC," fit perfectly over the large hole protected by the stones."

Tucking the blanket under her armpits, Tara rolled up her sleeves, baring skin of a less-tan shade than her hands. She hoisted the lid off the well and looked inside, sniffing. Nothing seemed out of the ordinary smell-wise. Turning the crank, Tara lowered the bucket deep into the dark abyss of the well. Would the bucket hit ice? A faint splashing sound confirmed that the precious commodity had not frozen solid. So the town did not die from the lack of water.

She let the bucket sit there for a moment, feeling the weight of the water filling it, before drawing it back up, full to the brim. Upon inspection of the water, she found no abnormalities. Breaking the surface tension with her pinky finger, she let her magic rush through her, detecting any metals or minerals that may have been out of place.

Typical water. She hypothesized that the disease did not seem to have originated or spread through the water source. Could she chance it?

"It's good water," a male voice spoke up. She looked left and right but saw no one.

"It's been a while since we've seen anyone new through these parts." A male spoke clearly through the fog. Tara turned her head toward the voice coming from behind her.

The mists swirled the snow from the ground upward, mingling with the white clouds. A faint sunset refracted through the haze. Through the mists, she could make out a healthy stature clad in a tailored suit with well-polished boots leaning his back against the posts of the house that stood about ten feet from the well.

The voice bore breeding, or at least some sort of education. Evidently from out east, not from this town originally, the precise, almost bored droning voice belonged in banks and courtrooms, not dusty trails and half-constructed towns.

"From my understanding, you all need a healer." Tara, fearing neither death nor man, spoke clearly. Even if he were both, she would not fear him either. A man, not much older than she, appeared in front of her. His hands found the pockets of his pin-striped pants, damp at the hem.

From five feet away, his eyes inspected her before using his fingernail to pick at his teeth. "I don't know where you came from or where you got an idea like that, but we're all good here."

Crossing her arms, Tara scanned the area. "Then why is this town not bustling at noon? And where are all the dragons?" Had he caused this mess? She had so many more questions with which to pepper this slick-haired blond, but she bit her tongue. Best not to make an enemy off the bat. She had no idea how many other people were around still, or if they would walk up behind him like the zombies in the penny dreadfuls that her niece would beg her to read.

He ignored the first question and responded to her second. "People decided that we didn't need them much. We're set up to take care of ourselves, don't want any outsiders coming in and changing our ways." The term outsiders struck her as amiss, as he seemed out of place in his fancy clothes, ill-suited to the climate.

Something was off, majorly off, about this situation. She had been led to believe from stories she had heard from the papers that entire towns this way were basically frozen over, with little to no survivors. Dragon riders did not dare stop, lest they never leave. According to her few sources, for which she had had to scour Titan's Creek in order to find, the scouts with the Association of Healers had had to beg dragons to fly them nearby to gauge if the towns were safe enough to send healers to.

How was this rosy countenanced person alive and walking around?

"What happened here?" Tara asked a question that she already knew the answer to in order to test his reliability. She was suspicious of this singular person living in a ghost town.

"They're all sick. Started getting sick and everyone gradually gave it to each other," he said matter-of-factly.

"So then you need a healer." Tara narrowed her eyes. Given how easily he provided her with the dictionary's summary of a pandemic, it was almost as if he had practiced the line or recited it multiple times.

The gears in her head turned like a water mill.

He interrupted the cascade of thoughts in her mind.

"Where are you from, Miss?"

"Healer," she corrected him. "I'm from out west of here. A small area known as Titan's Creek."

A sharp intake of breath from him discomforted her.

"So then you've seen dragons?" His spouted words relayed his excited interest.

"Once or twice," Tara waved her hand. "Nothing out of the ordinary. I was able to hire one to ride out here." His tone left many things to be discovered about him before she told him her background. She had had too many experiences with interactions gone sour once they heard that she was a Fuentes. People saw her differently—with money signs in their eyes and greed dripping drool from their chins.

"On second thought, please allow me to invite you to my home for a nice meal. You must be famished after such a journey." His sudden change alerted her that she may have something he wanted. She knew from her work with animals that one was best off following its lead to learn more of its den. Best to play her cards close to her well-endowed chest. But she had a funny feeling that it had to do with dragons.

The man led her up the stairs of the porch of a two-story wooden building with a flat front and sparse windows. Far too many boots greeted them on the porch, where everyone who wore them knew they should never be stored. She took the large-brimmed hat off her head as she entered the house, pushing back wisps of dark hair that stuck to her forehead.

Such an ample-sized home advertised that a large family dwelled within it. If he were a family man, he would have some investment in reviving these people. He could help her; maybe he had a child that she would heal first so she could appeal to his protective side. Or, perhaps he would have a plan of attack for how to best heal the town, as he had been there for what looked like some time before her.

Family knick-knacks lined the walls in the entry hallway. Photographs of a happy family. She stopped to inspect them further, hoping to find a way to connect with this person. They were, after all, the only two people walking around for at least twenty miles.

As she examined the sepia photos, she could not find one instance of this man in any of them. Maybe, she reasoned, he had been the photographer. But his blond hair was not traceable in any of the traits of the family members. The end of the hallway led into a small kitchen, where the man stood pouring a glass of wine.

"So, Mr. —"

He recorked the bottle and lifted the glass to her health. "Egoman. Dennis Brandon Egoman, but everyone calls me 'DB'. Do you often enter men's homes that you don't know?"

"I'm a healer. I have trained to expect to find myself in weird positions for the rest of my life."

"What's the weirdest one you've ever been in?"

"Missionary."

He choked on the wine that he had poured into his mouth, his face reddening with each cough.

"I should go wash up." She prided herself on having just rocked him outside of his comfort zone, taking note of his embarrassment. Nothing like acknowledging a woman's sexuality to test the waters of a man's mind.

A stained handkerchief collected the spew from his face. "Absolutely, you know where the well is."

Nodding her head, she walked through the family tree to the outdoors, placing the hat back on her head as a holder while she cleaned up.

The frigid water that she had recently drawn from the well sent goosebumps down her spine as she splashed it on her face and rubbed it on her hands. Though it was fairly clean, she noted that she would need to boil it before it could be of any use to her for drinking or healing. She wiped her hands and face off on the insides of her skirt and set off to find out more answers.

"So, DB ..." She walked through the hallway of pictures to the modest kitchen.

"Yes?" The man poured himself another glass of wine and sat at the head of an unset table in the kitchen area. She noticed that he had not poured her a glass. Her good breeding prohibited her from filling her own glass. She preferred to see how this scene played out. Each moment was a chance for her to dissect his character.

Pulling a honey-colored wooden chair out at the other end of the table, Tara noticed the man's furrowed brows. She would wait to see how long it would take for him to mention whatever was on his mind.

Instead, DB inspected his pocket watch from his ticket pocket. "Well, it's getting mighty late. Better get started on the dinner before we're eating at midnight."

"Oh, it hasn't been cooked yet? Hopefully it doesn't take too long."

"Depends on how quickly you move in the kitchen."

She raised a finger at him, processing the words that he had uttered. *No, she wouldn't jump to conclusions,* she repeated to herself as she took a deep breath.

"Oh, I'm more than happy to play your sous chef."

"Oh, ho, you know what a sous chef is!" Her rage-meter was slowly ticking up the thermometer toward feverish. Of course, she knew of the role of the sous chef; she had not been raised in a gutter. Didn't her riding a saddled dragon tell him anything about her upbringing? Plus, Titan's Creek boasted a higher socioeconomic status than most places out west.

"I suppose so, though I'm just a simple healer."

"That's alright, you can cook whatever you like. I'll eat almost anything except poorly cooked rabbit. I'm not a dragon after all."

Oh. Oh no. He did mean exactly what I had interpreted previously. He proved me right.

Tara calmly stood up and pushed her chair back into the table, pulling the blanket off it. Placing her hat back on her head, she took a deep breath to calm the roar inside of her.

"I suppose that is where we differ, Mr. Egoman. But unfortunately, we are both in a predicament, since it seems neither of us cooks. So I will be off. Have a good evening." She tipped her hat at the man and showed herself out the door.

Unbe-fucking-lievable. The man had invited her over to cook dinner for him. She berated herself for not having learned anything further about the cold sickness, but the angel on her other shoulder was about to steal the demon's pitchfork and attack the man's crotch in retaliation for the offense.

Outside the house, she pulled the blanket around herself and surveyed the general layout of the area. About to go left and start at the row of buildings across the street from Egoman's house, she didn't even notice that DB had crept up behind her, wearing a black hat and long wool coat.

"I'm sorry, did I say something to offend you?" he asked her. She startled, knocked out of her thoughts.

"No, my call was over for the day. I'll be happy to stop by again another time." She tried to keep the sarcasm out of her voice as she walked forward. The man followed her.

Tara's brother used to poke fun at her manly voice, which was, in all honesty, only on the lower end of the female spectrum. Reaching inside of her diaphragm, she utilized this tone to make a bigger impact on the mannerless ass in front of her. "Can I help you with something, or do you like lurking in my shadow?"

"I was wondering what your plans might be for the foreseeable future, ma'am."

"Sleep, sir, and no, you may not join me." She stepped out into the street.

"I meant your plans for this town. As you can see, it's a disciplined town and we won't have any of your witch doctor medicine coming in and disrupting our way of life."

She chuckled at his turn of phrase. "A ghost town can be a disciplined town, I'll give you that."

"Like I said, they're sick. They're all asleep. I'm sure they'll all be healing in no time by themselves. Fast passing diseases happen all the time out here." The man tipped his black hat at her. "As you just arrived, you'll probably want to stay the night before you head out on your way back to where you came from. There are ample places to stay here, but I'd recommend you and your dragon depart at first light." He implied an "or else" with his hands on his hips, near his holster.

"Hmm," was all Tara replied. She had no intention of leaving at first light, but she kept this information to herself. He did not need to know anything about her plans. She did not trust him in the slightest to think of anyone's well-being except his own. "Thank you for your *hospitality*," she added.

With a stupid nod that only men used to communicate, he turned and walked back to his house. Rather than go inside, though, he stood on the front porch. He pulled a cigar out of his inner jacket pocket and proceeded to cut the end with a cutter that he kept in his pants pocket.

How many pockets did this guy have? And what else could he possibly carry within them?

With the swipe of a match (from his coat pocket) on the house's post, he lit the cigar, puffing on it slowly. The red embers glowed in the dusk. She expected his eyes to glow similarly before she reminded herself that he was a man, not a demon.

Two

Tara

The sign on a larger building in her periphery touted itself as "Mercantile." Making up an excuse to ditch the man, she told him, "I need to get some food and get to work."

Inside the shop, dust matted on shelves. A scent of rotting emanated from some barrels. She would have to take care of that, or the mold would attract insects and other scavengers. Walking in, she had meant to put a door between her and DB. Now, as she surveyed the shelves, she realized that there were no jars of preserves anywhere to be found. Though her bags would last her at least a month, she had hoped that she would find some food out here should anyone wake up or if she needed to stay longer than one month.

She wondered if someone in town had packaged up all the berries and vegetables and hidden them. Someone who had no idea what plague loomed on the horizon. Or maybe, Tara theorized, they had been hidden by a woman who did have an idea, but her husband did not listen to her, and he made her stay. Or maybe he had to stay because he had nowhere else to go.

Tara shook the whirling/scattered thoughts from her head as she walked around the large room, surveying for any forms of life.

She walked around the large room, surveying for any forms of life. No one was visible. No bodies in the unlit back room. No one lying out back. The whole shop seemed as abandoned as the runt in a litter of pups. She grabbed a broom from the corner and a bolt of cotton, figuring that clean material could come in handy with the healing. She also took some coffee from a large barrel, sniffing it to make sure that the aroma still held, though coffee technically never went bad.

A stack of newspapers occupied a shelf near the barrel labeled, "sugar." Dated from a month ago, the headline read "Dimin Greystock wins mayoral election by a landslide!"

She tore a corner off a newspaper from the bottom of the pile, this one advertising that a company named Man, Man, and Man would buy up houses of anyone wanting to leave the area before they grew sick. How thoughtful of those poachers, Tara thought sarcastically.

Grabbing a pencil from atop the register, she wrote a list of the items that she had taken. She would settle up with the shopkeeper if she ever found him. Otherwise, she would thank Mother Maker for the donation to her non-profit healing situation. Though this venture inside had led her away from the stalking eyes of the misogynist she had met, she knew that she would eventually need to broach him for more answers.

She walked outside, surprised at how it seemed a bit warmer out there than in the shop. DB still stood on his porch, puffing on that cigar, except his eyes were on Camelia when she stepped outside. They quickly followed Tara as soon as she made a movement toward the next building.

Looking in the frosted window, she caught the sight of an adult body slumped over a table, frozen in time, a slight blue tinge to their face that would not have been noted by a non-healer. She stepped back aghast.

Growing up, Tara's older brother had often tried to scare her with ghost stories that her sensibilities tried to refute. The scariest parts of those stories stemmed from the desperation of the folks who were about to die. Those ghosts, she knew in her gut, would never compare to the raw reality of the physical leftovers that she would have to deal with in this town. *Would the occupants be dead? Alive and salvageable? Alive but in need of an escort to the next life?* That third kind haunted her nightly in her preparations to journey out here.

She knew from her education the generalities of what to expect in this place: disdain, death, destruction. All of the pains that hit her so deeply in her heart and why she disliked her gift of healing so much. She could not stand to see the suffering; her heart broke when she could not save someone, and suffering was brought upon their family.

In the quiet moments on the back of Camelia as she flew them east, Tara had mentally prepared herself to see everyone dead and to smell that putrid scent of decrepit bodies as she had read could happen in a pandemic, as the newspapers had termed it. Towns had started to go silent. Travelers would arrive and never be heard from again. She should have steeled her heart for the compassion that would flow from seeing these victims.

She shuffled away from the entry of the house wondering what other pathetic scenes she would find that would be the same. *Please,* she begged Daughter Dreamer, *don't let me find any children.* She would surely see the face of her six-year-old niece, Marjorie, in each victim. She would not be able to handle seeing the children.

Her eyes filled with tears, the scenes' possibilities peppering her imagination became almost too much for her to bear. How could such evil exist in a world with the wonders of petrichor, ice cream, and dragons?

She ran toward the clearing where Camelia was working. Thankfully, her packs were still tied to Camelia's back.

"Come on, Camelia, let's go." The tears streamed out of her eyes. Camelia reached out and awkwardly rubbed her paw over Tara's entire face. "This is so sad, it hurts so much. They were just going about their everyday lives, and this man came in and stopped their existence. And not all at once." Her voice shook as her body heaved a shaky breath. "Some took a while. And some saw others go. What if children saw their parents—" she couldn't bear to finish the sentence. With her hand over her heart, she shook away the thought.

"Camelia, I wasn't made for this." Though her healing powers were a blessing from the dragons, in times such as these, her empathic abilities were a curse. She felt too much in the face of such a demon.

Time, forever unbiased in its merciless toll onwards, tormented healers. Many said that healers fought against the Trinity to seize back life. Tara knew better. Time stole lives and deposited them at the Trinity's doorstep.

She would not win the war in this town against cold-hearted Time.

She could not help them all. The weight upon her soul made her feel unworthy of her powers. Why have them if she could not heal everyone? She clung to Camelia's foreleg, rubbing her smooth scales against her calloused hands. Reminding her of home and her family.

She motioned for Camelia to bow down slightly. Stepping into the saddle with her left leg, she flung her right leg over the back and onto the other side.

"Hee-ya!" she said in the loudest voice that she could muster through her sobs. Camelia launched up, turning toward Titan's Creek and the sunset.

The two had not been in the air for more than five minutes when needle-stabbing pains pierced her hands and feet. Maybe she could ignore the sensations.

As the tingling spread toward her torso, her legs and arms began to lose feeling entirely, making it difficult for her to hang on to the saddle.

Shit. The Oath. Was ignoring the summons worth forfeiting her life? No, considering she actually liked being alive. She wanted to see her family again, laugh with them. She loved the feeling of rolling in the hay with her lovers. Every day held a new sunrise that she looked forward to. It would seem that the Oath actually was binding, and not a tale to scare medgical students.

"Camelia," her voice cracked. "I'm all tingly. We have to go back to Grogtown. I need to heal these people or the Oath will take me."

And so they flew back to the place she least desired to be in Cosimo, at a more rapid pace than the dragon had taken to leave.

While returning, the tingling dissipated, and sensations returned to her extremities. She still felt sad, though. Tara mourned the moments before she had learned of her healing gift. She prayed that her niece, Marjorie, would come to terms much quicker when she finally discovered her wayfinding abilities. She knew that her brother would share with Marjorie the words that their parents had shared with both of them.

"You are from the dragons. And like the land, you thrive with the dragons," she remembered these words the most.

With that gift came responsibilities and expectations. Without that gift, Tara had individuality and free will.

Of course, all the healers in Cosimo derived their power from different sources. But the Fuentes power came from the dragons, the most ancient and Trinity-touched creatures of all. Tara had always felt strongest and the most connected with her power in the dragonlands, those lush places where the powerful creatures roamed free. Unlike her brother, Ignacio—or Naz as his family called him—whose power was replenished by the sun, she never could venture too far without her home of Titan's Creek calling to her. Camelia was her tether to the earth and her powers.

Tara knew nothing about saving a city. Naz would have been a better choice to fly out here. Though looking at the sky, she reasoned that his energy would deplete completely without any sun. She dug her heels into the ground Camelia had breathed upon, feeling the slippery squishing below her soles of the thawed land.

She considered the clouds. This entire city needed spring. As a member of the Fuentes family, she could manipulate the weather, but even that took time to work with the patterns.

She covered her face with her hands and inhaled deeply. The world often fell upon her shoulders. She had needed to help with Marjorie once Esperanza, Naz's first wife, had departed. She was there to help rally the troops to save the dragons when evil stretched to Titan's Creek. She would now be here attempting to inject life back into a cursed town, full of strangers.

Switching gears, Tara started reasoning about her sleeping situation. The next day would be the best time to get to work, as her energy would be as high as the sun. Though her initial plan had been to sleep inside the house of some friendly patient, her experience with the window earlier made her not want to go back toward the victims until the light of day was upon them. After further consideration, she determined that outside in the fresh air would be the best spot for her to sleep that night. She could build her magic up from the ground, and Camelia's warmth could surround her to protect her. Laying the broom and bolt on the front porch of the house, she said a mental prayer that everyone in the town would make it through one more night.

Something about the lone man did not sit well with her gut. She tried to sort it out as she unloaded the packs from the saddles on Camelia. The story to the town must not have been that Dimin arrived, everyone fell under a cold curse, and the town simply needed to be awoken, as she had learned from the information she had pieced together. Nefarious deeds had transpired here.

The kind-hearted dragon, used to Tara's needs, had thawed a small green patch in the clearing. Tara curled up in the grass, her cheek feeling the stems poking into her face like acupuncture. "Just like we used to do when I was at school in Lesea and needed to reenergize," Tara recalled with a smile at Camelia.

Once the warmth of the magic started creeping in, she took a deep breath, relaxing into her surroundings. She buried her head into Camelia's side. Camelia curled around her, the dragon's backside and tail blocking Tara's vulnerable sleeping self from view.

"How do I choose where to start? What do we do here? I am just one person." Camelia's wing curled around Tara's back in an embrace, a blanket hiding her from the world, not unlike when she was a little girl hiding under her blankets until her big brother came by to logic her out of them.

But no one was there telling her the order to save people. Where were the other healers sent? Why was she here in this town with no one to help her?

She was alone, with only Camelia here to save her. Though everyone knew that dragons, like healers, could not kill.

On the verge of sleeping and deciding that everything would look better in the sunlight, she remembered.

"Damn it, I meant to get the water."

Camelia's stomach shook with an acknowledging laugh before they both fell asleep.

Three

Tara

Tara stood in the clearing, peering at the mountains, wondering if those people who dwelled so high had escaped Dimin's blanket of evil. With her bare feet firmly on the ground and a cup of warm coffee (courtesy of the percolator and matches she had packed on Camelia and water she had drawn first thing that morning) in her hands, she felt less caught off guard.

Focusing on the energy as it wound up through her legs distracted her from the haunting image. Soon, acute awareness of every hair on her leg that stood on end as the energy traveled directly to her heart and dispersed throughout her bloodstream.

She missed her home already: the dragons roaming freely, the calling of dragon hands around to one another and jesting, the calm sureness of how it had stood there throughout time and would continue to stand there. The energy of the land and its inhabitants flooded her soul there, not like the slow trickling of it in this desolate place.

But no, she would do what she always did: Take a deep breath, make her choice, and stand behind it.

The sooner that she could assess the town, the sooner she could be home, so she threw back the remainder of the coffee that had grown lukewarm in the cool air and headed off toward the town. A plea to any of the Trinity to listen for the caffeine to pump to her brain and counteract her emotions with logic emitted from her lips as she ventured out of the clearing.

Tara brushed the windblown hairs from her face into her low braid, retying them with the brown leather cord that had been failing her the whole trip out east.

Every step forward into the narrow street was an acceptance of her gift and a defiance of her natural proclivities.

The Healers Association had delivered no metrics for the completion of her task. No numbers of how many to save, what the current status was, what working state the town needed to be in so she could leave with the Oath satisfied.

The collaboration that she knew between healers, the research she often had access to, was gone. She had no clue what others would do; no way to know what would actually work to heal a town. Every single healer was cut off, yet trying to solve the same problem. No dragons flew the post routes between towns. Even if they did, the time that would be lost in communication could be better used for healing. Some towns had been completely destroyed, and she knew from the papers that this problem pervaded the eastern half of Cosimo.

As she breathed in the cold air, she wondered to herself about healers of the past. What had others done in the face of old pandemics? What was the morally correct way to respond to such a conundrum as whom to save first?

As she had been taught to read from left to right, she figured she would start on the left. A homely-looking abode with windows and a second-floor balcony. Stepping up the steps of the first house, she looked to either side of her. On her right, the swinging doors to the saloon blew in the slight breeze, hinges creaky with disuse. To her left, the dragon clearing stood unoccupied save for Camelia. Turning the bronze knob and pushing the front door open, she closed her eyes and said a silent prayer to Mother Maker that there were strong people around who would be able to help her with this herculean task.

"Hello?" she called in a half whisper, afraid to waken the dead. She did not believe in ghosts, but she did believe in maintaining a quiet reverence for those who had traveled to the Staircases. Goodness knows she had been around enough death before her training and during it that the concept did not frighten her. The death of the stories saddened her. The ones that ended before they could be truly rounded out and read. The adults who were still children in their hearts and taken before the time when they could see what their sacrifices would mean.

Normally a stickler for taking her boots off upon entry, she thought it best that she keep her feet covered in the chilly, dank house. Perfumed dust immediately tickled the hairs lining her nostrils. She walked through a pretty front parlor, decanters full of whiskey. She lifted the top off and took a whiff. It reminded her of home and her brother's study. She could hear his calloused hands rubbing over his whiskered cheeks as he turned pages in the books, learning new strategies for getting the most out of the earth, for keeping the dragons safe. She wondered if he was learning about any new whiskeys on his adventures with Grace and Marjorie, or if he had finally figured out how to quell the burning in his chest that he pretended not to get when he drank red wine or ate tomatoes.

She walked up the stairs. Peeking into the room to her right, she found a bed bare of its blankets except for the bed sheet. Stacks of books decorated the corners of a dressing table. A framed photograph of a smiling light-haired woman and a tall mustachioed blond man stood front row on a heavily occupied bookshelf.

Glancing around, she walked to the next room. Whiskey bottles—empty and full—fishnet stockings, corsets, and a dressing screen inhabited the room. A tiny window about the size of a toddler child was sealed shut. Despite the dust on the sill, Tara could spot the dragon clearing from it. Camelia was walking its perimeter, smelling the ground.

The third room on the right housed more furniture, lavishly decorated with textiles and oddities from a past life. She opened a waist-high wooden cabinet to find a set of porcelain dolls from many years ago.

Exiting this room, she noticed a bare room across the hall. Walking into it, the bed stripped completely of its clothes beckoned to her. As if its owner had made a journey out of this room into her own future. A blue corseted showgirl outfit lay on the empty bed. Her fingers brushed the satin, only a small layer of dust jumping onto her finger pads. More dust covered this area than the other rooms, as if it were a shrine to the one who had once lived there. Tara tried to imagine a happier ending than the cold sickness for that person. Maybe she had escaped. Walking out of the room, she turned her head toward the last doorway.

A large open room with windows beckoned her entry. The corners of the windows were not completely occluded by the curtains; the triangles from the sunlight, dulled by clouds, pointed toward the middle of the room.

Everything was better with a bit of light, yet Tara was not so sure in this case. So, she steeled herself for the anguish of the reality of Dimin's powers and strode to the windows. She threw open the heavy curtains, overly pungent with stale air. She glanced to her right, catching sight of Camelia once again. Her breath melted the dreary gray winter into a hopeful green spring as Tara watched her roam.

Then, she turned around to survey the room in the daylight.

Three women huddled under the mound of blankets on the sofa, blue-skinned despite their varying skin tones, clutching one another around their waists, heads buried into each other's shoulders. Her eyes watered at their holding each other in their final moments.

The scene overwhelmed her. The dust. The cold. The desperation. The determination. Swallowing tears, her boots led her out of the room as her lungs cried for air. How many other rooms would be filled with similar or more ghastly scenes? Back in the hallway, she caught sight of the blue dress on the bed, again. Bright blue mischievous eyes. Taffeta that was trained to do one thing but often did its own, wrinkling in the process. Black lace that showcased feminine strength. Tara thought of her friend, Grace, and how that fierce firecracker held off that cold curse. She remembered the strength of women and steeled herself.

Returning to the large room, she touched the women's icy wrists in search of any sign of life. There, beneath the veneer of death, life faintly pulsed through them. All three were still miraculously and defiantly alive. When moving the blankets around, she saw the one with her arm across the other two and knew that this woman would care enough to help her manage the crisis.

And here, with these women, she would help the world remember that women inherited the best part of dragons: their spirits and their never-ending fight to mother humanity.

Four

Sadie

Ten years ago, Hamber

Oh, but Justin's eyes twinkled when he looked at her! Much like the gold coins her father provided in her dowry would do in the sun. But she didn't see this comparison. All she saw were his hazel irises radiating like ivy toward her heart to ensnare it. And they couldn't stretch out soon enough. She wanted to be in love, wildly in the throes of passion, to embrace all the sensations of this long-eluding state of rapture.

"Sade," he whispered his nickname for her in her ear as his clean-shaven cheek rested on her head, a contrast to his gravelly voice. "Marry me."

Tears welled up in her brown eyes, blurring her view of the riverbank across from where they sat, arms entwined around each other's waists. The effect led her to remember the artists who painted in Lourde; she longed for him to take her across the sea to visit the city one day.

"Today and every day after, my answer won't change," she blubbered happily.

She should have known by the number of trysts that they had had before the ceremony that something was off. But it never crossed her mind that there would be any problems between them. One doe not think of snowy winter nights in the middle of a sunny spring day.

The day they said their vows to each other and she became Mrs. Sadie Hoff-man was the happiest day of her life.

Each morning, they would rise with the sun, entangled in each other's arms. After supper on warm nights, the two promenaded arm in arm around the square, as people would whisper about what a handsome couple they made. And as time went on, the whispers crescendoed. Until one night, five years in, the whispers became questions to their faces. Questions that they themselves asked each other through tears every month.

"When will you be expanding your handsome family?" Society found mul-tiple ways of implying this question.

As if it were anyone's business what they did.

Five years and their arms stiffened as they trod their worn path, nodding their heads at the new faces, full of hope. Their friends had long since ceased to be able to meet them on walks, as their circles now contained others with extended families.

Sadie wanted children. She knew it was her place to provide them for her husband; but every month, he spoke words of support, "It's just not our time yet." And on the weekends, they would send prayers to Mother Maker that their family would grow. They had so much love for each other that they could not wait to spread it with another.

Or so Sadie had thought.

One fateful afternoon, she was going over the budget with the contractor for the furniture and renovations she was making to their home located in the park square of Hamber. She had poured cups of tea for her and the contractor and had only sat down five minutes earlier to discuss the paperwork spread across the giant wood desk that spanned the study. No books decorated the walls, as nei-ther she nor Justin had time to read with society benefits and business meetings to attend. Instead, framed deeds and contracts with important signatures, like Man, Man, and Man, adorned the places of high visual. When Justin worked in here, he preferred to be reminded of his past accomplishments, in which he so prided himself, rather than the tomes of accomplishments of others.

"Sade! Come down here!" Sadie sprang to her feet from behind the wooden desk, as her husband's early arrival surprised her. Excusing herself quickly, worrying a death had befallen a friend, she glided down the stairs, eager to answer his call.

Justin, upright citizen and friend to all, slumped in the threshold of the front door of their townhouse. The door stood wide open, and passersby stopped to gawk, hoping to catch a "casual" glimpse of the inside of the stately Park Avenue home. Justin's collar, always freshly starched, stood popped in disarray. His normally well-oiled hair was a mess, and the thighs of his trousers had oil stains on them as if he had been running his hand through his hair and then rubbing his hands on his legs. In all the years that she had known him, she had only seen him in such a state after nights at wedding celebrations.

Sadie quickly shut the door as undramatically as possible to save their face in society before asking, "What on earth is going on?" She stooped down to assist him in standing up by his armpits, but he was a heavy rag doll. Tall as she was, he was still a bit taller, which made the overall situation awkward. The whiskey on his breath betrayed his irregular afternoon activity. As she was about to call the butler for support, her love cut her off.

"Enough." He pushed her away in a weaving motion with his back. "You've done enough. Here." Reaching into the inside pocket of his jacket, he pulled out a small wad of cash and threw it at her face. She was taken aback. What sort of game was this? Justin continued to reach into different pockets of his coat, finding other wadded-up balls of money which he continued to throw at her. Confused as to what had occurred to make him act in such a manner, she took it all without flinching. The money hurt nothing in comparison to the words he was about to fling at her.

"You've done nothing but been my whore for the last five years. What do we have to show for it? There's your payment, be gone." He spat the last words at her before wiping the wet droplets from his chin, still clean-shaven from his morning ablutions six hours before.

Sadie felt as though her sternum met her spine as all air escaped her full bosom. This speech could not be coming from her rock of love and support.

"Excuse me?" She stepped back, giving herself space from the now drunken upstanding citizen, a wall of confusion blocking her heart from the hurt. Searching his face for a smile or a tear or some semblance as to what feelings could be causing his actions, she found none.

"I can't do this anymore, Sade." As he carried on, the slurring of his words became more obvious. "I thought we'd have a dozen children by now, the way we've gone at it. We were bound to hit it at least once."

She blinked multiple times, hoping to revive her brain that had frozen. "We'll hit it sometime." She echoed the reassurances that he had given her before. A repeated refrain between them that would keep them bonded in hope together, much as the recitations at the weekly services.

"Sade, you're not getting any younger. And that's not what the doctor says."

"You saw my doctor?" The admission stunned her. Why would this have happened?

"Yes, I saw him today in the hallway at work. He told me that I was a better man than anyone he knew for sacrificing my place on the Fourth Staircase for you."

What was this new information? How had the doctor never shared it with her? Stabbings in her chest had her pulling at her stays. She desperately needed air.

"How are you sacrificing for me? We're in this together ... oh." Having children guaranteed a spot on the Fourth Staircase after death, for it pleased Mother Maker, Daughter Dreamer, and especially Granny Good.

"I'm out here working my ass off for the next life, Sade, it's all about the endgame. And you're not helping my cause."

"But we love each other." The statement rolled off her tongue as simply as "the grass is green."

He puffed out his chest, bobbing a bit in his drunken demeanor, and placing his hand on his lapel as he would pose for a picture to hang in the corner office of a bank. "It's a sacrifice I'm willing to make for eternal salvation," he replied.

Bewildered, she cried out, "But I'm not willing to sacrifice you, and I'm half of this marriage!" He didn't respond. The moment gave her pause to take a deep breath. "You're drunk and feeling downtrodden about the whole thing. We'll figure this out when you're sober. We all have down moments. I'll lift you up through this one."

"Sade, I got drunk after I made the decision."

The admittance hit her like a slap in the face. Her eyes slit with realization that he had numbed his own senses, or whatever feelings he had, in favor of making an objective decision completely devoid of concern for her well-being. She could see the man for who he was. A self-serving coward who cared more for his soul later than for the souls he was with in the present.

Justin couldn't even discuss with her how they would handle the doctor's information. *He* made the decision. *He* was making her leave *his* house.

"I want you to have everything in this world," her father had said as he helped her onto the guide plank up the boat and kissed her cheek goodbye. The gold coins rattled in her bag as she waved from the deck as the boat departed her continent of Quinda for Cosimo.

And now she had nothing.

Her father had passed away in her home country shortly after he had transferred her inheritance. Everything that had been hers now rested as her husband's claim to this world.

A throat cleared behind her as the contractor gingerly descended the stairs, his bag in hand, ready to walk out the door.

"Do you need any help, ma'am?"

The hand resting on her chest that had been tugging at her stays tapped her there, realizing that she could not give in to hysterics in this moment. She inhaled, regaining her composure. "No, he can find his way to his room, thank you."

The man leaned in closer, whispering confidentially. "I meant in packing your things to leave? I can send my wife over."

"Absolutely not!" The man's siding with her husband outraged her. How could he think that she would be leaving at all? This moment was a dot in the larger painting of her life. Yet, Justin was completely within his rights to terminate the union due to her. The purpose of marriage was to elevate one's soul. And as he had just informed her, all she had done was elevate his dick.

What was she going to do? Her society friends would find out, and then she would know who was really her friend as she became an item in society's papers.

"On second thought, yes, please have her come over."

When the butler showed the contractor's wife into the dining room, Sadie raised her glass of whiskey from the head of the table and offered her one.

"We need to get you set," the woman, introduced by the butler as Fortuna, said, "and quickly before news of this spreads. You can carry on drinking, Maker knows I would be trying to deaden my senses in your position. We can do this."

Sadie had responded exactly how Justin had to the news: pouring a big fat drink and blaming someone else. She threw the whiskey glass at the wall behind her.

"My stays were a little tight. Seems they're better now. Thank you." She straightened herself up.

Fortuna cracked a smile before she took her gloves off. As Justin lay passed out upstairs in his wedding bed, Sadie and Fortuna laid out a plan to funnel all of the money that had been deposited for the renovations into Sadie's hands. By making a massive withdrawal, Fortuna would turn the money into gold coins and pass them on. She could not open a new account without either's husband knowing.

Sadie, in that moment, had no one else to trust. Except for this woman whom she had seen with a variety of women about town. This woman, whom she hardly knew, would save Sadie as much as a female in this society could.

Society would scorn Sadie for not living to provide children and would scorn her for trying to survive when she couldn't. Her best chance at survival in this predicament was moving out. Tears trickled down her face, mirroring those she had cried when she accepted his proposal to join his life. Now she was accepting his proposal to leave his life.

"I think we have it all settled," Fortuna said.

"On second thought," Sadie's brown eyes, known in circles for their intelligence rather than their friendliness, calculated the money that stood in the room as well as the others in the house. "Would your husband like to purchase anything on consignment? Perhaps to remake for a new project?"

A big smile spread across Fortuna's face. "Oh, send your man for Missy Salver, the local antiques dealer. Tell your man to have her come in through the back door. She'll know what that means. We're going to make this fool you married pay."

When Justin would return from work the next day, the house would be empty. No butler would answer the door. No cook would prepare his meal. No furniture would exist to sit upon. No Sadie to fuck. Just him and his echoing house of dreams.

Sadie had never ventured outside the city. She had never wanted to go further than her heartstrings could stretch from the self-righteous Justin.

The clothes on her back, her satchel of the change of clothes, and her money, firmly tucked in various parts of her person, all as she had arrived on this continent. She had built herself up earlier in her life, and she would do it again.

And finally, her chest reinflated as she inhaled the unknown. She had no further luggage. Heading outside the city, she approached the meadow where the tender beasts grazed.

Eyes of every color stared at her. "An offering," she announced to the thunder. Her voice shook as she came within earshot of the dragons. "I have myself, some money, and a will. Will you provide the way?" She held up the coin,

A female dragon with swaying hips and long eyelashes approached her and nodded her head before blinking slowly at the lone traveler.

"You are truly the best of the dragons, *Anaveh*, you sweetheart." She paid the man to rent the saddle and deposited the gold coin in the small bag hanging around the dragon's neck. That gold would be for the dragon herself. "Let's go west, take me somewhere that I can figure out who I am outside of a man's property."

The dragon spread her wings and headed west.

Five

Britt

Four years ago, outside of Grogtown

B ritt's ma held open the door to their dirt home that Britt's pa had make-shifted out of some juniper trees he decided to hack down one night. But juniper trees were sacred, so the Uriah family would be forever dodging the disdain of the Trinity. Britt did not understand why she should bear the brunt of her pa's mistake, but there it was. Cursed never to find happiness in his own home after chopping them down so unceremoniously, Uriah also no longer found a home in society, as the townspeople respected their religion much more than Uriah did.

Every morning Britt would wake with the dawn, that damn rooster crowing outside, beckoning any dragon in the nearby vicinity to swoop overhead, damn near taking the thatching off the roof. The beasts were gorgeous. She dreamed of dragons as she tidied up the house and pumped water from the outside well for the morning coffee that her ma would scold her for burning. She was not a coffee queen. The acid from the coffee would be a welcome treat to the smell of the dirty house. She was not a cleaning queen, either, though she did her best.

One day, she promised herself, like she had every morning for the last ten years, that she would leave, just walk outside one morning, and follow the path of a dragon wherever it took her. Anything had to be better than the mud shack with caustic language that she was living in.

Britt heaved a deep breath, rubbing the sweat off her forehead with her right forearm. Another scorcher of a day that would most likely end in her ma's complaining about her aches from her day out bartering.

One day, Britt told herself, she would be known as more than the hot-headed daughter of Crazy Uriah, and she would have more people to talk to than the dreams within her head.

Maker knows she was not always hot-headed. But those damn men with their damn condescension.

The times she would walk with her mother, hoping to barter with the men at the mine, the whispers would always trail. "There goes Crazy Uriah's wife," and "His girl's pretty but just as crazy as him," and "I wouldn't touch those vermin with a fifty-foot pole." Good Granny knows her mother never did much to dispel the mutterings.

Could they not see that Britt was as desperate as they were to move forward in life? To own a piece of their own world? She had as much agency as the pickaxes in their hands, though—that is to say, none except for whatever the man holding onto the handle bid it to do.

She needed to stop considering these foul men, or she would work herself into a frenzy. The day wasn't about to afford her any relief from the heat.

Her ma limped in, hand on her lower back, skirts introducing outside bits of rocks, dirt, and dust to what would be their indoor companions. A dilapidated wicker basket dangled from her opposite wrist. The outdoor debris clung to the loose twines like barbed wire.

"What did you get today, Ma?" Britt asked cautiously. The worse the day, the bigger the bite.

"Nothing for you, you good-for-nothing blight on this continent," the woman deadpanned the tired retort.

Sandra Uriah's beauty had never blossomed past the initial blush she had at sixteen, or so the people nearby would whisper. By the time she had turned thirty-five, she had about exhausted all avenues of available men and had turned to the men ready for second marriages. Her parents offloaded her onto Garrett Uriah, who cared naught but for her breeding body. Once Britt entered the world, he was content to wander the hills while the women strove to survive day to day.

The indignation in Britt rose as high as her eyebrows. "Excuse me?" She threw the rag that she had been using to wipe her mother's gatherings clean.

"You heard me." Her ma pointed her forefinger at Britt's chest and pushed. "I'm sick of this, working day in and day out, and what do you do?"

"I'm pretty sure that I make certain that this house is taken care of and food is cooked." Britt huffed back at her.

"Do you? Because I didn't see anything cooking out on the fire." Her ma waved her hand in the direction of the fire pit that announced their shack.

"Because you're home way earlier than normal, and I haven't gone out foraging and hunting yet."

Three solid knocks on the worn front door interrupted them. Her ma looked at her, daring her to prove her usefulness by answering the door that her ma stood next to. Balancing the broom against the wall, she wiped her hands on her brown muslin skirt before walking the ten steps to the door. A cotton dress would have been a luxury.

"Howdy, Miss Britt," the feeble-minded Rusty from across the ravine greeted her as she opened the door. Rolling her eyes, she threw the dusty rag into his eyes and slammed the door in his coughing face.

"You should ask him in, you rude cretin," her mother chided. Obviously, a word her ma had learned that day out because she never would have picked up a book to read. Britt doubted her ma even knew how to read. Luckily, Britt had spent some time with local school kids growing up, so she knew enough to do numbers. Letters had forever missed her, though. Or she had missed them, as she would sneak out to go to school and rush home in the afternoon before her ma returned home.

Her ma must have forgotten that she brought these important life skills to the team.

"You are nothing but a suck off of me. You're old enough to be married, and you're not."

Britt had had enough that day. Her body was so warm, her brain had lived in an imaginary place where she was not berated on a daily basis. "I do NOT suck off of you. We do this thing together."

"Oh, really, then why do I feel like I'm doing this alone with a good-for-nothing twenty-something daughter who still acts like she is ten?"

"Do you even know how old I am?" Britt inquired.

"Do I even care?" Sandra spat.

That last retort hit Britt hard. Fiery rage burned in her chest, the taste of blood from her cheek where she bit it as she tried to think of one thing to say to her ma of the many that were floating around inside her head. The insides of her mouth were scarred from the number of times that she had bitten her lip. Her arms were scarred from the number of times that she hadn't. Her ma was right. Britt had lived twenty-plus years off her sleeping dreams. She dreamed of leaving and having some peace, maybe a home where she could be respected.

Her ma's rebuke told her that she had no ties remaining. Her ma sure did not care about her, and she would be damned if she let her own self-worth be dictated by someone who negotiated prices on a daily basis. She stomped to the doorway, snatching the sunbonnet and a large flask of water. Nothing else in this sad excuse for a house—because it definitely was not a home—called to be saved.

"No, you don't care." She said, tucking a hunting knife into her boot. "And neither do I. Goodbye."

Rusty stood outside the door, still. "Your ma said that if you slammed the door, that I should just keep waiting. That your 'no' really meant 'yes'."

Oh, fuck OFF. She turned and swung her fist into his nose. As he recoiled, he dropped his rifle to the ground to cover his bloody face with his hands. Of course, he would be there still, waiting for her to go hunting. She would help him load one of the many rifles that he brought with him out to the forest, where she would help him quickly reload but never shoot one herself. And she was faced with a choice—stay here and end up as Rusty's wife in a never-ending cycle (repeating from her ma) of doomed marriages, or leave and end up as Maker knows what—-but at least she'd be breaking the cycle.

"Really, Britt? I just healed from the last time." Britt had endured Rusty's whining for the last time.

A dragon flew low and slow overhead, catching her eye.

"Owww, I think you broke my nose," he whined.

"Do I even care?" she echoed her mother's sentiment.

Heaving a breath, her eyes left the sky and traced the path in front of her. She made up her mind to follow that dragon wherever it may take her. That would be the best plan. And off she headed, leaving her dirty work behind.

She did not mind being alone. Maker knew that her ma had been leaving her for days on end long enough since she was small. Plus, having foraged and hunted for small animals herself, she was rather good with a knife and knew which mushrooms would not kill her. Her ma had taught her that much at least. She supposed she should be thankful for the survival tips. Britt was pretty sure her ma had just wanted to make sure she was self-sufficient enough at the earliest age possible. Staircase forbid that her ma actually care for another being.

A rustling in the brush behind her stopped her calloused feet's trek across the dusty mountainside.

"Where do you think you're going?" the ragged male voice announced her pa's presence.

"I'm done, pa." She tracked the dragon in the sky, making sure that she did not lose sight of its path to her freedom.

"Well," he moved his ragged hat off his sunburnt, hairy face. The sweaty smell of decades wafted toward her. She had once waited for that smell, missed it as a child, thinking of her pa as a king. She knew better now. He was a pauper, only reliable at being poor. But the one time out of one hundred that his eyes twinkled at her, her inner soul glowed. Much as she imagined that dragons' hearts beat when they saw one another.

"I'm sure you could blame this on me. If I'd only been home more ..."

"Pa," she held up her hand to stop him. "I'm done with everything. Ma's yelling. Your abandoning us, showing up whenever you feel like you need to shove your dick into her. Leaving her with nothing." She took a breath and thought for a moment. "I don't know what you ever had, but if it was me, it's not anymore. No use in beating a dead dragon."

What did she want from her pa? She did not even know what she wanted because she had no idea what Pas actually did.

Once she saw an older man who wore a blush tie pick up a little girl in the same color dress and hold her on his hip, helping her onto the dragon they must have taken a break from. She spied on them through the bushes where she foraged one day. Their similar head shapes and smiles told her that they were related. What would life have been like if her pa had cared a little bit more for her ma? A little bit more for her?

Pas, she deduced from that interaction, kept you safe. She had only herself. One day, maybe she would learn what it was like for someone to keep you safe and for you to do likewise. Simply because love existed.

"Seems like you've made up your mind," Uriah said.

"Seems like." Britt wanted to carry on following the dragon.

"Best of luck to you," he tipped his hat at her and turned back toward the drab pit she used to call home.

Fuck that guy.

She followed the dragon's path to a dusty little one-street town. It landed in a clearing just outside the street, where wooden buildings of a variety of heights bedecked each side. She took a small swig of water from her flask. Interested, she walked over to the group. She had never seen dragons up close. Four majestic dragons of different sizes and colors had their tongues out as they licked from troughs that collected rainwater. It hadn't rained in quite some time, she noticed, and it seemed as though no one had thought to put more water in for these creatures.

"Here, drink some of mine," she offered to them. She poured a bit of the water into her hand so she could show them it was water. They walked over to her, and she raised the receptacle high, pouring a stream. Four forked tongues stuck out, lapping to catch all of the desert nectar before it hit the ground.

The stream quickly turned into drips. "Oh, it's all out," she told them. "I'll work on finding you more."

She walked up to the first house, where a middle-aged woman with brown skin answered the door. "Can I help you?"

Britt pushed her shoulders forward, lowering her head as she used to when speaking with women of a station above her. "Please, ma'am, I'm out of water, and ..."

"Oh, of course, please come in, and I'll get you a glass."

"It's not for me. The poor dragons are thirsty. Might I have a bucket or something to fill up their troughs?"

Brown eyes twinkled. "You may, and in fact, I'll help you." She brought two metal buckets to the well down the street, where they helped each other pump the water.

Careful not to splash any over the sides, they slowly made their way to the clearing.

"You seem to care a lot for these creatures," the woman commented.

"I care a lot for many creatures; they just don't seem to have time to care for me," Britt replied. "They're the only ones that seem to care throughout the ages about what we humans do to each other. Maker knows the Trinity don't. Or she's leaving all my prayers unanswered, anyways." She had stopped going to weekly services years ago on account that she had too much work to do at home. She also stopped as she grew to have trouble believing that the Trinity would make such people who hurt others, like her parents, and such creatures who provided love, like the dragons. The duality confused her. Then again, it was a simple case as her ma used to tell her pa that he was "talking out both sides of his mouth."

"Some people are too busy with the staircase of the dead to concern themselves with the land of the living," Britt observed quietly as she expertly tilted her bucket into the empty trough. The other woman nodded in agreement as she emptied her bucket. How was this woman with clean, well-trimmed clothes so capable of pouring a bucket into a trough in the middle of a field? She did not look like she lifted a finger for anyone.

"And where are you headed to?" Her rich voice continued asking questions of Britt, as if she cared about her livelihood.

"Just following the dragons out of the living's version of Below the Staircase," Britt replied, hesitant as to the line of questioning. She had not traveled very far from her home. Though a woman of thirty years, she did not want her parents to find out that she was a short stop away. As far as she was concerned, they were dead to her.

"Were you hurt?" The woman's eyes blazed, her tone denoting retribution was on the table.

"No, ma'am,"

"Enough of calling me ma'am. It's Sadie." Britt felt the woman regarding her as so many seemed to do these days. "How do you feel about earning your own way in this world?" Sadie posed to Britt.

"I reckon I'm going to have to now that I'm on my own for good. I can hunt, can't shoot worth a damn." Britt did not know what she had to offer to this world. She only knew that she did not deserve to be shat upon regularly.

Sadie put an arm across Britt's shoulders. "I'm going to lay this all out for you, and when I'm done, it's your choice. I'm very pro-choice, you see. And you always have a choice in this world, even if you need to clear away some stray branches to see another path."

"Oh, me too. Very pro woman's choice to throw an axe in a man's face should he try anything on me."

Sadie gave Britt's shoulders a squeeze as she guided her back to her house. "We are going to get on splendidly."

Walking into Sadie's for the first time felt like walking into a palace. The floors were planked, not made of dirt. Translucent chandeliers caught the light through clean windows, accentuating the cleanliness of the home.

"You must be cleaning all day," Britt murmured as she thought about her days trying to keep that dirt thing they called a "house" clean. This building, this was a house. That other thing she had dwelled in was a mound of dirt where they lived until they died and were moved to a different mound of dirt.

"Ha! Definitely not. I make money all day. And when I'm not making money, I'm resting until the next time that I start making money." Sadie motioned for her to sit on the couch, dirty clothes and all. "I pay a woman to come round once a week to keep the dust off the chandeliers and windowpanes. She also cleans the furniture."

"Are you the only one here?" Britt could not believe she was standing in a house this size. Ten of her dirt home could fit inside of it.

"I've become as much a part of this building and this community as it has me. Girls have come and gone, but this is my home."

Britt filled with hope at the word "home." "I don't tend to leave those that I am loyal to, Madame Sadie."

"You know what a madame is and what is expected of you?"

"I have the basic idea."

"Well, that'll get you by til it doesn't," Madame Sadie replied.

"And then what?"

"Then we'll figure it out." Sadie's warm smile melted Britt's remaining defenses instantly. Sadie seemed so wise. With her arm across Britt's shoulders, she showed Britt the kitchen and finally to the room that Britt would rent through her wages. The small space held a brass bed, some shelves, a screen, and a wardrobe. How magnificent would she be if she had at least two sets of clothes in that wardrobe? And stockings! Whenever women rode by in carriages and stopped outside the small sign in the road near the center of their fifteen-person town, the ankles that appeared out of the carriages before the garments fascinated her. Along with the men's salacious eyes at the ankle.

Did being a lady mean that one held the key to men's hearts in their ankles?

Back on the first floor, sitting behind her desk, Sadie motioned for Britt to sit down. In a handwritten page, she set forth the terms of the agreement in the contract that she laid out for Britt.

Britt watched Sadie's face as she read it to her. She could not do anything about her background, but she had control of her future. Eventually, the words swallowed her up like a flood, drowning her in intricacies and numbers that made no practical sense.

"Miss Sadie, if you please," Britt interrupted. "You have a kind, trustworthy face. I'm going to use that as all that I need to sign this contract with you. I'll trust that you have both our interests at heart." Writing a circle with a line through it, Britt made her mark and held out her hand.

As she lay on her new bed with clean sheets and a blanket, having bathed in warm water for the first time in she couldn't remember how long, she baptized the pillow sham with tears of joy.

A knock on the door preceded Sadie's entrance. "Is everything to your liking?" She held a book in her hand.

"More than to my liking." Britt sat up, palming the tears off her cheeks. "I'm sorry, I don't cry. But then again, I don't have happy moments like this."

"Well, you're going to have men's wangs between your thighs, so I don't know if many more happy moments will be yours. Theirs, yes, but yours? Maybe not."

"They *want* to be with me. They will *pay* for my company. I have some value other than as a doorstop. I can demand as much respect as I want and not have to worry about the terrible things they will say to me."

"The worst they can whisper is the truth," Sadie advised wisely. "You are a whore who makes her own decisions. And if you hold your truth, you'll find that others will respect that in you."

Britt considered the words for a moment. She had been called a whore for so long, and she had not chosen that. Taking ownership of her life put the power back in her hands. That word was hers.

Sadie stepped inside and handed Britt a book. "It's a primer. I'm going to teach you to read tomorrow afternoon before the evening crowd starts. Nothing more dangerous than a woman who can find information out for herself. And you're going to need to know how to read to do some research, because some of these men get creative." Sadie said with a wave as she closed the door on Britt for the night. And for once, Britt climbed into bed looking forward to what the next day held.

Six

Tara

"I thought I said that I hoped I wouldn't see you in the morning." The male voice popped up behind Tara.

"Hope has abandoned this locale. All you have is me." She didn't take her eyes off Camelia's scales as she rubbed her down, checking for anything that might have climbed over the dragon in the night. Now that the sun was high, she had more decent light to use to check the dragon over.

"You're all set, love." Tara pat the dragon on its back. As it walked away, to where Tara presumed it would find something to eat, she noticed DB's eyes following it.

"Have you never seen a dragon before?" She was wary of his leering at Camelia.

His attention snapped back to her breasts. "Of course, I've seen a dragon before. I'm not destitute. I know something of the world. You hadn't mentioned that you had a dragon here though, when I mentioned it earlier."

Tara rolled her eyes. "Eyes up here." She pointed two fingers at her eyes. This guy was as bad as a new dragon hand who hadn't yet been introduced to the family, who didn't know how these dragons would do anything except kill for them and her. In fact, she sensed Camelia's breathing getting closer, the warmth easy to detect upon Tara's relaxed fingers in the brisk morning air.

His stupid blue eyes, that only reflected light as they were incapable of producing their own, roamed from her chest to her face and hair. A cocky, entitled smile pressed itself across his stupid lips. She had seen that look before. She flexed her hand, twiddling her fingers, her magic jumping between them in a quick dance. She started thinking about ways that she could heal that asshole that would pain him if he started anything with her. Healing that chiseled jawline so that it was softer? Taking away the headaches that obviously created the lines in his forehead so that his skin was so tight it couldn't move? She would need to learn more about him to find his weaknesses. She could stand down, but her mother had always taught her to never back away from a challenge. Plus, she had magic. What did he have besides arrogance?

Go on, try me. Her eyes surged with the dare. He would be out of her way, no harm done.

"Good luck resurrecting the dead," he told her, nodding his head in farewell, before he turned to walk away. "May your mission be successful."

"I'm no subsidiary of the Trinity. I carry no qualms about disobeying you," Tara quipped.

"That may be true, but you are a healer who took an oath to do no harm so I will not be hurt by you when I toss you out of here." He was right and she had no rebuttal for this accuracy. And Oath breakers suffered for breaking their medgical Oaths.

"I'm a healer. I wasn't taught politics. I was taught to answer my call, wherever that led, magic or not." She cocked her head to the side. "Do you have a problem with my upholding my Oath to Granny Good?"

"I do actually." He stiffened his back. If he had hoped to come across as taller (and more formidable) than she, he did not accomplish this by more than an inch.

At his posturing, she blinked rapidly a few times, trying to cast away the laughter that kept threatening to burst from her. She searched him over top to bottom before wetting her bottom lip, thrumming with excitement as to what she would do next. The corners of her lips pulled into a half smile. "Okay then, what are you going to do about it?" She put her hands on her hips, tucking her thumbs into the holster that rested there, and undoing the loop around the handle. If her challenge did not come from her face, it emanated from her stance. The male's increasing wait time for a response made her chest giggle, though her face never displayed this movement.

Wisps of her dark hair blew across her face despite the tan hat that held the sun at bay from her brown eyes.

"I suppose that you have a choice," he replied. "Either deal with me or deal with whatever bogus lie you've been fed about your oath taking over your body in consequence."

"I'm attempting to deal with you, but you're full of empty words!" The frustration mounted inside her. She did not need to tell him how the Oath was real, with tangible consequences. The man did not need any more power in this situation.

"I don't deal with women, especially those prone to emotional outbursts such as yourself."

Tara's mouth dropped open.

"I'll let you carry on with your business. Please let me know when you leave, so as I may extend my fond farewell and watch your dragon ass leave."

Tara bit her tongue with her back teeth, holding back any retort. His presence delayed her from her task, anyway.

While in "medgical" school, as everyone called it, she had dealt with men such as he. Men who came from money and expected the world to fall at their feet because they were born with dicks. Just enough smarts to read a book, extrapolate all their own theses on life from one sentence, and then live by that manifesto for the rest of their lives. Without ever letting life's vicissitudes change or alter their credos.

Stagnant at age twenty.

Of course, her background, once they learned her name, only served to threaten them more. They would become stubborn, overly competitive. If any showed the slightest bit of healing ability, that man would talk it up and down the hallways at her as she passed them on the way to different classes. Typically, a female with lesser ability would gravitate toward his bold black-and-white speech, claiming he was so sure of himself and his values.

Any man that set in his ways and his ideas was no more sure of himself than a bottle of wine that forever hinged on the possibility of changing to vinegar.

"Since you're leaving so soon, though," he added as an afterthought, as if pretending that he was surprised that she would be leaving, "perhaps you wouldn't mind sending out some post for me? It's been a little while since we've seen any dragons around these parts. I count on your discretion not to go through the personal communication."

He handed her a letter addressed to Dimin Greystock. *How odd. He had not heard.*

"I feel the same way about you, sir. So long as you stay out of my way, we won't have to see each other anymore."

Though as much as she thought about it, she could not figure out why he wanted her out of the picture so badly. If she could bring at least one person back, perhaps she could find out a bit more about what happened here so she could do her work, fulfill her summons, and be done with this place.

Seven

Sadie

Off the dragon, Sadie held the brim of her hat down to shield her eyes from the blowing wind that whipped left and right, threatening to leave her blind. Placing her hand in front of her eyes as part screen, part sieve, she could barely discern the goings on around her.

The man at the carpentry shop, whom she later grew to know as Nicholas Charles, stood outside waiting for his shipment to come in with the stagecoach. His skin shone in the daylight, a shade lighter than hers, as if someone had mixed in the color of old book pages with her deep brown. He wore his hair close-shaven to his head, much closer than the men out east had. Beside him, a young woman stood, wiping her hands on a rag that could have used a soak in water with some heavy lye. Her eyes betrayed a wisdom beyond her years; her carriage boasted a rebellious spirit.

Sadie relayed a half smile to the carpenter as she lowered her lashes. Mentally, she noted to return to that man later.

Her eyes scanned the street. Two small contingencies of men relaxed on a break from erecting the sides of a building that she could not yet distinguish. They had wasted no time. Yes, this place needed a spark of life. The coins jingled at her side. There was just enough for now, but in no time, there would be more in that bag. She moved her head, taking in the street before her eyes landed on the empty spot next to the saloon. Already, a small cemetery occupied the space beyond it to its left. Nobody needed to be reminded of death; it crept up constantly to the front door. Her house would stand in front of it, as if to remind everyone to have fun today. And she would make a fortune turning tricks on this whole town.

Walking over to the site, she stuck her parasol into the ground. "I claim thee as mine, land." With a prideful smile, she pulled off her gloves and threw them into the wind. Time to get her hands dirty.

Ten spots had been marked off already in two lines by various means. She had a trunk and two large carpet bags. She put the two bags in a perpendicular corner. With a heaving breath and an upward prayer, she walked fifty good strides of her long legs. Straight, or as straight as she could, toward where her plot could end: some freshly dug graves. *Great, people would love fucking while their death stared at them,* she thought. *But maybe it would make them think they should be fucking before their time runs out. Let's go with that.*

Next, Sadie walked down to about where she thought the bag could line up with the back corner of the plot of the building next door before measuring out more paces. At its perpendicular finality, she placed another bag down. With three pegs down, it was no chore to find the last. When she did, she ran to her trunk. Reaching inside its densely packed contents, she pulled out one of many blankets. She banished the memories from her mind of when she knit them while in one set of her fourteen days of purgatory, waiting to find out if she would become a mother. Now they would hold together her home and her future.

As she unraveled every skein that she had invested a dream within, she stretched the yarn across the four points with a new dream. Once the four corners were looped with stretched yarn, Sadie stood in the middle, admiring her work. She could not see the full picture, but she felt safe within the four sides. This rectangle was all hers. No one would take it from her. No divine providence would elect to steal it. Land stood the test of time.

Boots clunked behind her. Her hand immediately reached into her bodice and wrapped itself around the small pistol hiding there, ready to defend her holding.

Taking a quick breath and whirling around, she addressed the man, holding out the gun at him. "This area is mine."

His hands flew upward in the universal sign for surrender. "Whoa, lady, I wasn't doing much. Just asking if you might like a hand."

"And what, pray tell, makes you think I can't handle myself?" One of her hands flew to her hip, doubting his simple answer.

"I never implied that at all, but I'm a carpenter looking for work, and you look like you're able to pay."

His arm muscles showed that his words held truth. A snide smile crossed her face as industry recognized industry. "Oh, honey, I'll pay you as handsomely a sum as that reflection you see in the mirror each day." The man smiled back, tilting his hat at her less cautiously as she put the gun away.

"Sadie," she said, holding out her hand, "and I'm the owner of the finest female establishment in this town." It was the only one in this town, yet to be constructed, but she believed in self-fulfilling prophecies. Plus, she'd bone some guy in the middle of that square if she needed to in order to make ends meet.

"Nicholas Charles.' He smiled through his gold-patterned teeth. "Here to meet *all* your needs."

She scanned his pauper's outfit, stained with sweat, and his hat, obviously used for Maker's Day only.

"Oh, I very much doubt it," Sadie said, more to herself than him, "but that challenge is for you to pay to play."

Shit. Walking through the first floor's joists and laid out timber, Sadie realized that she had not built it quite wide enough. She had wanted an office and a spot to conduct business. Why had no one advised her on what her business would need as she grew?

Well, up they'd have to go.

"Excuse me, miss?" The jean clad girl in her early twenties who had stood next to Nicholas Charles days before interrupted her thoughts behind her as she gazed at the sky.

"Hm?" Sadie had been looking above the ropes, trying to visualize the upstairs and how it would work with the rest of the house. She had decided on the trip out here exactly how she would sustain herself—a brothel. It would not be a large establishment, goodness knows her pocket money would not pay for a seven-bedroom house. She would prefer to invest the money in an upscale situation. But it would be enough to feel like an upscale home. She wanted to be around nice things, anyway. Just because people would see it as a lowly profession did not mean she would live in squalor.

To Sadie, sex work wasn't a lowly profession; though the town was dirty, her life didn't have to be. She would elevate it to an art form, an experience. Men would come in desperate for her, and they would pay. Much more than that asshole Justin had. They would pay for her gift of being able to practice making children without actually creating them. She would make them pay more than their wives' dowries. Her success would be at the cost of her high standing. But by Granny, she would have respect and wealth, and in gaining such, she would have vengeance upon every person that had demanded a price on her had delivered a number for her dowry.

The town must have only had about twenty people there. Arriving one day too late to be considered a founding member, her name lay off the Declaration of Townhood that hung in the sheriff's office at the heart of the street. She could see the potential for growth, though. A town not far from the base of the mountains would attract travelers to the city of Puntos that dwelled on one of the peaks. This new town also sat halfway to Lackluster Lake from Puntos. Travelers would need to restock provisions at the mercantile store and relax at the saloon. And they would need a good fuck at her brothel, even if they did not know it when they walked into town.

The throat clearing jarred her out of her planning. "My pa sent me over with the blueprints. He said that if you needed a place to stay while you were constructing, that you were welcome to stay with us. It might be safer for a woman, he said, to stay with others." The girl rolled her eyes.

"Honey—" Sadie started in a sugary voice to the girl.

"I sure as hell ain't your honey, ma'am. You can call me Thalassa, like my mama named me." The girl's hands flew to her hips. Sadie detected a small amount of sass in the statement and she cracked a smile. This girl had gumption.

"Well, Thalassa," she took a more straightforward tone. "I thank you and your pa for your concern. However, I claimed this land, and I'm not about to let some man steal it from me because I couldn't sleep on it. If I can't sleep on it now, then I certainly won't be sleeping in the structure alone. This town will never respect me."

"I fully agree, ma'am, which is why I was reluctant to come over here with his message." A thought dawned across Thalassa's face. "How about I sleep here with you? We can take turns keeping watch. I'm a decent shot, and I don't mind a bit of hard work."

"Why would you do that for me?" Sadie asked skeptically.

"Well, you can think of it as protecting my pa's investment. But you can also think of it as we women need to stick together in such a barren place. You're right. I've never seen a man around here help a woman when she could be used as a stepladder instead. Plus, I'm a sucker for helping people who look like they need help."

Sadie decided that she liked the girl and her honesty. "Then you're welcome to stick around."

That first night, Sadie awoke with a start to a shot going off near her head. About to scold her for her idiocy, Sadie realized that another person was present when she opened her eyes. Sitting up, her eyes raised from his boots to his shoulders to his face. Nicholas put his finger over his lips, tasking her with keeping quiet.

"Alright, I see you mean business. I'll let you go."

"You should, and tell your friends that I'll be shooting them next if you try anything sneaky again," Thal replied.

Nicholas tipped his hat and walked away.

"What was that about?" Sadie whispered to Thal, who uncocked the shotgun.

"Pa suggested that we show the town that you mean business and that we are not to be messed with. You can go back to sleep. I'll wake you in a couple hours."

So Sadie fell asleep that night, and no one bothered the women until two nights later, when Sadie was forced to put a bullet in a man's stomach. She had no regrets except that the state of man required her to police their animal urges.

After the town found the girls burying the body in the cemetery, word went round that Sadie would shoot a man in cold blood if he looked at her wrong. The legend of Sadie had begun.

Building the house was a labor of love. The three people worked on that house day in and day out. They took turns fetching water from the communal well near the edge of the town.

Their finish was anticlimactic. Rather than putting the final nail in, the three wandered around wondering if they had finished everything.

Finally, Sadie broke the trio's work to say, "Well, if someone falls through the floor, I'll blame it on good sex."

When the structure held overnight, Sadie stood outside it in the sweet light of dawn. She had built herself a new life.

Eight

Eve

Three years ago, just north of Bleak Harbour

Eve Rothman looked at her husband, Archibald, from beneath her lashes. She stretched her arm as she brushed the red lock off his forehead, marveling at his stillness while his gray eyes peered at her from a foot above her. He was tall; tall enough that he was like a lighthouse, always looking for the next best thing. Well, maybe now that they had finally married, he could settle himself down.

He stood in front of her, utterly frozen. The crinkling of her skirt was the only sound between them as they were lost in one another's eyes.

Finally, Archie cleared his throat. "There's a new opportunity for investment."

"Fabulous!" She clapped her hands in excitement. The two speculated quite well together, always scheming to find what would be a money mine. So far, their latest bonanza had included denim jeans.

Eve had inherited early, when the elderly Mr. Hammersmith widowed her. Her heart did not mourn him; twenty years her elder, she lost no love for him. But he had taken care of her. Though she had not borne him any children, she was forever his "pet." She had spread her legs when appropriate and thrown parties for the social calendar.

She had met Archibald during one such ball. Hammersmith tended to stand in the corner, preferring to watch the men drool over her. The two would talk about who had lost their hearts most to Eve that night, giggling together. He would be so pleased that he had made her his when everyone wanted her, that when they arrived home, he would have a quick thrust in her and be done.

She only wanted one when she met Archibald Rothman. The Hammersmiths did not laugh in the carriage that night. The husband saw the blushing and stolen glances of his wife behind her fan. Instead of making it to the next social gathering, he sent their regrets, telling her he wanted a quiet night in. Eve looked wistfully out the window at the carriage before nodding her head softly in agreement with her husband and walking back upstairs to her room to change out of her pink silks.

The next night, Mr. Hammersmith mysteriously choked on some under-cooked meat. If the healer had been called but five minutes earlier, he would have made it. Instead, Eve's "hysterics" prevented this from occurring. The cook was sacked (she was sleeping with the butler anyway), and two weeks later, Mr. Archibald Rothman showed up for dinner with a bouquet in his hand. The two promptly married in a small courthouse affair.

"We need to take a trip," he explained, staring into her eyes oddly, as if having practiced this speech before this moment. (Indeed, he had, multiple times on his way home from the meeting, to tell her.)

"When are we off? I'll have Hattie get started packing. She and I will go and get set up at the new house."

"That's the thing," he slowly supplied. "We don't have a new house."

"Hm?" She tilted her head at him, much as her Pomeranian would do when she would say the word "treat."

"We need to head west to meet with some other investors to investigate creating a better way of using the land. Some new equipment to make farming a bit easier. But we have to be able to see it to know if it actually works. Plus, we have a few more ideas in the works that need to be negotiated, and those things are best done in person when that much money is involved."

"What other investors?"

"Some gentlemen that I've never met. The other two men in Man, Man, and Man. If it works, it'll help ease the dragons' lives on the land, especially out this way. But I need to go see for myself how it works. So we need to go out there."

"But why do we need to move?"

"I have no idea how long it will take. Plus, all the open land means open opportunity for investments in things to make life easier. New technologies and new people to possibly work with. I have a few other partnerships that I would like to pursue that I can only do from out there."

"That does sound exciting. And you're not wrong, it does seem like our money could go places out there."

So, Eve packed up their necessities. She had never packed before, so she never had to discern what items were necessary to bring. She loaded as many bags as she could with all of her treasures.

"Do you really need all these books?" Archie asked her, dragging the fourth bag into the front yard where a hired dragon waited for them.

"Do you really need those boots?" Eve retorted. "Of course I do! What other forms of entertainment will there be out there? Do you want me to talk to you incessantly?"

A clever smile spread to his eyes. "Hm, I can think of ways to both entertain you *and* keep you quiet." He pinched her bottom as he helped her onto the dragon that he had rented to carry them and their things out west. She was excited to ride on a dragon for the first time, especially with Archie.

"This is Lurien. He has made this trip so many times," Archie reassured her when she commented on how weary he looked. "He knows where he is going, and he will get us there safely."

"But I doubt quickly."

The day passed as they flew overhead. After they left the city, Eve counted the number of cities that they passed. At first, the number quickly ticked upward. Gradually, as they moved west, counting cities became as counting sheep, and she fell asleep with Archie's arms wrapped around her stomach.

That night, Lurien's less-than-smooth landing into a dragon clearing jostled Eve awake. Other travelers' tents decorated the area around a small creek.

"You'll feel more yourself if you clean off. You might have slept half the day, but Lurien didn't. He'll need his strength to get us through to tomorrow," Archie told her. As she performed her evening ablutions in the cold water, she dreamed of the house that she and Archie would build in this new land. A large mansion with marbling throughout the interior that they shipped from out east. Gold leaf on the moldings. Their home would be a monument to their love for each other—and to their success together. Indoor plumbing. She could endure the rural life as long as she had the endgame in close sight.

After a rocky night of lying on the ground, tossing and turning due to weird noises and snores in nearby tents, Archie loaded Eve and their things on Lurien's back. She marveled at where he could have learned to tie everything onto a dragon as he did.

In the sky, her eyes closed as air rushed at her face. She drifted off to sleep rapidly, which she knew Archie would be sure to tease her about as soon as they landed for the night. She had just settled down to a cream tea with the mayor's wife when her stomach bottomed out. Eyes flying open, the clouds whirred past her as she plummeted through the sky. All of the belongings that had been tied onto Lurien rained around her. As she took stock of her surroundings, she glimpsed Archie below her, also falling fast. Maybe, despite his confidence, her husband had not known what he was doing when tying the items onto the dragon. Something must have gone wrong in the balance or the weight to cause them to be careening toward their deaths. She wanted to be with Archie through this terror of death. Outstretching her arms in a diver's position, she attempted to move her body weight so that she would fall faster to catch up with him. He noticed and stretched his arms out toward her as if to catch her. They were ten feet away from their final moments of being alive together.

All of a sudden, a claw wrapped around her stomach, yanking her upward, and she screamed. Throwing her arms forward, she struggled to join Archie in the air. Alas, she was high in the air when the man hit the ground. And as Lurien made a rocky landing, with her safe in his arms, she continued to shriek and kick. Rolling out of his claw, she ran to Archibald, who was but a splatter upon the ground.

Silence blanketed her surroundings, dulling her vibrant world in gray grief. She moved as though sprinting in a vat of oil—slowly, with effort and regret.

As she approached Archibald's disfigured body, Eve's hands flew to her thighs as she bent over. Vomit surged up her esophagus and out of her mouth. She turned back to him and could only look at the man that had once held her body so close to his.

Everything to say and no way to say it. No final I love yous. No thank yous for being the best parts of their lives. No tender caresses. No final touch of their lips.

Pages of her books drifted on the breeze, falling around her as ashes from the volcanic eruption of her heart. The tears poured down. Her heart breaking into as many pieces as her crushed husband. Late husband. She was a widow to a beautiful love story; the kind one had only once in a lifetime, while others imagined it all their lives.

Her sobs overtook her stomach, crushing her onto the ground. The midday sun evaporated her tears and the liquid from her vomit. The flies flocked to the stench and subsequently, her warmth. As she grew more aware of the smell, a muzzle nudged her side. She sat up from her forlorn state. Tears pooled halfway up the old dragon's weary irises.

The repeating refrain of shock had begun to play in her mind. *He's gone, he's gone. No more, he's gone.*

Lurien huffed a quiet apology to her. She wanted to reassure him that it wasn't his fault; Archie should have asked for help in hitching up their belongings to Lurien. Nothing came out of her mouth, though. The dragon took a few steps backward into the dirty clearing. A single tear escaped his eye. He nodded his head. Then, aiming his muzzle at his tail, he breathed fire.

She had only heard of the wonders of dragon fire, as it was seen so infrequently. But this was not wondrous. For the tongues lapped up his scales, burning him to a pile of ashes in front of her eyes, as all she could do was scream. The horrors of his cries would haunt her dreams.

Standing up and backing up, Eve covered her mouth. *Would water put out flames? Where was the water? No leaves to fan out. Fire will burn my skin.* Eve faced death, yet again helpless. The embers floated around her, catching on her dress and a few book pages. She barely felt the small burns as they left scars in the fabric and her skin.

Instinctively, Eve walked away from the death in a trance, gripping the skirt of her tattered dress. She no longer cared. She had no idea where she was. She couldn't even form a sentence to think of what she needed next. As she dragged her feet into the town, eyes fell upon her slowly as she passed. She saw the dragons from their traveling group in the clearing ahead. Maybe she, too, could burn. As she drew closer, she could just make out a beautiful alto voice. Four dragons rested in the clearing there, with a black-haired girl sitting with them, drinking happily from a bottle of whiskey, singing to her audience.

The singing stopped with Eve's appearance. "You look like shit," the corseted girl said. How deliciously scandalous and freeing it must be to lounge around in one's undergarments.

"You look like someone who doesn't care what she looks like," Eve replied.

The girl's eyes assessed the scorched dress, and what Eve could only imagine was a rat's nest of her hair. "And you look like someone who used to," the girl countered.

"I don't care about anything anymore." The black-haired girl sat, arms over her knees, in calm silence before she held out the whiskey bottle to Eve. Eve took it and sat down next to the girl.

"I'm Britt, and you're my new best friend."

Happiness briefly visited her one morning in the form of green eyes accentuated by smile lines. Her blue eyes opened into a friendly, weather-worn face standing in her room. His grin spread to his green eyes, accentuating the smile lines around them.

"Look who decided to open her blue eyes," the man said, putting down the book that had been in his hands.

"Lots of stories to be read still." She yawned, covering her mouth and stretching herself upward.

"Lots of stories to be written, still," he added. "Trees are ready to be sacrificed as pages for your legacy."

"Well, aren't you a charmer," she chuckled.

"You don't seem at all distressed by a man being in your room."

"Sir, I am in a house of ill repute— "

"But one with the best reputation." She regarded him as he shot her a shitass grin.

"You're going to have to return in an hour after I've had my coffee and read my book." Walking over to the door, she took the book from his hands. He eyed her pink silk nightie that barely graced the tops of her thighs.

"Why yes, your majesty." He bowed dramatically. She pushed him and his good spirits out the door, closing it behind her. Eve was disheartened to see him go. Quickly, she remembered that she had no idea who this man was. Throwing the door open and calling after him, Eve teased him for the information.

"What name should I put on the wait list if I have a free slot in my day suddenly open?"

"Verdis." He turned and continued walking down the stairs.

Eve waited a beat, expecting him to ask her in return. Confused, she prompted, "Don't you want to know my name?"

Without turning around, Verdis answered, "No. I want to fantasize about what word could possibly contain your beauty."

Verdis returned that night, slipping into her room as he buttoned his pants. Curious, she put her book down onto her blanketed lap, holding the page open with her thumb. She reached over to her bedside table for the cup of tea that sat there.

"That Britt sure knows how to blow a man's memory clear outta his head … both of them."

She coughed up the tea that had gone down the wrong pipe at his frankness.

"You're not used to this life yet," Verdis said to her gently. "You will be soon. Then you'll wonder how you ever dreamed of anything else except brutal honesty, heartfelt sentiments, and morning's potential. But as for now, be comforted in the fact that you're fucking alive. Meanwhile," he grinned, "I'm alive fucking." He put his hands behind his head and swiveled his pelvis in circles and thrust them, accidentally crushing them on the doorknob.

The absurdity of the sight tickled her soul until giggles escaped her. Giggling turned to garumphing turned to heaving. She had never laughed so hard in her life. Oh, how her stomach hurt in such a pleasing yet upheaving manner! Tears streamed down her face as the man, bent over his crotch, and his hands cradled his delicate sex as if it were a newborn babe that had been dropped from its mother's arms.

"Do you laugh with your crotch?" she managed to shove out.

"Oh, what I don't do with it!" he said to her. At this comment, their eyes caught, and they both buckled further over. Taking their moments to guffaw, and heave and haw, they finally pushed the tears out of their ducts and looked at each other.

"You know," Verdis said with a hiccough. "You women were made much tougher than we men were. That's why your jewels are inside your body. You're not showing the world your hand at any moment."

Eve looked at him with incredulity. "That's because my hand is hidden up my snatch half of the time." The voiced thought escaped her in her comfort. Verdis laughed in response.

"I like you …"

"Eve," she said. From then on, Verdis would stop by whenever he had finished with Britt. Occasionally, he would hang out in her room, and they would end up fooling around with a coin exchanged. Those moments did not happen as often as she would have liked, on account of his being out peddling. Sometimes he would be gone for longer stretches, like during the cholera outbreak. He would always return, though, with a book in hand to hide on her shelf as a surprise.

Nine

Britt

"Eve! Have you seen my fishnets?" Britt called from the bottom of the stairs one late afternoon.

Eve's head peeped out of her room. "They should be outside on the line. I did them with all the other ones."

"Just take one down from the line," Sadie called from her office.

"But we're not the same size—her thigh is the size of my wrist," Britt whined.

Eve stuck her nose in the air. "I'll thank you not to comment on the shape of my body as it's the same as that of my mother, whom I loved dearly."

"But it's true!"

Sadie entered the hallway and walked silently to the bottom of the stairs. With her teeth clenched, she threw a pair of fishnets at Britt, hitting her square in the face. Britt caught them in her hands.

"And when she puts on a few extra pounds because someone gives her a box of chocolates and she decides to indulge, and her thighs become the same size as your head, Britt, will you comment on her body then? And in doing so, are you saying the change is good or bad? Leave your mommy issues at the door, Britt." Sadie rebuked her. "We support each other in this house, for we are all we have against that world out there." With that, Sadie turned on her heel and returned to the office, slamming the door behind her.

Britt appeared properly chastised and quietly apologized to Eve as she darted up the stairs and past Eve's room. She stole to her window, where she had a view of the colorful dragons in the clearing. Leaning her arms on the windowsill, the tears in her eyes blurred the colors together like the beautiful painting that Sadie had hung in the parlor.

The guilt ate her insides. Eve was like the younger sister she never had. Ever since the day Eve had stumbled into that dragon clearing, Britt had felt a protective instinct for her. She should be the one sheltering her, preparing her for life, not wounding her in it.

A knock from the door stole Britt's attention from the dreaming out the window. "I brought you some coffee, because I know you have a late night ahead."

Britt wrung her hands. She had never felt so properly rebuked in her life. She had learned to tune out her mother's criticisms; never would she have wanted to hurt someone else the way that those hurt when she actually listened to them, though. "I didn't mean to hurt you, Eve."

Eve smiled. "No harm done, Britt. I know you were doing it in jest and out of caring for me." Eve's big heart did not belong in that brothel. "I need to go back to my room before Frumo makes off with one of my books."

"Would you even notice? You have piles and piles."

"Of course I would!" Eve put her hand over her heart in fake performing dismay. "That's like asking if I would miss a finger!"

"I think you'd get by." Britt did not doubt the resilience of her friend, who had already been through so much.

"Not without my middle finger, silly." Eve daintily showed it to her. Britt threw her pillow at her, which Eve evaded, running back to her room. Britt stalked her across the hallway with another pillow, which she launched at Eve, who had thrown herself on her bed, covering her head.

"You wouldn't be able to get by without it either!" Eve sputtered out between giggles.

"I do like to use that finger."

"Yeah, inside yourself."

Britt laughed at Eve's joke and stood in the doorway. She fingered the leather-bound objects, fanning the pages. "Where do you get all your books, anyways?"

"I have my ways," Eve said mysteriously, cracking a small smile and lowering her eyelashes. Try as she may, Britt had never been able to capture the demure flirtation style that Eve could pull off. Her brand was much more brash and forward. To each her own.

"Well, if you ever need to borrow one of *my* books, all you have to do is knock to let me know. Mighty educational."

Eve laughed, thinking about the books with poses that Britt would study during her downtime. "My clients tend to only want a sweet song, or a pretty face to stare at while they come." She paused in silence, thinking about the common trends between her clients. "They want to pretend I'm the girl in their lives that got away. I don't get many females. I think they feel inferior to my looks, which is so funny to me. If anything, I feel inferior to them because there is no way that I could possibly choose to start a new life out here like they did."

Britt cocked her head. "You do know that that is exactly what you did, right? Even if Archie made the choice and Grogtown wasn't meant to be your final home, you were going to live out west. So maybe those women around town can't look at you in the eyes because you do handle life here so well. You've had it just as rough as they have, and you never let anyone hear you complain."

"Except you."

"Well, that's what best friends are for."

Ten

Sadie

T he cold whispered dark secrets in her ears that she had repressed for years. Those insecurities that she dealt with long ago. The grief of her womb. The hatred for the one she had considered the most loved. The happiness she had at leaving her father.

She had been warned what was coming: The sickness. Then the forgetting. Then the death. Or at least she had pieced together what would happen from the stories Grace had told her while she had lived there. Perhaps if the town banded together, they would all make it through. Grace had tried to pull them together; but she was an outsider. Sadie had lived in this town from its inception. She believed they would be able to find common ground and cast out this evil before it infected the town.

In case they did contract the sickness, Sadie had stocked up on blankets, firewood, matches. Anything that could make some sort of heat. She began writing in a daily calendar, taking clear notes, any way to remind herself of what was occurring, should she begin forgetting and still need to take care of her girls. Her last will and testament sat safely in a safe at the bank, should she not make it through untouched, as Grace had. As a captain on the high seas would, she was prepared to go down with this ship that she had so lovingly built.

She counted on all the physical symptoms of the cold sickness to take over the town. She was not prepared for the hostility to grow between neighbors.

For as much as the cold brought her insecurities forward, someone else was experiencing their own insecurities brought to light.

With Dimin and his suave way of talking came the smarmy DB, always next to him. When she first met the two, she happily invited them into her home. How bad could they be? Weren't they men at their core, filled with their own needs and desires that she could learn? But Dimin was obsessed with one person who no longer lived there, and DB was obsessed with Dimin's power.

The two would confer together in her front parlor. At first, she had thought they were just talking, and others were joining in. Then, she realized they were bringing others in to meet them there. She eavesdropped enough to hear about their hatespeak. Widows down the road being targeted for their belongings. Children were being lured away from their parents to go and work at the mines. Dragons being beaten in the middle of the night and driven away from the town. The town was essentially cut off from any supply chain except those that Dimin secured exclusively with his exorbitant tariffs tacked on. She learned that he would cut deals for those who did dirty work, such as watering a family's supply of firewood so they could not keep warm.

As soon as she heard of this talk occurring in her house, Madame Sadie kicked them out.

"I don't know who you're fucking over today, but it's not my girls. So, unless you care to pay up, I suggest you leave. This establishment is one of comfort." No one would cross her threshold with a threat in mind.

"You're a businesswoman." Dimin attempted to negotiate with her. "Allow me to pay you for the use of your parlor, Madame Sadie. I'm sure we can come to a lucrative solution."

Her wariness had no evidence, yet her instincts held tough. "I'm an honest businesswoman, Mr. Greystock," Sadie commented. "I promise pussy, you're getting pussy. No games. And that's how I intend for my house to remain. I'm sure you can respect that our mission statements are not simpatico."

Greystock stood up, tipped his hat, and moved out. DB started to say something from his seated position, but Greystock held up his hand to silence him. "Madame Sadie has made her point. We shall find another domain in which to conduct our business so it does not interfere with hers." With that, DB stood up and followed his boss toward the door.

"We understand one another, Mr. Greystock," Sadie said as she nodded to him. As soon as the two men had made their way across the threshold, she shut the door behind them, barely slamming the door on their asses.

She felt a slight twinge of guilt when he took over the front of the saloon next door. Annie, the barkeep, had never stood a chance. But they had all made their choices to do what was best for each of them.

If they had stood together, maybe they wouldn't have all fallen individually.

Her vision muddied, and she wiped it away. She must be having sunstroke, she thought, as she wiped her brow. Sweat continued to run down her face, though.

She walked inside the house for some solar reprieve.

Britt stood there with her hands on her hips.

"Well, what do you say?"

"To what?" Sadie replied. The whole two minutes felt like some weird fever dream.

"To my proposition of bringing men over from the saloon," Britt reminded her.

"If you think that'll work, I'm all for expanding the business. And maybe they need to see the wares to know what they'd be shopping for. Especially since you sleep all day," Sadie gently ribbed her.

"I don't sleep *all* day, but I'm not quite sure how I wouldn't since I'm awake all night." Britt stuck her chest out proudly.

Sadie thought for a moment of the best way to compromise the needs of the house with the needs of the individual. "What if we institute a lounging hour? You can take your naps in the big open room down the hall from your room. If customers come in, though, you need to service them."

"I don't want to be all ready in my outfit though," Britt started.

"So don't be ready and charge half the fee," Sadie negotiated. "You don't even need to bring them into your room. Just one and done 'em in that room. When some men show up, they don't even care where they get off. They'll be happy to escape the heat and receive a happy ending to their break here."

"Hm," Britt considered. "I can live with that."

"You can start spreading the word tonight, and let Annie know too," Sadie said.

"Are you coming back?" Britt asked.

Sadie looked at her, confused. What a weird statement that had nothing to do with their current conversation.

"Coming back?"

"Are you warming up?" The voice did not quite match up with Britt's mouth.

"Hmm ...?"

The haziness that had taken in her vision outside seemed to have moved into her front field of vision from the periphery during their conversation.

Shaking her head clear of the scent of lemongrass that had taken over her senses, Sadie said, "I'm going to go lie down."

As she turned out of the back room, she walked over to her room.

"Hey, pretty one," the female voice called after her.

What? That was a new one from Britt, so she decided to ignore it. Britt must be talking to herself about a new dragon that she could see out the double doors lined with windows. That woman loved dragons and would often watch them there from the balcony during the day. If someone were to offer her the opportunity to become a dragon, Britt would be the first in line.

No sooner did Sadie close her eyes than she opened them again to find herself peering into brown eyes and a tan face of a beautiful woman. Much too young for her forty-three-year-old ass.

She looked around her at the furniture in the lounging room. But hadn't she just walked into her bedroom?

"Hey, pretty lady." The calm smile facing her felt like sunshine on her face, and she closed her eyes to bask in it.

"No, no, don't go back to sleep." Strong hands cupped Sadie's cheeks, and an energy surged through them, hitting her brain like a poorly made mug of strong coffee. Like when Britt made it. "Open your beautiful eyes again." Sadie lifted her lids barely enough to show part of her irises to the new woman.

"Hi, there we go. Just a bit more ..."

Sadie acquiesced. A woman with a long, messy braid stared at her excitedly, though her voice communicated with gentility.

"Hi! Welcome back!" The woman clapped her hands merrily and giggled.

"Back to where?" The setting looked familiar, but as her senses returned from her nap, the sting of cold hit her face.

"I don't know. Grogtown, I suppose, or the physical structures of Grogtown, anyway. The community spirit of Grogtown is at a bit of a stalemate with life right now."

Sadie noticed that she lay atop a giant mound of pillows and blankets. Moving her arm off the mound, she disconnected it from another hand and put her hand on her head, attempting to sit up.

"Whoa! I don't know how long you've been down with this but be careful. You'll need to readjust."

"Been down with what?" Confusion painted her dark, finely sculpted brows.

"The cold sickness."

Eleven

Tara

The strikingly beautiful woman could have passed for a blackout drunk. She had no idea what was going on. Best to tread carefully, Tara surmised.

Remembering her days in the training clinics, she recollected one man who would suffer from episodes of forgetting. He would be conversing with a loved one, and the next thing, in the middle of the sentence, he would be talking to his sister as if she were in a different time and space, or as if she were his wife.

The trouble came when man's sister would try to explain to him that she was actually not his wife. Or she would try to clear up his brain fog. He would quickly descend into panic and become seriously disturbed.

Messing with one's consciousness and understanding of their place at a particular moment should be a torture reserved for Below the Staircase. Or maybe it was more of a torture for those who knew the man and prayed that he would come back one day. Who deserved such a Below in the Now?

Because of her prior experiences with amnesia, Tara broached the woman carefully. She barely moved her body, not wanting to upset the woman with sudden movements.

"What's your name?" Tara asked, in as calm a voice as she could muster.

"Sadie."

"Sadie ...?" Tara implied the question for the woman's last name.

"That's all that matters," the woman snapped.

"Sorry," Tara put her palms up out in front of her chest. Evidently, this woman's memory was moving quicker than she had anticipated. She tried another route, hoping it would keep her patient calm. "Can you tell me anything about what you remember?"

Sadie's eyes moved about, grasping the layout of the place. Then, her arm tried to move before she looked down at herself. Sadie's eyes flew to her stuck hand ... and what was at the end of it.

Another hand grasping it.

Seeing the situation unfold and the woman's discomfort, Tara peeled back the layers of blankets from the mound. When the face of a girl with long black hair, sun-kissed skin, and full lips came into both of their views, Sadie gasped.

"I remember everything," Sadie croaked.

Covered in blankets, water in a mug in her hands, the woman finally removed her eyes from the mound as her healer spoke again.

"You looked like you were the closest one to knowing what was going on here," Tara told her, "so I started with you."

"Why did you decide to start with us, though?" Sadie asked. "We're a brothel. People trampled us underfoot as we stayed. Women and children are out there."

"I didn't see your job, I saw your closeness. I saw your commitment." Tara's heart did weigh with the mention of children as her thoughts jumped to Marjorie. "I saw someone who looked like she would have a handle on commanding a situation." She took a breath as she finally admitted aloud, "I can work, but I'm nothing alone. I need help. *Your* help." Tara looked at Sadie straight in her eyes.

Tara wasn't sure how to convince this woman that she had no ill intent. She bared the honest reasons to this unknown person, hoping the truths within the statements would do them both a bit of good.

"I didn't know if you were a family, or if you were just three women trying to hold their shit together in this world. I'm not going to rue my decision or have any regrets. I'm out here doing the best I can with what I have, and who knows what staircase I'll end up on, because that's not how I go about things. But I can tell you that at least my soul will be at peace with my choices."

Sadie popped an eyebrow at her. "Are you saying you saved me first because I'm old?"

"What the fuck—-NO! Out of all I just said, where did you get that idea?" Tara's eyes bugged out of her head. That response had been the furthest from her mind, and it left her reeling.

"Just checking," Sadie said with a cocked lip. Tara could only stare as she gathered her own thoughts before she decided that she would see what Sadie would do with her own medicine thrown back at her.

"I saved you first because you're the prettiest girl, if anything," Tara retorted, attempting to take Sadie off guard. Alas, the owner of a brothel was not surprised by much, and there wasn't much that she hadn't heard before from desperate men.

"Charming," Sadie garumphed.

"Just wanted to see those big brown eyes open up at me." Tara smiled at her. The effect was typically mesmerizing to others.

"You're laying it on thick," Sadie said, as she looked around her, not taken by this layer of conversation, apparently.

"Like my thighs," Tara said. With that, Tara pointed at her thighs and made them vibrate in and out in a sort of dance to music that no one could hear.

The laughter burst out of Sadie. The rich alto giggle flooded the quiet of the room. Once Sadie started laughing, she looked like she couldn't stop. The tears started coming down her face, in drops, as she must have been dehydrated enough not to be able to spare much water.

At being able to provoke Sadie's raw emotion, Tara smiled brightly before letting slip a "Good girl."

Sadie's eyes zeroed in on her. In a low, calm voice, she uttered, "Hey, that's my line." Tara would have been uncomfortable had Sadie's eyes not twinkled back at her. Sadie's gaze brought Tara's attention to the person next to her.

"Can you bring them back, too?" The brown eyes were full of fear and pain. Yet slivers of hope shone bright through Sadie's irises, like the hopeful cuts through a birthday cake, in wide, generous dealings.

Tara shook her head, clearing it. "Who?"

Remembering her healing moment not long before, the time with Sadie in her arms came to mind as she thought about what she was doing when this woman started stirring.

"Oh, the others. I don't even know what happened. It all started when I blew your curl out of your face," Tara admitted sheepishly. "I held your hand and blew the curl off your nose, because it looked like it was about to fall into your mouth." She had. She had not known what to do, so as she racked her brain trying to come up with a plan, she stared at the woman's face. Her stillness made her wonder how the patient could be alive without breathing, yet blood still pumping. The sickness defied medgical logic. In her wondering, Tara's face had approached the woman's, checking for signs of life. Breathing deeply to remain calm and present in the moment, Tara peered closely at the blue-tinged face. As she had looked in closely, at an almost microscopic angle, the blue in the skin seemed to dissipate. Tara had to turn her head away and back several times, checking to make sure her mind was not playing tricks on her. But there it was, the woman's skin was thawing.

"Hey, pretty lady," Tara had coaxed the patient awake.

Now this pretty lady lay helpless and confused, as if she had been living a different life until this moment.

"Your breath smells like lemongrass," Sadie broke the silence. "It reminds me of spring."

Tara smiled. "You wouldn't believe how I taste." She winked at her as she held her wrist, taking her vitals. One down, two to go.

Twelve

Eve

"After what I just did to you, you should be in bed." Frumo eyed Eve as she threw on her robe and stood up from the bed.

"Healer Frumo, I'm pretty sure that you've done this enough to me that I know how to recover quickly." The medgical man used his magic to suck up the blood and disinfect his scopes.

"Are you sure you don't want me to tie your tubes, like I did for Britt?"

"Shouldn't you be keeping that quiet?"

"Britt has told everyone in the saloon at some point or another that fact. She uses it as advertisement. It's public knowledge by now." It was true that she spread it; she just hadn't imagined that the doctor's tongue would be so lax about spreading it, too.

Eve's body felt tired from her ordeal; her mind raced, though, as it typically did after one of these procedures. Eve stumbled on her way to the bookshelf.

"Get back in bed."

"I'm grabbing one book!" The lightheaded Eve giggled. She reached out and grabbed a book off the shelf before Healer Frumo could get to her. She flung herself onto the bed.

"And no, I don't want to be tied, yet. I don't want to rule having children out of my life yet. I don't know if I'll ever want to be a mother, but I still want that choice."

"Seems a rough choice to make, but it's your body. I'm just here to help." He held his hands up as if he relinquished all his opinions. "Alright, well, you know the rules. If you start bleeding, let me know. I'm going to take a quick nap in this chair." The man sat down in the wingback chair that Verdis had brought up to her room one night. Positioned between the window and the bookshelf, the location had the best view of both the bed and the door. A perfect spot to play lookout.

"You're going to stop all my clients from spending time in here by sitting right there. No one will want to stay once they see you." Eve positioned the blankets carefully around herself, trying not to jostle herself too much. The tonic that the healer had given to her before the procedure helped only slightly. She wished that it numbed the pain more.

"Good. You need a day before you take on clients again," Frumo spoke through closed eyelids. His hands clasped across his chest reminded her of a corpse. "I've learned the hard way that you need babysitting so that you don't overextend yourself and permanently damage your body. That pretty pussy needs to heal. Now, two chapters, then lights out."

Quickly, Eve dove into the land of the miniature cream pies, bucolic mansions, and unrequited romances. All of her romances boasted unrequited love or unhappily ever afters. Nothing in books would ever compare to the love that Archibald and she had shared, though.

She nestled under the covers, content with the knowledge that she would be back on her feet tomorrow. Back to pleasuring men that would never hold a candle to her Mr. Archibald Rothman.

Eve had never felt the need to be understood. As long as she had her reasons, she was perfectly at peace to go about her ways. Therefore, she never questioned Sadie's reasons for dismissing DB and Dimin. Her house, her rules.

But a part of her, a very small part, wished that someone would look into her eyes and see the grief that rended her soul. Day after day, she woke up and relived the terror of the day that she and Archie were pitched from Lurien's back.

Some mornings, after Healer Frumo had performed the procedure, she would wake up, and the aching doubled as the physical pain inside of her reminded her that she would never have a child with Archie. Those mornings, her routine welcomed her into its embrace. In the gray moments, she would wonder who would have been the father. What a turmoil that would have sent the town into! Though she would probably have an uptick in clientele wanting to spend time with a pregnant woman. Once the child was delivered, though, her life would be over. Not only would no one want a woman with a child in tow, but a brothel was no place to raise a child. Plus, to worry about the life of a child would be no walk in the park! She knew that she would be prone to anxiety for what scrapes the child found him or herself in. She would not live with worry for another person in her life leaving her.

She bore no shame for what she did; she would have no more regrets in her life.

Thirteen

Sadie

I n the darkness of the big room, the stale air stifled her. Her body ached with lack of expenditure. She needed to leave that room, ground herself in something real—a time, a place, a new memory that she had not formed yet.

Gripping the banisters of the staircase, Sadie gingerly stepped onto each stair, rather pleased with the construction that had held up through the unplanned elements.

At the back of the house, the kitchen stood unused and dusty. She tried to recall how to make coffee as she approached the percolator, only to find it hot and ready. She knew the caffeine would keep her awake, though it was evening; yet she wanted a hot drink, and she'd had enough sleep for a century. After pouring herself a cup, she pushed the back door open, looking at the view ahead of her.

Seated with her back against a gravestone in the cemetery ahead, another figure watched the same sunset. Sadie gathered the blanket from brushing the ground, hoisting it higher around her shoulders to protect her neck. Her throat ached from disuse. Clearing it alerted the healer to her presence.

"Never caught your name," Sadie said, not taking her eyes off the beautiful colors. All her sunsets lately had been a repeat of one. Watching this one was like she was a newborn, opening its eyes on the second day of its life and realizing there was so much new to explore.

The tan-skinned woman played with the handle of her coffee mug. "Tara," she said, not taking her eyes off the sky.

"I'm Sadie," the as-named woman replied. "I don't suppose I'll ever be able to thank you."

"It's not necessary. I won't be able to save everyone. Maker knows that I don't even know how I saved you."

What an odd admission to make! Most healers would puff out their chests at their assertions of their powers.

A tug inside of her compelled Sadie to place her hand upon the woman's soft, plaited hair. "You sit out here with the dead while you are tasked with keeping people out of here. You are not lost, so do not throw yourself to the land of the lost."

"I'm not lost, I'm just not home. I need to be home. I get my energy from home, from the earth there. This ground here is haunted." The woman heaved a tired breath. "I presume that Camelia will require months to resurrect the environment to its everyday state."

"Maybe your energy isn't enough to fix this whole town," Sadie offered. "Took a lot of evil to bring it down."

"If my magic's not enough, all of these cities are doomed. My magic is some of the strongest around, since I'm directly descended from the dragons."

"A bit high thinking of yourself," Sadie raised an eyebrow.

Tara shrugged. "Perhaps, but not if it weren't backed up by fact. Watch."

With a cute confidence, Tara placed her hand palm down on the ground. While lifting it slowly, Sadie noted the water droplets that clung to Tara's palm, flying up from the soil. It looked like a small rain shower under the palm of her hand. Sadie had never seen anything like it. Most magic that she had seen in her life had been tiny little movements. Or more intricate spells that took days and ingredients to perform. To be able to control the elements through a simple hand movement indicated a strength that most did not have.

"Only Mother Maker knows the reason that I was the one sent out here and not some other healer. According to the newspapers, we healers were all dispatched to different towns by the Association. It was luck of the draw. But luck was in your favor, for I have seen the evil curse defeated. Your breathing excites me that by some grace of Granny, your friends and your town might be resurrected."

"Hm." Sadie took a sip of coffee and continued to stare out at the horizon, contemplating the woman's reticence. She had seen magic before; she was no fool. This woman in front of her wielded it as if it were as commonplace as cooking upon a stove. As Sadie watched, she held herself with a calm that her words communicated did not occupy her mind. As if also coming out of a trance, Tara shook her head and stood up.

"Well, let's move on," Sadie announced, dumping her coffee into the dirt.

"Well, let's get you back in bed," Tara announced simultaneously, not hearing Sadie. "I'll get back to trying to heal your friends. Maker knows I'm not making promises. The sooner I can figure out how to breathe on everyone, the sooner that I can head back home."

Sadie, as always, followed the Healer's commands, though she was learning that she had a voice in their dictations.

Fourteen

Tara

The morning after she all but resurrected a patient, Tara sat in the front room filled with the decanters, reading one of the books from the unused room as she drank her coffee. Down the stairs, Sadie bolted, skirts hoisted high and nearly falling over her own pretty ankles, still thick from their disuse. "Ahh! The calendar!" she shouted.

Sadie's bustle was no different than Tara's niece's at seven in the morning.

"What about it?" Tara calmly set down her book and mug onto a side table before bestowing Sadie with her attention. Sadie's eyes were so much more white than iris, that Tara could not tell where the information was stored. All she could do was follow Sadie to the back of the house.

As they walked toward the back door and the kitchen, Tara noted a small room to her right. Tara would have missed its importance had Sadie not turned into its small space. As Sadie maneuvered around the large desk in the middle, Tara spied a large leatherbound book spread upon it. It was not displayed; the book sat as a missive for daily reading and writing. The ink next to the book looked as if it had been used daily, and Tara surmised that it might be dry based on her finding the bodies all frozen. As she watched Sadie authoritatively flip the book closed, Tara wondered what this woman was thinking.

With another flip of her wrist after closing the book, Sadie flipped the book off the table. Tara realized that the book had been covering a marked-up desk calendar. Tara stepped forward, watching as Sadie murmured to herself about the marks. Between the louder murmurs and the familiar marks, Tara could make out a bit of the ledgers' stories. She did enough bookkeeping at the ranch to know the universal symbols and that paydays typically happened every two weeks. Some of the marks were completely foreign to her, though. She stepped closer to hear what was actually being said, trying not to disturb Sadie's thoughts.

"Each day that passed, I marked off before I went to sleep. I started to lose track of things, and I wanted to remember time. I don't know why, it just seemed like the only thing I could hold onto." Sadie finally acknowledged Tara's presence as she waved her hands across the numbers in an almost waft-like motion to her brain.

Tara nodded, agreeing with the logic. "Makes sense. Time measures life. You probably wanted to make sure that your life had some sort of start and stop, some sort of edges to it to show that you were here for a moment."

Sadie stood, mouth ajar, now staring at Tara, who moved to stand beside her.

Looking over Sadie's shoulder, Tara pointed at the calendar. The roughness of the paper contrasted with the softness of Sadie's face that her fingers were so close to caressing once again. If she could bring life into Sadie's entire face, she began thinking about where else her dexterous fingers could bring life to ...

"That was a week ago." Sadie calculated, interrupting Tara's thoughts.

Sadie flipped through the other pages of the calendar, noting three symbols, while Tara reoriented her brain to the calendar and not Sadie's fingers. "This symbol stops a week or so before, and this other one stops a good two weeks before that."

Sadie's hands flew to her mouth. "Oh, poor Evie has been gone for a month!" Immediately, Tara's mind started processing what this meant, when a knock on the front door preceded a door creak and a lower than tenor, "Hello?"

"I'm sorry, do I know you?" Sadie asked as she stood up from the desk. A presence pushed its way into the small office where it must have heard them breathing. Tara felt Sadie's fingers squeeze around her bicep in a move that Tara understood to mean "shush."

"Why, Miss Sadie, it's me, DB, your favorite client. I used to come in here all the time, don't you remember?" The shady man strolled into the light.

"I'm sorry, my memory is still a bit hazy. I don't seem to recollect any of that." Sadie touched her head as if she still had a headache.

"It's alright. How miraculous that you were able to wake up from such a frightful sickness! I myself only woke up a few days ago. We should really be working together like we always did. We don't need any outsiders coming in and telling us how to run this town."

"I'm sure I don't have any plans other than to recover, Mr. DB."

"It's Egoman, E-GO-man. But Mr. DB is fine for you."

"Did you need something? I'm afraid we're not quite ready to open for business. I'm going to need a few more girls, and this town needs to be in proper order before anyone comes in."

"Might be worth just heading out and starting fresh in a new territory," he suggested.

"Might be, but I won't know for certain. Now, if you'll excuse me, this kind healer was just about to help me upstairs to rest unless you needed something."

"I kept seeing lights on in the house, and I wanted to see what all the activity was about, especially since this here healer informed me that the town was not worth saving and she was headed out."

Tara opened her mouth to speak, but Sadie interjected. "Oh dear. I sure hope I didn't detract from your plans to get anywhere else by deciding to wake back up. I'm certain that we can all get on the same page once I've had a moment to be able to think."

"Well, you know where I'll be, if not ..."

"I'm afraid I don't."

He flashed a white smile at her. "Just the end of the block of houses by the well. Maybe when you're better, you can stop on by for dinner and dessert."

"That sounds lovely, now if you wouldn't mind showing yourself out."

He tipped his hat at Sadie, ignoring Tara.

When the door shut, Sadie grabbed Tara's hand, whisking her out of the kitchen and up the stairs. They watched through the parted curtains as he walked toward the clearing and surveyed Camelia.

"He needs to get away from—" Sadie shoved a hand over Tara's mouth.

"Wait until he leaves," she whispered into her ear. After a tense minute or two, DB turned and walked past the brothel, not giving it a second look. When the women could no longer see him, Sadie pulled Tara down onto the floor.

"That asshole is the biggest fucking liar. You mark my words now, he is scheming something. He always is. He is the very opposite of Mother Maker. He is what happens when the lackey gets too powerful."

"Always?" A realization dawned on Tara. "You clever minx, you didn't forget."

"No, no, I didn't. But we're going to hold this as long as we can. If we can get the other girls and the rest of the town back with their memories, then we can devise a plan to kick this man out of my home. He needs to not know that we're amassing power against him, or he'll strike before we're ready. Mother Maker is creating a new place for him below as we speak, and if she's not, I will do it for her."

Fifteen

Britt

"You just go ahead and take your time there," the man said, shoving Britt's head closer to the apex of his legs. That was fine. She had been having difficulty getting closer to the appendage she was meant to be massaging with her saliva. Small dicks were not easy blows.

As he relaxed a bit into the chair during lounging hour, Britt took her damn time listening to the news of the town.

The man whose member was in question sat with his arms behind his head, talking to her, trying to make her think that he was someone big and important.

"Dimin thinks he has his act together, but DB, he's the one with the true vision. Dimin is so obsessed with that hussy that told him 'no' that he can't see the bigger picture. He's taken over towns; they are in his power. But what does he do with that power? Nothing. He just sits there and builds it up for himself."

"Now, DB and me, we're tight." Britt truly doubted it, as she had never seen this guy by DB's side. "We're real close, you see, unlike me right now, you wanna lick a little faster, honey? I'd like to come before tomorrow. I have a hot meal. Yes, ma'am, DB's promised us all the fixin's tonight. We gonna celebrate the mayoral election of Dimin. And when Dimin leaves, DB will run this place, so it's as good a win for DB."

Is that what he hoped he was? The second's second? The votes hadn't even been cast yet. How could there be a winner? Britt finished the jerk off in her hand. Grabbing the towel from the floor that she had knelt on, she rubbed the nasty-smelling cum off her hand before she held it out to the man. He dropped a few coins into her palm, not realizing in his headiness that he had paid the normal fee, not lounging hour's typical half-charge. Before he could figure out his mistake, he was sent on his merry way. Britt jingled the coins in her pocket, making up a song in her mind as she headed off to the back of the first floor, to Sadie's office.

In her floral upholstered desk chair, Sadie pored over a heavy book. Her hands framed her face. A sharpened pencil decorated the top of her ear. Deep wrinkles formed between her eyebrows, despite her age of forty-three.

Britt was not sure if she should break the woman's concentration. With the sense of a mother, Sadie's eyes moved to hers through her hands.

"Is everything okay, Sadie?" Britt asked timidly, waiting for the onslaught of language that she was used to her mother using at her during times of frustration. Though Sadie had never given her reason to believe she was anything like Sandra Uriah, the fear had been sown into Britt like a weed that returned every time one thought it had been pulled.

"Can I pay you this month's room rent now?" Britt did not want to forget her obligations and burn through the money that Sadie collected on a monthly basis. She never had before, and this month would not be the one that she started.

"You absolutely can." Sadie pulled out a small book from the side drawer in her desk. She flipped a tab over quickly. Holding out her hand for the coins, she asked, "How'd you make out upstairs?"

"I'd have had that moron out quicker if he hadn't been so yappy. Kept going on about Dimin's winning the election and how great DB is and what a feast they are having tonight." Britt clinked the coins into Sadie's outstretched palm.

"Feast?" Sadie's quick response sounded irked. Her fingers tried to wipe away the confusion that clung to her elevens.

"We're all on rations. There's hardly enough berries for canning as it is. I don't know how we'll make it through this eternal winter," she reasoned out to Britt. "And he's having a feast?" The elevens turned into tilted lines, physically asking Britt to clear their confusion.

"I hear you can get some rations from DB, if you go through the right channels." Britt did not feel great about holding this knowledge herself, but she had no idea how to act on it. She tried to imply this knowledge to Sadie. Luckily, Sadie picked it up and knew what to do.

"Oh, well, that's not fitting at all." Sadie stood and walked to the door. Britt could breathe easy knowing that Sadie had things under control. Grabbing her hat off the stand, she asked, "You coming with?"

Britt ran up the stairs and threw on her overskirt and bodice over her corset and pantaloons. A bite in the air had sent shivers down her spine the last time she had been out on the main town street. She ran a brush through her long, dark hair. Leaving her room, she darted into the lounging room, where Eve read a book with her legs propped up on a man who was on all fours on the floor. A quick whisper and a nod, and Eve was in command of the house for the next hour.

"Take your shawl!" Eve called after her. Britt grabbed it from the doorknob on the back of her door before she rushed down the stairs.

Sadie looped her arm through Britt's as they set off through the stares and whispers that followed them like a bride's veil through the street.

Search as they could, they could not find the smarmy man walking through the street. They retreated to the raised, boarded sidewalk that connected the fronts of the building on the side of the street. From the slightly elevated height, Britt spotted him. A slippery eel, DB wove his way through the small groups of people scattered about. His "Vote for Dimin" pin shone in the diffracted sun's rays through the clouds.

"Have you voted for Greystock for mayor?" Britt tracked his lips as he leaned into whisper to a man, weathered with time, sitting on a chair with a shawl wrapped over his shoulders.

Britt clasped Sadie's arm gently and pointed to their target. "He's over there, Sadie," Britt informed her. Her companion immediately bristled, elongating her torso and throwing her shoulders back.

"Mr. DB! I have a gripe to settle with you, sir," Sadie called as they crossed over to where he stood outside the sheriff's office, where voting was happening.

The vague blue eyes looked at her and Britt. His mouth set a bit firmer as they approached him.

"Mr. DB," Sadie started, "is your candidate aware that we have limited food resources?"

"He very much is, and he is working with neighboring towns to ensure that our trade will bring more resources to Grogtown." DB gave a curt smile as he tipped his hat and turned to walk away from them.

"Great!" Britt chimed in, stopping him from leaving their interrogation. "And when is that set to happen?"

"He's in the process of negotiation. Should he be elected, it will be one of the priorities."

"One of the priorities? Having food and water should be THE priority." Britt was aghast.

"As I said, ma'am, one of the priorities," he replied smoothly.

"You didn't say ..." Britt started.

Sadie interrupted her. "I hear that there are other ways to obtain food."

"Well, there are always ways for those that can afford it." His fingers rubbed together as if he were twiddling coins between them.

"And if one were to be in the way of affording such things, how would one go about exchanging for them?" Sadie bat her eyes to punctuate the insinuation. Britt hated the entire facade. Why couldn't everyone just say what they meant?

"Well, you would tell me, and I would make sure that a system was created for procuring and providing for yours."

"And if one couldn't afford such things but still required them? Such as for the children?" Sadie continued, talking around the issue.

"Why, I haven't heard of any such things occurring around here. As far as Mr. Greystock has heard, there's an open pipeline for goods to be brought in should they be wanted. It isn't necessary at this moment." He picked at his teeth, as if he had a piece of fresh lettuce stuck there, and everyone else was not eating bread and preserves. The nerve of the bastard.

"We're all on food rations, and you're hosting a feast. How does that demonstrate public service to its townspeople?" Britt knew that Sadie was reaching the end of her patience with this game. She would soon walk away, unsuccessful in her bid to help the rest of the town, though with a way to purchase more food for her own people.

"Why, everyone has been invited! Sadly, we did not receive everyone's RSVPs in time to make enough arrangements. When Greystock is elected and this cold leaves for summer, we will celebrate together once again!"

Britt could not take any more of the lies and the bullshit. Her fist hit that little fucking dimple. She would not have been surprised at all if her hand had slid off the oily git's face. Instead, she hit smooth and dry, and the friction tossed his head to the side with the impact. She exhaled a breath, releasing some of the tension in her body.

As the sheriff slapped the cuffs on her wrists, she tossed a satisfied smile at Sadie, who rolled her eyes at her. *I just did what we've all been wanting to.*

"You can keep her in for the night," Sadie told him.

"I left my mommy issues at the door. My daddy issues are sitting in a chair inside the house, though," Britt tossed at her.

"You put those issues in a cuck chair and make them watch as you move on with your life, then," Sadie whispered in admonishment. "This is not how we do things. I suggest you use the night to think long and hard about why you are choosing to stay here in this town."

Looking at DB, who had acquired some ice from an icicle for his chin, Sadie nodded and departed.

"You are more trouble than you are worth," the sheriff told Britt as he shoved her into the one cell. In the corner, Peter Bolsheim sat napping off his hangover. The poor guy had stomped into the saloon last night, reporting that his wife had come down with a weird sickness and couldn't remember him, before promptly drinking his memory away and getting into a fight with the swinging doors on the way out. The sheriff's locking him up for the night was a small mercy in a town where empathy seemed to have gotten on a dragon and left with the first snowfall.

The line for voting passed by the cell. Dimin himself helped oversee the balloting. As each person walked by him, he would give a cracked-tooth smile and shake their hand, reminding them to vote for him. *What a creep.* She would make sure to cast her vote for whoever was not the Dimin/DB ticket later. As a taxpaying citizen of the town, she had as much a right as any to drop in a ballot.

The room was frosty. The bars of the cell bore a cold film that threatened to glue her hands permanently to them. With the line made predominantly of men, this place was free picking for customers, though.

"Hey Lars, want a quickie?" Britt asked through the bars at the man who walked by her.

He looked perplexed and embarrassed.

"What, right here?"

"Sure, why not? I'll give you lounging hours rates." His trousers betrayed his interest in this scenario. She knew he did not care about being seen; he liked to perform a bit during lounging hours. She rarely saw him outside of that time. He had every right to brag with the sausage in his casing, though.

Kneeling on the hard floor, she positioned her head so her mouth was between the bars. The man made quick work of undoing his trousers. She could smell his arousal as he thrust into her mouth.

"Here," DB handed her three gold coins without looking her in the face. "That should cover the next ten. As you see them walk in, tell them if they vote for Dimin, they get a freebie." He turned to walk away, but Britt's laughter stopped him in his tracks.

"That will barely cover one mouthing." Pride burst inside her, and she straightened a bit. "If you want one of those diseased girls' jaws for half a coin, you can go down to Lakeside and get one. I charge high prices for a reason." His mouth opened and closed like a fish. The people standing around began to whisper about the exchange.

"Yeah, DB, them girls is the best part of life and worth more than every coin I give them," a bystander commented. Britt wasn't quite sure who, for she was focused on DB's discomfort and making sure it was prolonged.

"You are nothing but a pockmark on this continent," he announced loudly. No one jumped in to save her. Memories of her mother surged within her, and she set her jaw, wishing to Daughter Dreamer that the bars would disappear between them so she could pull out her fist and even out his other cheek.

Britt wished for a moment that Eve was there to throw some big words at him and make him shut up. Or Grace to verbally castrate him. "Go fuck yourself," she told him, unhappy with that being the only thing she could think to say in return. She threw the coins at his face and tossed her long hair back so he could have a clear view of her eyes as she stared him down. Daring him to open the doors, to cross the bars that caged her in. The rage flushed her face. Her chest heaved, at the ready to be unleashed.

"I certainly will go fuck myself, as I wouldn't let the likes of you touch me." The air escaped her body, rage turning to tears.

And in that moment, when she felt completely powerless, she decided that one day, he would have his reckoning.

"Aw, DB, why'd you have to go and make the girl cry? She's going to be no good now." One of the men in line, she couldn't place who through her watery vision, lamented.

"Sheriff, come let her out," DB said. "She's nothing but a distraction."

"Put her in, take her out, put her in, take her out," the sheriff said. "Seems like something you should be doing to her, Mr. Egoman, not something that she's doing to you. I said it once, and I'll say it again. She's more trouble than she's worth."

"Just do it," he said, using his finger to loosen his collar.

The sheriff unlocked the cell and released Britt from the cuffs. She smirked at the room.

"Looks like I'm not the only one doing dirty business around here," she said to DB as she passed him by, patting his cheek just hard enough to not be called a slap. "I'll see you boys later. I'm off to get some whiskey before this fucker takes that from us, too." She sashayed out, waving her hand behind her.

Sixteen

Sadie

Emboldened by their morning encounter with DB, Tara and Sadie made their way back up the stairs to the lounging room. Over the two sick women, they had tried various ways of recreating how Tara brought Sadie back to the present reality. Tara placed her hands on their cheeks. Sadie stoked the fire. Tara blew on their faces, as she had when Sadie had first stirred. Sadie spoke sweet words that she remembered Tara using to pull her out.

The patients did not stir.

"What, if anything, do you remember about the start of the cold sickness?" Tara asked the frustrated Sadie.

"It was the air." Sadie recounted the source of the plague that hailed with Dimin's arrival.

"The air?"

"It became harder and harder to breathe. And there was this pungency of dead roses. Everything smelled like dead roses." Sadie recalled the day that Eve baked a pie, trying out a recipe. "The pie started a fire in the oven, and the whole house smoked up. I couldn't smell any burning through the roses."

That must be it—the smoke.

"Tara, the smoke did it. I'm not sure how, but it's connected." She ran over to the fireplace, grabbing the billows, desperately opening and closing the tool. She looked back to see if her rapid efforts worked. Neither one moved. She heaved a breath and coughed, the toll of the movement taking its effect on her still recovering body.

"Smoke isn't magical, Sadie-girl," Tara said gently. Surprise filtered through Sadie. She refused to let anyone call her by anything but "Sadie" or "Madame Sadie" in this town. Not even the women she worked with knew her completely. Because she worked in the sex industry, she had been lacking real intimacy. Did the cold's arrival coincide with her missing human contact and decency? Or had that been missing before Dimin's arrival? Perhaps this new grip on life deserved a new outlook. She decided to let the name stick.

Putting her finger on her chin, she intended for her moment of consideration of her nickname to look as though she were still contemplating the smoke. "The smoke might not have been the sickness, but it could have helped spread the virus."

Tara raised her eyebrow. "This sickness is not quite a virus since it isn't spread from person to person like a typical germ ..." She talked out some of her thoughts, connecting dots that were not visible to her. Tara snapped her fingers in the air. "That's it! You're a genius!"

Sadie glowed from the inside with the praise. She had always been appreciated for her steadfast nature, her entrepreneurship, and her societal understanding. For the first time, her ingenuity impressed another. And not just any other—a bright healer with determination that would bring a mountain to its valley. Her cheeks were still a bit too cold, or they would have held a rosy blush.

Tara rushed to the double doors and threw one open. "Camelia!"

The dragon peeked its head over the edge of the roof and looked down at her with an inquisitive cock of its head. Then, she ran back and started pulling the remaining women off the sofa and onto the floor.

"You came back around when I breathed on you, Sadie. I'm descended from the dragons. My magic comes from the dragons. You weren't out as long as the other two, according to your calendar. What if they need a stronger source?" Understanding washed over Sadie.

"I need you to blow on them, Camelia," Tara commanded. "Heat. Dragon air. Your breath. Whatever it is that you've been thawing the ground with. I need you to exhale and warm the air and their lungs."

Tara hoisted Britt by the underarms and dragged her across the ground. Sadie dropped the blanket she had wrapped around her and picked up Britt's legs. They lifted her like a droopy bridge across a canyon to the balcony. The air remained cold, but it had begun to become less frigid since their arrival. After the women placed her gently in the outdoor air, Camelia drew closer to the patient.

"Don't melt her face, please," begged Sadie.

The dragon and healer simultaneously turned their heads and looked at her incredulously.

"I mean, first of all," Tara put a hand on her hip and scratched her forehead. "If given a choice between life and scars or death and beauty, I'd choose scars every time. Everyone has them, though some scars may be more noticeable than others. The idea here is that the scars demonstrate survival."

"Second," she held up two fingers from the hand that had scratched her forehead, "we saved you. We're healers who try to do no harm."

The big brown eyes rimmed with tiny hints of a green corona stared straight back at the muddy brown eyes. The madame nodded and placed her hand on Britt's ankle, rubbing it.

"They are women with lives ..." Sadie started. She worried they would get less than perfect treatment now that Tara knew what they did.

"I don't care what she does. My business is with making sure she has enough time here in Cosimo to prove her soul worthy to enter the Four Staircases in whatever way she chooses to do so. I judge blood pressures, not hearts."

With that, she directed Camelia to blow on the woman's face. The full lips, blue with cold, became purple as warm blood, oxygen, and dragon magic pulsed through her veins. "Blow again," Tara said, her hand on the woman's wrist pulse point.

Eyelashes fluttered. Lips twitched. Her ears turned red. A remarkable thing, this cursed sickness. She would have expected her to have had frostbite or some physical damage from the coldness. Her mind would remain scarred from reliving her terrible moments for so long, but her body would never show it.

Another exhale of the dragon, and a giant inhale raised the chest. After ten minutes of acute signs, eyelids fluttered open.

"Oh, Britt!" the madame gushed, flinging herself over the woman's body, next to her hand that lay on her stomach. Britt's hand moved to touch Sadie's hair.

"Keep the air going, Camelia," instructed Tara. She began taking vital signs as best as she could amid the tears that were shed.

"Eve," gasped out lips that barely moved.

Sadie looked over at the couch where the blonde remained. "Hopefully she's not living her worst days because she might be there a bit longer." To the newly revived, she answered, "She'll be better in a few. You need to keep breathing this air."

"Sadie," Tara walked in quietly that night, wrapped in a robe and blanket. Everything in the house smelled of dampness and stale air, but nothing could be done. The air had not quite warmed enough to be able to dry clothes.

"How are you doing?" Sadie looked sadly at Tara from where she sat next to Eve.

"I feel like I will never be untired again," Tara admitted. "When my brother's wife died, I would stay up with my niece some nights. He and I both took turns consoling her. I thought I was tired then, but now I am tired on every level: physical, spiritual, magical, emotional." She rubbed her hand across her brow.

"How terrible for your brother! I can't imagine having to go through grief with a young child."

"Believe me, he was better off. That woman was an absolute bitch who cared nothing about family and attachment, or another human." She bit her lip in thought. "Come to think of it, she left the ranch because she claimed she would be helping the dragons by finding more land, but the more I think about it, I think she just wanted to get off the ranch."

"Ah, the ol' I'm going to hide my selfishness behind a seemingly grand act of self-sacrifice."

"She was always pulling stunts like that. I saw it, but it wasn't my place to involve myself in that marriage. Marriage is a long time."

"For some," Sadie replied with a mournful look.

"I've done everything I can. I am so depleted, and I can't keep up. I keep coming back to Eve, and whatever I do, I cannot get her warm enough."

Sadie looked at Tara. "It's so hard to admit aloud, but I keep wondering if she even wants to come back."

Tara's eyebrows furrowed, having never considered this.

"What if her spirit is simply tired, Tara?"

She considered the possibility. Hadn't she just admitted she was more tired than she had ever been? Would she ever get to the point that she would say enough?

"So, we just let her go?" A lump of guilt hit her chest.

"Or we help her along," Sadie said.

Tara put her hands in the air, as if she were halting dragons. "Whoa, wait, wait, wait. Let's take a step back. How can you be so sure she doesn't want to come back?"

"I've known that girl long enough to know that she grapples with demons daily."

"Then best let her keep grappling til she comes out on top. At least give her the choice to."

"She's lost everything." Tears streamed down her face. "I tried everything. Every day, she seemed to come out of her room a few steps more. She kept mostly to herself, did her work, lost herself in her books. That gentle heart experienced a grief that she let paint her life."

"Sadie, give her a chance to find everything then. I won't be involved in letting a person go if they aren't ready for that," Tara pleaded. "I can't do it anyway. It's against my Oath to help and not harm."

"What if she'd wanted to go, though? What if we find her one day having made an exit for herself? I used to worry daily that I'd find her hanging from a hook. I'd check her books to make sure none had hidden compartments. No one knew, but I did. I knew how her heart bled."

Tara grasped Sadie's hands and fought the urge to wipe the tears off the madame's face with her thumbs. This woman, who bore it all for her girls, was slowly coming to her knees with the weight of everything in front of Tara's eyes. "And trust that a bleeding heart can be mended. For now, let's see if we can bring her around, shall we? Don't let this creature of a man rob you of all the people you love."

Maker knows that Tara had felt the pressure before, the daily feeling of trying to hold a family together. And that's what these women were to each other—the only family in a town of buzzards.

"Let's give her some of our hope, shall we? It seems we've grown enough lately," Tara whispered to her gently. She could not fight the urge to wipe the tears anymore. She reached out and touched Sadie's smooth, beautiful cheek and wiped them away.

Sadie's dark eyelashes fluttered at the touch. A small smile spread across her lips, leaving her tears to drip in a new path. She sniffled and inhaled a deep breath. "Thank you, Anaveh."

The word, new to Tara, must have meant "thank you" from Sadie's past. So she merely nodded.

"You're welcome. Now, let's wake her up." She took Sadie by the hand, helping her up off the porch.

Seventeen

Tara

Tara pulled the bucket up from the well. Sadie could use a bath; the whole house could use a good cleaning. For the first time since she arrived, she could not smell roses. The faint smell of dew on grass caressed her nose with the same love that it did back home. Home. How she missed the quiet strength of the earth. Life's little luxuries, such as dinner and running water. She poured the water into the bucket that she had brought from the house.

Soon, she would be home. And better yet, she would return having succeeded in restoring lost people to their lives.

"You told me you were leaving!" The mayor with the mussed hair shouted at her while pointing his finger.

"I can't kill, I never said I couldn't lie. You told me things, too."

"This is my jurisdiction!" he said angrily.

"I'm tasked with this job. Your people are DYING." If people were alive, they would hear the two butting heads for miles.

"You think I need people alive to run this place?" DB countered at her. The two were almost forehead to forehead in the middle of the road outside Egoman's house. Tara's arms were about to drop from the weight of the full bucket of water.

"I mean, I've flown over ghost towns. There's nothing there to govern. No resources being mined. This place is one step short of a full ghost town staircase. What do you, the one last living creature, have to live on? This town either needs to be resuscitated or surrendered."

His rage seemed to settle back to cool disdain. "I intend to do neither of those things." He breathed on his watch, polishing it with the humidity from his exhale.

"I'm sorry, do you have some big, important meeting to attend that you're checking the time for? A hot lunch date? A scandalous love affair with a painted rock that has a hole in it barely large enough to see with the naked eye to fit your microscopic dick?"

He pointed his finger at her, shaking it as he assessed her. "You have personality."

"I don't even know what that means."

"You've got spunk, girl."

"Judging by the receding hairline, you're not much older than I am, so you'll kindly address me as such."

"Yes, *ma'am*."

She would accept that response. Trying a different tactic, she called him out on his politics. "You're straight out lying to people here."

"I'm not lying to anyone—"

"Of course, everyone is brain dead or physically dead; you don't have to lie anymore." Her retort would have incited others, but he seemed to grow calm from it.

"If that's how you see it."

"That's how it is." What was this truth-bending he wielded? Some men did not need any magical powers at all; they were gifted through life experience with various tools of manipulation.

"Now, if you'll excuse me, ma'am, I must be on my way with duties to fulfill."

"What duties? There's nothing here anymore! Dimin is gone."

He looked at her suspiciously.

"Have you not noticed that this place seems to be brightening a little every day? That whatever hold on this town that he had is slipping? If the Association had feared for my life, they would not have sent me in." She bluffed, for she knew this was not true. Despite her medgical strength, her gender made her a second-class citizen when it came to healers. She would walk in, and her patients would expect her to play nurse to whatever male was meant to be learning from her that day. She had heard "I want a real doctor" on more than one occasion. She hoped that the people who threw her out of their room had that phrase etched into their tombstones. It would be a fuck you enough.

"That's right, he's gone. That love letter you wrote to him is fuel for a fire. I've had it from the very people who killed him. You don't fuck with Grace, you don't fuck with a Fuentes, and you don't fuck with dragons."

An animal's cry, followed by Camelia's appearance with a furry snack between her jaws, accentuated Tara's statement.

"Whatever little plan you had hatching with him is over. He's powerless, and without him, you are too."

"You know nothing about my plans," he said, secretively. "And you never will."

"I'm done with your little power games. I have people to heal, so you can go jerk off a monkey and turn it into ice cream. And now that I've healed two, they will very much know if something happens to me."

She did an about-face and headed back to the brothel and the mysteries that awaited her. This man had her fueled to heal by spite this time. She would worry about his plans as soon as she had taken care of her responsibilities.

"Grab all the blankets that you can find," Tara directed Sadie.

"We already did that, Tara. Every blanket and towel in this house is in this room."

"Oh, good, then on to step two. Cover the cracks. We're going to make this room a box of dragon heat."

"A very hot box. This building is made of wood. Won't that set it on fire?"

Tara grinned. "Let's hope not!" So the women, both depleted of energy but not spirit, found hidden stores within themselves to carry out the next step in the plan. Tea towels found homes in crevices. Blankets were draped from the windows. Skirts stuffed into the cracks of the double doors.

"We should have done this from the cold sickness."

"You would have suffocated then, which is why you didn't do it. Leave one window free. That one over by the piano because Camelia can get to that one easily."

Once the airways had been sealed, the women looked at one another and nodded.

"Camelia!" Tara put her head outside the window and called for the healer dragon. "Come—oh, there you are." The dragon tread air, flying in front of the window. "I'm going to close this window as much as possible, and I need you to blow warm air. As hot as you can get it without the risk of making sparks, or we'll all go up like barbecue on a spit." The dragon nodded in response and pursed her jaws together. Tara closed the window just enough for her mouth to creep through. The dragon lips touched the outside of the building. A steady stream of heated hair flew through the room.

"Ohhh, that's lovely," Sadie said, rubbing her hands in front of the air. As the dragon continued to exhale, more warmth entered the room. Fog painted itself in water droplets across the windows as the temperature between inside and outside contrasted.

"It's working!" Sadie yelled at Tara.

"Science," beamed Tara. "Now, we wait." After about fifteen minutes, the place began to grow hot. Sadie took off her shawl and the top of her dress, so she was down to her skirt and corset.

Tara began to feel hot herself watching. She wondered if she could get Camelia to make it hotter in there so that Sadie would have to take off more clothes. She undid the buttons of her own shirt.

Sweat dripped down their faces. Tara watched as Britt's breathing became easier. Eve's coloring turned from blue to pale. Then from pale to a bit more flushed.

"Come on, come on," Tara muttered under her breath. "Come out of it ..."

Tara could feel Sadie's eyes on her as she intently watched Eve for signs of coming out of the worst spell. She wondered what Sadie saw and wished she didn't appear so disheveled. She could look halfway decent if she had a few moments to shower. But healing always captured all her attention when she was in the midst of it.

Eve's mouth opened, sucking in air around her, with an explosive gasp.

"Eve!" Sadie's hands flew to her mouth in a prayer position; tears filled her eyes. "Eve! You came back."

"Fuck ... that ... guy ..."

Eighteen

Tara

B ritt remained in the house with Eve, while Sadie and Tara set off to survey
the town.

"You cannot enter those homes, ma'am. They are private property," that
dastardly voice interjected their path.

"We've been over this. I am Oathbound to care for them," Tara said. "The
Healers' Association on this continent of Cosimo instructed me to arrive here
and provide care in the aftermath of that GreyStickuphisass."

"Greystock." DB did not portray any offense as he casually corrected her.

"Potayto, potahto." Tara felt weary. She hadn't considered that anyone would
be alive here. She hadn't even considered that anyone would be here who could
be saved. But now that she knew that people were mere breaths away from
arriving at the Four Staircases, her powers obligated her to them.

He put his hand on his holster. "If you decide to enter those homes, I am
going to have to invoke the spirit of the law upon you."

Tara furrowed her brows at him. "Seems we're at an impasse then, with you
upholding your oath and me upholding my Oath."

"Seems so."

"Funny thing is, I don't see any star on your chest, and I've never seen any
sheriff who wasn't keen on getting his hands dirty."

"Seen a lot of sheriffs have you?"

"Seen a lot of men in general. You're no different." Tara raised her eyebrows at him in a challenge. Sadie chuckled beside her.

"If you lay a hand on any one of these good townsfolk—" He started to threaten. Her rebuttals must have been starting to irk him, for he quit trying to negotiate with her. Satisfied with her becoming an annoyance to him, she interrupted him, intending to deal a final blow. "My healing count is up to three."

"Whores." He rolled his eyes and waved them off with his hand, in an action that she had not anticipated. "A dime a dozen and quite insignificant to the well-being and functioning of this town. You will not be penalized for touching them. Everyone does."

Indignation rose up in her chest at his terming any human as "insignificant."

"I never did catch your name, miss. So that I know what I'm carving on your headstone when you undoubtedly disobey me."

"Fuentes," she said, holding her head high. "Tara Fuentes."

His eyes flashed with recognition. "Explains your dragons and where at Titan's Creek you're from."

"Not mine, and just one. She follows her own code."

He considered her quietly for a moment. "It seems we got off on the wrong foot, Ms. Fuentes." He offered her a handshake.

"A common refrain when people hear my family name," Tara replied as she ignored the outstretched hand. She focused on picking the dirt out from under her fingernails.

"Perhaps we can come to some sort of agreement about this territory and your dragons."

She was curious as to what his endgame was. He didn't seem bothered about leaving or bothered by the fact that his boss had been offed, cutting off the supply of the curse. In fact, since she and Camelia had landed, the area around the clearing where the blue dragon rested had begun to thaw. The air seemed not as thick.

"What exactly did you have in mind?" She tried to sound amenable, hoping that more of his plan would come to light.

"We'll both agree that you've revived three people, but let's say the rest were unsalvageable. Nine out of ten of them probably are, if they're like anything I've heard about in some other towns. I'll write a nice recommendation to the Association. Maybe they'll give you a medal for your work. You can move on. And I'll stay here, not bothering anyone, just little old me in this here town."

"DB, do you understand how a moral code works?"

"Sure do, miss. Just seems to me that your code doesn't quite line up with mine. We're a smidge off, but nothing a little compromise can't help." That smarmy sideways smile did not oil her up.

"When I make a promise, I intend to see it through. When I took my medgical Oath, that Oath was actually binding. The guilt will become a parasite within me, eating my innards inside out, so I will physically die if I do not help these people here."

"Seems a bit dramatic," DB pushed back.

"I thought so too, but then again, women have always been the more straightforward killers."

DB sighed and rubbed his brow, obviously tired of this conversation. "What can I say to get you to leave this town?"

"You can tell me why."

DB shrugged. "Would you believe me if I said this place is the only peace that I have in this mad world?"

The straightforward no-nonsense was poisonous. Tara slowly nodded, though she wasn't quite sure how his peace had the right to affect everyone else. She figured she would take the small win for the moment. "Alright, I'll see what I can do."

"I knew you'd come around." He held his hand out and Tara accepted it, shaking it.

"I appreciate that you only shook on agreeing to 'see what you could do,'" Sadie commented quietly as they walked back toward the brothel. Tara had forgotten that her new friend stood next to her during the exchange.

"That man gives me the ick. He would be asking me to give up my life for his, as if his stupid dream of living in a bubble has more value than my life—"

Sadie interrupted, "—Where you too want to live in a bubble." Tara stopped in her tracks and looked at Sadie, who shrugged and dared her. "Tell me I'm wrong." Sadie crossed her arms over her chest as if she were waiting for the argument.

Tara sighed. "Fuck, you're not." She hated being compared to DB in such a way. But she did, she wanted to finish this calling and go back home to her little bubble of Titan's Creek, where she could sit with her tea and her books and work with the dragons. Where her manor was surrounded by wards to keep unwanted visitors out. *Did that make her as selfish and terrible as he was?*

Looking over at Tara, Sadie explained her silence. "I believe in justice. And not one of them—not Granny Good, Mother Maker, nor Daughter Dreamer—not one seems to care about what is going on here." She paused to look at the sky, perhaps invoking their presence. "Who is going to care for us, especially us women, if not them? Why did they put us here first just to let the men ravage us?"

"Maybe they're busy with the influx of souls," Tara supplied. The two sat in silence, looking over the graves. "That over there," she pointed to one grave without the Maker's Mark on it. "That was a healer."

"Frumo," Sadie nodded sadly. "He worked in my home. He had theories, mind you. Especially after seeing the state of Grace, but no solutions. Sad man. He really seemed taken by Eve, though, and spent time with her the most. Like she gave him some softness that he lacked in his life."

"Think we all could use a little softness sometimes," Tara uttered. The coffee warmed her chest as it made its way to her empty stomach. Never mind that, though, the coffee would soon take away the grumbling.

She had known her share of healers in the past who shouldered too much. It was all too easy to crumble under the weight of curing a person. As a result, many healers took to dissociating between themselves and their patients. Tara had never learned this lesson.

Her first healings had been for her brother; she learned she was a healer when, in her pathos for his scratched-up cheek from falling off a dragon, she reached out and touched it, instantly healing the wound.

His amber eyes met her own in excitement. Four years her senior, he already had figured out his powers and, in turn, his responsibilities. "Try it again," he coaxed her.

With a high that increased her breathing rate, she looked around for something to work with.

"Here," Naz grabbed his gun and shot it at his foot, which instantly started bleeding. He sat down on the ground, with his legs out in front of him. He leaned back on his arms.

"You fool!" Tara exclaimed, jumping down to the ground. "Mama's gonna kill you!"

"It'll be fine. Pops stopped counting my bullets a while ago when he said that I need to spend time practicing. Now do what you did again. I made sure the bullet went straight through, so you don't have to pull anything out." His ten-year-old self grimaced as blood pooled at the bottom of his foot, making said appendage look like a weird statue fountain in the middle of a fancy pond.

"Okay, okay." Tara held out her hands, palms and fingers spread in front of it. "It's not working." She peered through her tightly shut eyes.

"You touched me last time."

Tara poked her pointer finger into the wound.

"OW, TARA!" he flinched back, whacking her hand away from his foot.

"You said to touch it!"

"Daughter Dreamer, help you, girl. Touch it as in touch the wound like a normal person—"

"Normal people don't touch wounds, Naz."

"Tara, this really hurts, as much as I'm not complaining. What did you feel last time?"

"So sorry for you, and I didn't want you to feel that way."

He paused in contemplation. In a moment, tears from her sweet brother's eyes started falling down his cheeks. Oh, her heart! The poor thing was just trying to help her, and he got himself into another scrape.

"Oh, you dear, let me help you." She instinctually placed her hands on either side of the foot, letting the energy from her heart flow to her hands and, in turn, to his foot. As she focused on how much she wanted him to not be sad or hurt, she watched his face.

Tears stopped flowing, and a smile spread across his face. "Tara, you did it! You healed me!" He gave her a big hug. After he pulled his boot back on, he grabbed her hand, pulling her back up to a standing position with him. "Let's go tell Mama!"

In their childish exuberance, they hadn't anticipated that their mother would give them a stern talking to, or they would have stopped to work on their story together ahead of time. Naz lost his gun privileges for a week and received a lecture from his father about wasting bullets and taking uncalculated risks.

Of course, Tara was given her moment. And in that moment, as a six-year-old, she felt one with her family, like she had a place that she belonged. She chased that feeling every day she dwelt outside her home.

Nineteen

Sadie

Sitting in a momentary silence with Tara reminded Sadie of how she had wished for times that she could simply sit in peace with her husband. Justin always had something on his mind. An aura of disconnect surrounded the two of them as their relationship ... grew? floundered? progressed in years? Whatever it was, the disconnect was there. They both knew it, but apparently only one of them was willing to fight for what they once had or what they could be.

A lovely calmness surrounded Tara, as if everything would be alright. Indeed, her world had gone to shit, and Tara had woken her up; this very fact reminded her that the sun would still rise in the morning.

Sipping their coffee, they looked out. Through the window, Sadie caught Eve's head in the kitchen, looking at the two of them before returning to another part of the house. The safe haven in this blasted, male-condemned territory. The structure was her stance against the world, even if she had used a man's help in getting it started. What was she supposed to have done? She would have preferred his daughter's help, but she was too young in her apprenticeship to take on building a house. Instead, she welcomed the time they spent together.

"Would you like me to get you more coffee?" Tara's voice broke through the memory that she had too often lived through lately. She stood with her arm outstretched.

Happy to be brought back to the present, she told her, "You don't have to, I can come with you."

"Sadie, I know how to pour a cup of coffee. Just sit in your reveries."

"I guess that's the problem, I did so much sitting in the past, that I don't want to. I physically feel uncomfortable, considering that I lived through the same moments multiple times, as if on a loop that I couldn't escape from."

Tara paused. "Well, then, maybe we need to create some new memories for you." Her lip cocked upward in a half smile. "What makes you feel alive?"

Sadie froze, shocked. No one had ever asked her this question. She had never asked herself this question.

"I felt alive leaving Justin. I felt alive building my house. I felt alive throwing people out of this house when they thought they could do what they wanted." She thought about what she had just said, replaying the confessions in her mind and their images. For once, analyzing the past that she had lived through so many times. "So, I suppose taking ownership of my own life, especially if I'm taking it back from someone. I feel like I have agency, and even if I'm not sure what that purpose is, it renews the feeling of wanting to have a purpose, even if that purpose is to not be commanded by another."

"Sometimes I've felt alive when I set out to do something and I do it. I make a goal and stick to it. I love balancing the ledger, especially when I've a new idea to bring in more business."

Tara sat back down in her chair, holding the mugs in her hands. Sadie became aware of what every part of her body was doing under the gaze of the woman in front of her.

"You've been offered another fresh start, Sadie-girl. You won't be letting any of these other two down if you change directions. You'll only be letting yourself down if you don't."

The words rang true in Sadie's ears. She felt them in her soul. Somehow, this woman could heal with both her hands and her words.

Searching in Tara's eyes, Sadie found a calm that she had always tried to give others, but no one, not even Justin, had ever been able to give her in return, let alone first.

"I suppose I should figure that out."

Tara shifted both mugs into her left hand and, with her right fingertips, tipped up Sadie's chin to look at her.

"One thing at a time." And Sadie truly felt as if she had the space to figure out one thing at a time, though there were so many things to figure out; which first?

Twenty

Tara

They sat on the front step, feet dangling in their stockings, bared ankles in the ghost town, cupping their crappy coffee that Britt had burned again.

"Where does he even go all day? I haven't seen him out at all." Tara peered down the street, searching for sight of her nemesis. She avoided gazing too long in any one spot lest she should catch sight of frozen people through windows.

"He lurks in the shadows," Eve said in a spooky voice as she sipped her coffee. The women had taken to drinking way more bean juice than they should have based on supply and caffeine content.

"I've wondered this myself," Sadie mentioned as she shifted the blanket across her knees. The knife-like cold had left the air, no longer piercing her heart.

"The way he talked to me," Tara said, "I half expected him to come banging the door down with a shotgun pointed at my head and command me to leave."

Sadie thought for a moment. "Hm. DB doesn't work that way. He'll make big ultimatums, but then he'll come at you behind the scenes, in ways that you don't expect it. He always delivers on his threats, though."

"He ran everything in this town once Dimin left," Eve said.

"He looks like he's taken up residence in Ben Thatcher's house," Britt observed.

"Explains why none of the pictures look like him," Tara said. The mystery from earlier had been solved. He did not belong in that house any more than a candle belonged in a bale of hay.

"Thatcher and his wife were some of the first people to go," Sadie supplied. "Britt found him face down by the well. His wife was inside in her bed."

"Terrible."

"That's a gross understatement. It was like he was a mangled tree." The black-haired girl reenacted the frozen body on the floor, fingers frozen in claw shapes.

"Britt, that's morbid." Eve tossed her napkin at the girl, who jerked in reflex before relaxing into her typical position.

"Oh, I know. I saw it. And I wish I could share it with all of you so that I'm not alone in reliving that nightmare every night before I fall asleep," Britt said.

"What do you think he's doing in that house?" Tara wondered aloud.

"Hopefully crying from loneliness and freezing his eyelids shut," Britt said.

"Maker!" Eve exclaimed.

"Well, then he'll have to leave!" Britt explained.

"How? He won't be able to see! He'd be stuck here worse," Sadie countered.

A mischievous smile crossed Britt's face. "Let's go look and see what he's doing!"

The stillness of the air would not make the expedition of creeping down the street easier. Daylight shining through the clouds, stronger than the day before, also would not obscure them.

Who was backing this man at this point? Would he be missed if they offed him? Would anyone send out a jury to hold him to justice for his part in the systematic takedown of an entire town, tiny though it may be? Could they awaken enough people to give evidence for his participation? They needed more intelligence, and fast.

Tara's intuition told her that he was to blame for this town's annihilation. Though she did not need hard proof for herself, based on the threats he had made at her, solid evidence would be helpful in proving the story to the rest of the continent. For who would believe four women?

Camelia started following them, and Tara shooed her back toward the brothel. If they were to act stealthily, the dragon's large size would give away their position. The dragon hopped atop the roof where it scanned the area, watching its friends as they sallied forth into man's land.

The women scurried from shadow to shadow, which was harder to do than it would have been three days before. She wished that one of them had had the idea then.

As the four of them approached the house, they realized that they had not formulated a plan. Nor had they quite understood the scope of the height that they would need to spy on him if he were in his room.

"I say let's look and see if he's in his room," Eve said. "I know if I were alone in a town like this, I would be lying under the covers with a book and a box of chocolates."

"You did that even when you weren't alone in this town," Britt muttered under her breath. Eve's elbow suddenly found a home in Britt's ribcage.

Sadie held her hand out, palm to the sky. "Really?" she said in a hushed tone to Eve. A raised shoulder shrug from Eve was the only reply Sadie received.

Tara rolled her eyes and beckoned them to stand against the side of the house closest to the well. She pointed up and gradually made eye contact with each of them. A weird, out-of-tune singing could be heard with various fricative rhythms from the top floor.

Britt raised an eyebrow. "Bring that dragon back here."

After a low whistle, Camelia started to tiptoe back to them. The women covered their mouths and tried to swallow their giggles at watching as a dragon, at least one-and-a-half floors tall, tiptoed down the street with her wings tucked in close to her body.

Tara rolled her eyes before twisting her finger in an upward corkscrew. The dragon flew high above the clouds.

"Where did she ...?" Britt mouthed.

Without a sound, Camelia landed gracefully behind the home. She flattened her body against the ground and slithered like a snake until she was under the window in front of Tara.

Tara made a climbing motion with her hands and feet. She grabbed onto the side of Camelia and scampered up with ease. She had been climbing up dragons since the day she was born, so she knew the ins and outs of where to put her feet. Britt climbed up next, also lithe from her muscle memory of climbing, foraging, and hunting in the woods. Sadie needed more assistance with hands up from the girls and then a hoist from Eve, who waited on the ground, shaking her head at getting on.

The three girls held on tightly as Camelia slowly lifted them to a point where one crouched below the window, and two stood on either side of it. All peeped in.

DB stood in front of a mirror that was thankfully angled in such a way that he could not see out the window behind him.

"What is he doing?" Britt whispered.

"He's looking at himself in the mirror and getting himself off," Tara whispered.

"To himself?" Britt upturned her lip in disgust. "That's a whole new level."

"Self-care," Sadie said, shrugging.

"That's revolting," Tara said.

"The self-care?" Sadie asked.

"Maker no, the narcissism," Tara replied.

Britt made the universal "jerking off" sign down to Eve, who shot back an affronted look in return. "While singing?" Eve mouthed. Sadie turned and nodded her head, switching her legs into a different position as she did so. Eve stuck her tongue out in response as if to say "ew." In Sadie's movement, her balance shifted. Suddenly, she was sliding down and off the dragon. Eve reached out to grab her, and they both fell into a heaped thud onto the ground.

The singing and grunting stopped. A chair scraped across the hardwood floor.

"Shit!" Tara mouthed at Britt, who had a maniacal smile on her face. She was used to getting into trouble and getting herself out.

Camelia dropped them to the ground so fast she almost flung them off her.

With a confident, sprightly step, Tara jumped off Camelia and ran to the door, where she feigned having fallen while tripping over the front step.

"What are you doing here?" the man asked, running his hand through his disheveled hair.

"I was coming up here to ask you a question," Tara made up on the spot.

"You're supposed to be gone."

"Surprise! I'm not!"

"Well, aren't you the lumbug that wouldn't quit," he rubbed his temples as if she had given him a headache.

Tara smiled in response.

"Unfortunately," he continued, "I'm rather hard up at the moment, so a chat isn't in the question. My best advice to you is to get some snow and pack it around that ankle before it starts swelling."

DB turned and went back into the house after providing the healer with medical advice. As if she didn't know how to treat a simple sprain! What a self-important wad of phlegm!

As soon as the door was closed, Tara pretended to limp off the steps rather slowly, holding onto the banister for extra dramatic effect. Glancing to her left, she noticed that the women and dragon had left. She hoped a wind would blow away their tracks so that he wouldn't realize they had all been spying on him from the side of his house. Either that or she would have to make a dramatic show of landing Camelia there and flying her around the town.

Back at the brothel, they regrouped on the porch.

"How are we going to cure all these people? Drag them all into the house? It'll take days to lug them in, and we're not exactly built to be carrying hundreds of pounds of meat." Tara gnawed on her bottom lip, trying to wrangle out a new solution. Saving these three women had seemed so easy in comparison to the herculean task ahead.

"If, as the papers claim, the sickness originated from a dragon curse, logic holds that it needs to be healed by dragon magic."

Sadie wrung her hands as she thought. "How can you be so sure?"

"I know what halted the spread, or should I say who and how that was done," Tara supplied. She had not heard of any other area being resuscitated yet. Then again, she had not been very forthcoming with sharing her knowledge of how to heal the land.

Not every healer derived their magic from the dragons. Some merely borrowed it. Some called upon Mother Maker in exchange for a vow of servitude. You couldn't compare the strength of the different magics any more than you could compare the severity of a killing disease. They all got it done in the end. But this curse bestowed on the hatred of man called for the benevolence of the magic of dragons.

"We're gonna need more dragons," Tara thought aloud.

Part Two

Twenty-One

Sadie

"Get on the fucking dragon, Eve," Britt commanded from atop the blue dragon. She wrapped a shawl around her arms. Though the air had lost its bite, Sadie also felt a bit chilled after her time with the sickness, despite the effects having worn off. Or maybe it was just an overall reaction to having been revived that had given her the shakes for a day or two. Perhaps, she thought, Britt was feeling this as well.

"I can't!!" Eve's blue eyes overflowed with tears as she sat in the moist dirt like a petulant toddler, reminding Sadie that Eve was the youngest of them. The dragon rolled its eyes, its patience dwindling after having sat through ten minutes of her hyperventilating. "Last time, the dragon picked me up and did the work. I don't know this one." Sadie noticed that Eve wore two colored skirts and two shirts awkwardly, but could not tell if she shook from the remnants of the sickness or her sobs.

"You didn't know Slewja, either!" Britt tossed back to her, her greasy hair falling about her shoulders. They all needed baths, which Tara had promised for them as soon as they arrived.

"Yeah, but he was different." Her cries were rapidly deteriorating into whines. "He had kind eyes and worried so much about someone that he barely knew!

You should have seen his tail swish when I told him he had saved Grace by bringing her out to us!"

"You do realize that this dragon just worked to save your life, and so it has a vested interest in making sure you stay alive, so it didn't waste its time, right?" Britt countered. The dragon nodded its head, accentuating this remark, shaking the three women on its back.

"I very rarely have seen a dragon lose its patience," Tara inclined her head and whispered from in front of Sadie.

"Are we about to?" Sadie leaned her head in closer and replied out of the corner of her mouth.

"Granny, I hope so," Tara replied, sucking in her cheeks, her smile still peeking through.

Sadie's grin expanded freely across her face, calmly and without hold as she took charge of the situation. "Eve, you'll be fine, love."

"He fell," she bawled, hands and chest on the saddle, feet halfway up in midair.

"We both know that's not the case," Sadie said, dismounting the ride. With steady and sure paces, she walked to the back of Eve. Interlocking her fingers below Eve's right foot and hoisting the light girl up, Sadie exhaled. Tara grabbed Eve's hand and pulled from above, while Britt laughed about the scene. Sadie rubbed her hand on Eve's lower back in a motherly assurance that all would be right.

Sadie had no idea if all would be alright, but it could not be worse than the prospects of the situation that they were facing. She glanced back at Tara, whose eyes quickly roamed upwards over the madame's body. A small smirk crossed Sadie's face, thinking that Tara had no idea what that ass could do.

Sadie sashayed back to her spot on the dragon and attempted to get back into the stirrups and hoist herself up. Unfortunately, all eyes were on her, which made her ultra-aware of her having an audience. Her stage fright made the mounting of her dragon less than graceful.

A chuckle to her upper right gave rise to her fury.

"Shut your pie trap, or I'll make you shut it!" Sadie reprimanded Britt, landing with her stomach across the beast. She shifted, swinging her right leg over her dragon, careful not to kick Eve behind her. The pommel, stiff in her hands, gave her some semblance of grounding on the rocky steed. The saddle was big enough for Sadie and Tara to ride in, but the other two were stuck on the end, riding bareback.

"And how are we supposed to get our friend to fly?" Britt called out to Tara, who was in front of the crew.

With a sideways smile in her eyes and a soft pat to the creature's side with her right hand, Tara said, "Hee-ya!" Off the dragon walked, toward the clearing. She made the dance steps seem so simple. Sadie marveled at the synchronicity between the two.

Tara held the reins in her left hand at the front, with Sadie seated almost on Tara's rear end. Eve clutched onto Sadie's stomach for dear life. Poor girl must have thought that she would be able to save her from the unknown. Past Eve, Britt lounged on a jagged scale thing that jutted out from Camelia's back, looking as if there were no place that she would rather be.

When she reached the clearing with more room, the wings spread out to either side of the women in majestic beauty. The icy-blue dragon lurched into the air with a start, her body bouncing to and fro, every time those padded feet hit the ground on her take off. Forward and forward Camelia propelled until she arrived at the very end of the road—the worship house—and she blasted overhead, knocking the shingles off the roof. Why anyone prayed to the Trinity when dragons held the magic of the moment would forever defy logic.

Up the dragon soared. The air that seemed to rush toward Sadie's lungs, filling her with a new sense of acuity with every gasp.

The glint in Tara's green, haloed brown eyes caught the sunlight and reflected back at Sadie as she turned around and checked on her fellow riders. The effect was magical. And the stare held. What Tara saw, Sadie had no idea. But to be truly gazed upon in a steadfast, accepting manner, without judgment, without expectation, comfort dwelt within that gaze ...

She reflected that gaze back as a smile. Wholeheartedly given. Distributed to one. And only one. And Tara smiled back.

They soared up and up above the heights for hours before they stopped in the shelter of a hill for the night.

Britt brought kindling over to the group.

"How did you know where to find that?" Sadie asked her.

"I'm simple, not simple-minded. I grew up having to make fires," Britt responded.

This far from the enchanted town, the temperature seemed to have elevated by a few degrees. Sadie spread the blankets over the rocky ground to sleep on, as if she were preparing a picnic in a meadow. "Thought you only stoked fires in men's hearts, from the way you tell it, Britt."

"Oh, you know you were a heartbreaker in your time, Sadie," Britt teased her.

Sadie smirked, smoothing out the corners of the woolen creations they had borrowed from the general mercantile before leaving. No sense in not sleeping as best as they could; they would need their energy the next day to get through hanging on for dear life. "I didn't break hearts; I ripped them out and stomped on them."

She remembered the men who had greeted her upon her departure from the boat. The "aunt" who had greeted her and hid her in an ultra-dramatic, attention-grabbing way at the port. The way the men had lined up outside the door for the next calling hour. As if she were fresh meat for the dragons. What she wouldn't tell her past self about how to command that sitting room now.

Britt cocked her head, seeming to consider this image before she asked, "Really?"

"No! I'm not you!"

Britt threw a thickly circumferenced stick, no longer than her forearm, at Sadie, hitting her squarely across the chest. "What was your biggest conquest, then?"

"A lady never tells," Eve rejoindered from the edge of the fire, repositioning her knees under herself as she jumped into the conversation.

"Fine, what was the weirdest thing you ever had to do for a client?" Britt smirked as if she had painted Sadie into a corner.

"Oh!" Eve's squeak punctuated the turn of the conversation.

"We all know that yours has to do with that guy with the chair in the corner who wanted to watch you, Eve," Britt told her.

"Yeah, but you have it wrong! He wanted to watch me sew, and then he took out a knife and cut his finger off. He then wanted me to kiss it better and sew it back on."

"You never told me this!" Sadie's eyes bulged.

"I didn't need to. Healer Frumo was in the hallway when I peeped out for help under the guise that I was looking for more thread. He got everything sorted and cleaned, and the man passed through town and we never saw him again."

What else did Sadie not know about that had occurred in her house? She thought she knew everything. She marveled at her friends, though. If men's secrets were gold, these women would be rich. A more vindictive soul would have extorted the men for more money. She knew that a blackmail scheme would catch up with her and eventually kick her out of her place and her town.

Sadie had seen many clients over the years. Her rates were higher than the others based on her experience. She maintained a small client list in order to balance her time with managing the business aspects of the brothel. She racked her brain for one of the more interesting stories. Kink-shaming was prohibited in her house, but that did not mean that she had not seen some bizarre shit.

Sadie caught her thought and chimed in. "One time, a client wanted me to reenact his birth with him. Like full on, he started sitting on my stomach stark naked with my knees bent high and my feet on the bed near my back." She lied down on the ground to demonstrate. "Then, as I made pushing and grunting noises, he turned his head forward toward the ceiling so it was between my legs. He slowly sidled down me, and I pretended to push him out through my legs. At one point, he yelled, 'Give it one more big one!' He sprinkled water all over everything. There was so much water that if I had urinated, he would not have known. So there he was, lying so his naked butt touched mine, and I don't know where he had hidden it, but this golden colored gelatin thing that wiggled appeared in his hands. He put it on my stomach and yelled, 'Afterbirth!' Turns out it was this gelatin placenta that he had had his sister make for him under the guise that it was a joke for a friend. So that's now sliding down my stomach and over my front crack before he tossed it across the room, as if my vaginal muscles were that powerful. After all this, he stuck his thumb in his mouth, curled up at the base of the bed where he was lying, between my feet, and he proceeded to sleep. I was so dumbfounded by what had just occurred that I remained there motionless. When he woke up, he paid me triple my fee, then told me that he could move on with his life now. Never could look me in the eye in town."

When Sadie completed her story and her demonstration on the ground, she returned to a seated position. All three women's jaws were dropped.

"Who was it?" Eve broke the silence. Normally, Sadie would not have given the client's name away, but the man was probably holed up frozen with his sister's gelatin mold.

"Louis Gavulier."

"He never could look me in the eye in town, either, so I don't think his birthing had anything to do with it," Britt added.

"He probably thinks that I told you, which up until now, I hadn't!"

"Couldn't look at me, either, but I know it's because I look like his sister from the back," Eve added.

"Britt, what about you?" Tara piped in before glancing back at Sadie. Sadie hoped that Tara did not think any less of her after sharing her story. Hopefully, Tara had a story of her own, so Sadie would not feel as though she were the only one with weird men in her life. The smile on Tara's face showed that she was enjoying the banter of these females. Sadie reasoned that their lives were colorful, and they were not dumb to the intricacies of the human condition; perhaps Tara saw that, too.

Britt stretched her legs out in front of her, leaning back on her arms. "Weirdest I got was a client who wanted me to put all these strange things in my mouth." She licked her well-renowned lips, bringing her audience's attention to them better than red lipstick. "He had brought a bag of food and other items, and he eagerly watched me insert them through my lips and pull them out. Then, after each time that I did this, he took each spit-covered item and rubbed it on his cock. Just rubbed. I was going to get Healer Frumo involved at the end because one of the items was covered in rust, which I only noticed when I tasted the metallic tang in my mouth. But the client didn't want me to talk at all, even as he was leaving. I tried to mime that his dick was covered in orange rust, but I think that he thought I was waving my hands around my crotch, asking him to put it inside me. He was adamant about leaving with his hard-on. So, I couldn't tell him that, hey, he might want to see the Healer. Frumo told me that I would be fine, but the man was in big trouble if he had any open wounds on his cock. The way that I saw him rubbing those things on himself, he must have torn skin. If only those standing graveside knew that Mr. Jack Wiesterman had con-cock-ted tetanus."

Eve chuckled at the pun.

"No laugh, Sadie?" I thought you would enjoy that one."

She did not always get to exercise her silly side, so she was delighted with the opportunity to play. "It was ri-dick-ulous." The four laughed. Sadie noticed that Tara's eyes made beautiful moon crescents when she laughed.

"What about you, Tara?" Sadie asked, hoping to learn more about the lovely healer. "You see any weird sexual exploits?" Her imagination created a scene in her mind involving green grass and sexy female dragonhands, all while dragons roamed about. Maybe a tail would join in. Could be fun. *What would make Tara moan?*

"Nah, nothing really besides the occasional greenhorn dragonhand who tries to get frisky with a dragon only to find out that a) his cock isn't big enough and

b) dragons can pick up and fly away, leaving you holding your cock in your hand while others stare at you."

Sadie wondered if Tara were holding back or if she were inexperienced. But no, she had to know what she liked. Though Sadie was ten years older, Tara was not a child. Thinking back, Sadie thought about all the innuendoes that had passed between them. Tara had never backed down from one. Perhaps she was savvier than she appeared.

Back on the dragon the next morning, they flew over ravines and meadows. Everything that was frozen appeared as frosted as a cake on Trinity's Nigh. Finally, they reached a vertical sheet of hazy film that stilled before them. Tara yelled, "Sit back a moment!" as she outstretched her hands to either side of her, palms facing the film. The layer seemed to fall to the ground like a theater curtain cut from its rods. Through they flew, the sensation as of a thick waterfall that wouldn't drown them, yet they all held their breaths because three-quarters of them didn't know otherwise. But they had nothing else to lose. They had been this close to death before. Wasn't everything that happened since then merely a taunt at it?

Once the mist cleared, Sadie could make out green. Emerald carpets of grass speckled with kelly clovers. Deep forest shades of evergreen. Peat coated the bark of trees, climbing up the trunks to reach the sun. Fronds of fern and sage decorated the flatlands. The few rolling hills wore a velvety hunter color that reflected more of an artichoke color when the light bounced off it at the right angle.

It had been so long since the vibrancy of life had caressed her pupils that the strangeness caused the joy to tear up and fall to her cheeks. A warm handful of understanding captured the middle of her hand. Through her tears, she saw Tara turn her head to turn back to her and nod, as if to say, "I completely understand." The tiny, calloused hand found hers and slipped around her soft palm, giving it a gentle squeeze.

She did not quite know why she found the touch so calming. Or those eyes so beguiling. Or that mouth so tantalizing. She only knew that they would face this together.

Twenty-Two

Britt

The four of them carried on a short way. Until they swooped and landed at what appeared to be a large house, possibly the length of half of the street that Sadie's house dwelt upon.

Camelia landed smoothly, as if she understood that she carried precious cargo. As soon as the women had their feet upon the ground, the creature leapt into the sky, bound for only Tara knew where.

"Now what?" Britt said, exasperated. "We came here for dragons, and the one we have left us." She truly had hoped to see a yard with at least three grazing within it.

Tara grinned, shaking her head. "She didn't leave us. She went to the meadow to go and find the others." Britt raised her eyebrow in response to ask Sadie for further clarification, but Sadie deferred to Tara.

"Let's go inside."

Britt would have preferred to have gone with Camelia to find the other dragons.

The vastness of the manor astounded her. The building itself could have held four of Sadie's houses within it. With its immaculate white front porch and solid brick exterior, the house did not look to have stood there for four generations, as Tara had informed them on their way. She could hardly hear the information over Eve's whimpering, though.

Bless Eve's heart, the woman had held on to Sadie for dear life. All four of them had smashed so close together on Camelia that the stains from their sweat were indiscernible from one another's. The saddle had almost remained on the ground back in Grogtown, where Tara had tossed it amid her mumbled swearing about the only other human inhabitant in the vicinity. Sadie had talked her into putting it back on the dragon.

Was DB a problem to Britt? Yes, but nothing that she couldn't handle. He was merely a gnat in the sky, swarming around her head. She would shoo him away here and there; sometimes she would ignore him. Pestering him did not place high on her to-do list.

She recalled that, before the town froze, the man had visited the brothel to demand an audience with Sadie.

Britt, who had stepped in for Sadie to answer the door and to welcome clients, told him that Sadie was eating her one large meal of supper for the day, and that Eve was available. The man refused to have anyone except the "original." She guessed that the man was very particular about his pussy, though he didn't have much of a past record at the brothel as far as she knew. She shooed him away that day with her hands on her hips as she ensured he walked well away from the house. "And if you come back, choosing to demand things out of a woman who has too many men to contend with already, I'll get that shotgun from the wall of the saloon next door, and you will never get the option to come back again."

Snapping out of her reverie, Britt's eyes refocused to track the dragon, yearning to accompany it to what she assumed was its thunder. She did not want to desert her own herd, though. The travelers stretched their backs, dampened from each other's sweat and closeness. Though it had taken a few days, that last leg of the trip seemed the longest. Tara had to keep taking out the map to check it to ensure they were on course. The move did not quite inspire trust in the navigator, but Britt did not mind. Seeing dragons was worth it.

Britt shuffled behind Sadie and Eve into the manor. Both had been proper members of society at one point; she marveled at their poise as they approached the home. She pictured them in their daily town clothes, hair tidy and boots cleaned, calling on a high-ranking society member. Would they have even looked at her if they had passed her on a street out east?

Sadie and Eve differed in every way on the outside, though. Where Sadie was tall, Eve was shorter. Sadie was more than fifteen years older than Eve, with a mature shape and a calm that came with dealing with the daily chaos the world threw at her door. Eve wore less clothing than Sadie, but mainly because she was expected to always be at the ready. Plus, she had the prettiest undergarments. Eve had confided to Britt one day that she elected to spend her money on items that would make her happy in the moment, much as the reason that men spent money on her. Whereas Britt preached the motto that she was not here for a long time, just a good time, Eve tended to display it.

As soon as they all discarded their dusty shoes in the front foyer, Tara called for fresh clothes. A woman in her sixties brought tea, ushering them to a beautiful front room with paintings on the ceiling and white furniture. Peeking around a corner, Britt noticed that the room seemed out of place in decoration from the wooden paneling they saw in the front foyer. The older woman poured out four cups, adding a sugar cube to each. Britt hastily slurped the divine concoction, accidentally burning her mouth. The cool cucumber sandwich that she picked off the platter acted as a balm. She had devoured four finger sandwiches when she finally looked at her companions. The other three women also engaged fully with the food. Out of the corner of her eye, she noted that several dresses of various prints and sizes hung over the railing of the stairs. She stood from the chair, wiping the dust off the seat cushion and hoping she would not be in trouble for spoiling the nice furniture. A printed sundress halfway down the pile attracted her attention, and she pulled the others off. Cotton! The dresses were made of luxurious, light, and breathable cotton! She stripped bare next to the staircase. Slipping the garment over her head, she breathed in the freshly laundered scent. It draped loosely around her curves, big in some areas. But she had never felt so comfortable. Her face hurt from smiling, and she closed her eyes. When they opened, her friends smiled back at her.

After the others had changed and finished their tea, Tara led them around in a tour of the house. For her having been gone a good week or two, the house was immaculate and dust-free. Aside from the sand they had emptied out of their boots that speckled the entryway. Tara's pistol and belt hung from the second hook in the entryway.

The whole time the tour occurred, Britt kept peeking out of windows, trying to find the one with the best view of the creatures. Where were they?

As they approached a pretty sunlit room, she thought she detected movement from out the four-paned window hidden behind lace. She wanted to run into the room to see, but felt as if she would be trespassing on an innocent childhood that she did not belong in.

Elaborately painted, delicate dolls lined one set of shelves. A checkerboard and markers peeked out from the lace-edged quilt that did not quite reach the floor from the top of the bed. A toddler-sized white felt hat, blazoned with the initials "MF," adorned a hook on a door that Britt suspected held ornate pink gowns and white cotton sundresses.

"Here's Marjorie's room. My niece is super sweet and mischievous. Also, her insights on the world around her blow me away. I miss hearing her talk. I bet she would love to meet all of you one day!" Tara narrated as they passed by.

Jealousy twinged throughout her body. This little girl, whoever she was, had the opportunity to play with toys and grow up with dragons.

Britt's thoughts were interrupted by her blonde friend's exclamation that brought new information to light.

Twenty-Three

Eve

"You're a Fuentes!" The claim burst out of her mouth, as if it were vomit from a stable hand on a Saturday night.

The swirled moldings on the doorframes. The intricately carved stairway balusters with small, tasteful dragons on the newels. The crystal chandelier fixtures in every hall with their matching wall sconces. Eve knew the manufacturers of them all from the big houses out east. She knew that she was not standing in a poor house. And when she passed the family crest with the "F" etched into the stone fireplace in the main living space, she could not keep her deductions in.

All three women turned and looked at her. She covered her mouth, embarrassed that the realization had bolted out of her mental space and into reality.

"You good?" Tara replied. Eve could only nod her head up and down rapidly, hoping that her assent proved that Tara could continue, and Eve would mentally move on with her.

The Fuentes family was legendary across the circles of folk who wished to involve themselves in the business of dragons. Business. If you could call it that. Everyone dreamed of having a Fuentes dragon, but everyone she knew who had one had obtained it in a different manner.

Her uncle had bartered with a drunk who seemed inclined to beat his dragon. Why the dragon hadn't burned the drunk straight up out of self-preservation still baffled her.

A suitor had claimed to have a dragon from the ranch, but when he displayed the dragon to Eve, he showed off an intricate F. True aficionados understood that the Fuentes family would *never* brand a dragon.

Once, she eye-flirted with a man in her theater box, whom she had seen mouth the word "Fuentes" to his cohort. The sheer look of arrogance that followed the word turned her off completely to the remainder of the intrigue.

The one time she fell in love, she heard Archie wish that he understood the power of a dragon and that of a Fuentes. Alas for him, he ceded to the fact that he would die forever musing on their mysteries and powers. Little did he know how correct his prophesies would be. Maybe dragons lived on the Staircases, and he would see them in his eternal dreams.

So when Eve realized that the hardwood floor upon which she stood had been made of timber burnt down by dragons, that the flooring had been sealed together with the heated breath of dragons, on glue from epoxy made from dragons, that the leather skin had been made of dragons, she realized that she had not fully understood the reverence that the Fuentes family carried for the creatures.

Everything in the house spoke of the family's devotion—-some said relation—-to the magical creature. No wonder this woman was a healer with strong powers!

Eve's stockinged feet slipped on the polished wood in the library. She bent over a deep leather sofa, holding on to the arm for support with her left hand as she pulled the stockings off with her right. The warm air did not necessitate them, anyway.

"I can't believe you're here all by yourself," Eve murmured as she stared at the books in the wood-paneled study. The cool floor stuck to her bare feet, making a Cckk sound as she moved around between shelves.

"Well, aside from my brother, his daughter, and I'm assuming eventually his lover, and then all the staff, sure, I'm alone," Tara smiled.

"Where are they at? Can we expect them anytime soon?" Eve turned her head momentarily from the shelves to look at Tara for her reply to Britt's question. Tara sidestepped Britt, who had entered the room completely and now stood at the window.

"Maker knows. They're off traipsing around the world." Tara shrugged, looking at Sadie, who nodded in acknowledgment of her speaking.

Running her fingers along the tops of books, she skimmed the ledges for the oldest-looking tome. Eve spied a browned, frayed spine. Inserting two fingers into the top edges, she tipped it backward before the rest of her hand pulled it out. She opened *On the Foundations of Dragon Magic* to the endpaper and then held the book to her nose. Thumbing quickly through the pages as one would a deck of cards, she inhaled deeply that old book smell, immediately transported back in time to those moments nestled in bed as a teenager with her book and cream tea. When she would dream of love and her own happily ever after. How close she had been to having those happy moments forevermore!

Sighing, she put the book back and turned her head to return to the tour. Everyone had left her to her own devices. Reluctantly, she stepped into the hallway, scanning the sounds for which room her companions were in. Tara's head peeked out from a room on the left.

"You can stay in there, Eve. When supper is rounded up, I can send it up to you. Don't know when that will be, because I need to find the cook and tell her that we'll be here a couple days."

Twenty-Four

Britt

When Eve split off to investigate the books in the study, Britt felt the urge to also separate herself.

"Tara, where are the dragons?" She had checked every window that they passed on the tour, yet could not tell where these beasts were. *Had Tara lied to them? Was this all a ruse to get them to go back with her and abandon Grogtown?* Though Britt could not see a clear reason why Tara would do that. She had an Oath to upkeep. Healer Frumo would mumble about his Oath in his sleep.

"What do you mean?"

"Are they out back, or where are they kept?"

Tara's brows furrowed indignantly. "They're not *kept* anywhere. They come and go as they please. And believe me, they go *everywhere*."

"Is there a best spot to see them? Why haven't I seen any yet?"

Tara looked at the wooden grandfather clock. "They should be out by the creek. Do you want me to take you?"

"If you point me in a direction to start walking, then I'll be good."

"Go out the front door, hang a right so you walk past the side of the house, and keep going. If you see a man with a rusty colored mustache that you badly want to snip off, that's Mr. Milton, the overseer. He would be happy to answer any questions, but also, if you see him, can you let him know that I'm home temporarily and can answer any questions he might have?"

Britt smiled and nodded. She turned and headed as quickly as her feet could carry her. Once she got past the corner of the house, she started jogging and then broke into a sprint. Her heart would burst with excitement. How many dragons would there be? Would they let her touch them?

Running in the sun, she began giggling.

She ran over a small hill and jolted to a stop with a gasp. Shivers painted her skin with the realization of what lay in front of her.

Dragons. Every color, every size. Some rested, some flew. Dragonhands speckled the meadow around the creek, tending to the creatures and looking like nits in hair.

Their majesty accentuated the vastness of the lands.

She longed to go down to see them. Walking slowly, so as not to scare them like a pack of geese that would fly away, she made her way down the side. She stood in a grassy spot. Five feet away from her stood two dragons, making guttural sounds and moving their heads at each other in some sort of communication.

A laugh escaped her chest, alerting the two creatures to her presence.

The sun shone off their iridescent scales. A light purple highlighted the browns of their exteriors. Their amber eyes searched her before bowing their heads in a genteel fashion of greeting.

"They're brothers. You can tell by the colors. Their mama's got a gorgeous purple to her and their pa's got this shoeshine brown color." The mustachioed man who fit Tara's description of Mr. Milton walked up to her.

"I'm Britt," she said, holding out her hand in introduction to the man. "Tara brought us back to round up some dragons and save the world."

"Oh, did she now?" His amused face lit up at her straightforwardness. When she nodded in reply, he told her, "I'll be heading up to the house to check in with her, then. I wonder what her plans are. That woman never likes to be away from the dragons for too long."

Taking Britt's silence for listening, when in fact she was watching in awe as the two dragons began to wrestle with each other, Mr. Milton carried on in his conversation.

"Has she said anything more? What kind of mood is she in?"

Britt could not quite say. Sadie would have a better read on Tara, especially since she had been behind her for most of the journey. As far as Britt knew, Tara had one emotion: determined. As long as Britt was on that train with her, the two of them were on good terms. Otherwise, she needed to get out of the way and let Tara through.

"Well, any of the men out here would be happy to show you around—"

"I bet they would," she laughed.

"They'll only get handsy if you invite it. Perfectly safe here. Though contrary to popular belief, you're the safest around the dragons. Especially the females. They are the best of the dragons." He thought a moment as he ran his fingers over his lip hair. "In fact, come this way." He wound around several dragons before he placed his hand gently on the shoulder of one that was lounging.

"Retta, dear," he sing-songed at her. The big eyes popped open and assessed the situation. "I'm leaving Britt in your care. She's spirited." How had he gathered such an impression of her already? It was almost impertinent of him.

In response to her unvoiced question, he said, "I'm around these wild creatures every day. I know when words are spoken without them ever being uttered. I know the feelings shared by the mere twitch of an eye. I recognize another spirited creature when I see one. You'll be good with Retta."

He walked away, leaving the two to examine one another.

The large amber eyes looked at her straight on, as if they watched her every move, yet did not expect a motion. Most dragons, she was learning, had amber eyes. Much like Tara's. The sunlight painted them gold.

"You're beautiful," Britt gushed at Retta once Mr. Milton was out of earshot. The dragon nodded her head.

"You can understand me? I thought that was something made up in books." A toothy grin spread across Retta's snout.

"May I touch you?" She always asked for consent in the clearing in Grogtown whenever she sat with those dragons. She tried not to develop firm feelings for them; they were transient creatures, moving from place to place as they wished. Sometimes they would accompany a particular human that they liked; sometimes they would dump whatever human they had carried into the town, only to depart immediately thereafter. Even the messenger dragons that delivered the mail and packages never stayed.

Retta pushed her snout towards Britt's outstretched hand. Raising her head up and down in a scooping motion, she pet Britt's palm.

A huge smile spread across the girl's face. "You're remarkably smooth," Britt said. "I bet that helps you fly." Though she read the chapter on aerodynamics, she had not quite grasped all the concepts. School had not been a priority growing up in the Uriah household. Finding and making dinner had been.

The dragon dropped her snout and pushed her eyes so they were looking directly into Britt's. From Britt's periphery, she noticed some movement. One of the dragon's claws gently pushed Britt's dark hair out of her face and tucked it behind her ear. Maintaining eye contact, Britt reached her hand towards the dragon and hooked it on her giant arm. Pure exhilaration rushed through Britt's veins. With that, the dragon scooped Britt up between both of her claws.

"Whoa! What are we doing?" Laughter sprang from her diaphragm. A dry tongue licked Britt's face.

A gust of hair blew into Britt's face as the dragon flapped its wings, lifting off the ground.

"We're flying!?" The dragon winked back at her. The strong claws kept her tucked in, as if in a nest. The trees and grass became smaller. A few other dragons looked up as they made their way overhead.

The loud wind gusted around them, silencing even the laughter that escaped Britt. Retta kept them moving horizontally once they reached an altitude of her liking. Probably keeping it gentle for her. But Britt had never been a gentle girl.

She twisted her body to look up at Retta. The motion grabbed Retta's attention. Britt patted her back, motioning that she wanted to climb on.

As Britt trusted this creature to switch her from both claws to one claw midair, she also trusted her own safety when she was transferred by two talons gripping her around the waist to the animal's back.

She momentarily gripped the scale that protruded from Retta's neck. Her legs tucked instinctively around the dragon's body. She could feel the motions of calm breathing between her thighs. Sweat made grasping the protruding scale difficult. She kept having to take turns wiping each of her hands on her backside.

Retta took a sudden drop, and Britt's stomach tickled with the sensation. Tears streamed down her face. Here she was in the middle of a beautiful landscape, sunlight sparkling on the water, riding on the back of Mother Maker's greatest creation.

It was everything and nothing like she had ever imagined. The breeze whooshed against her face, yet she could still see. The swooping and turning of the dragon scared her at first. As they continued onward, Retta would cock her head left or right a moment before she would turn, so Britt could brace herself better and move with the dragon rather than in contrast.

When they landed, the overseer approached her to help her off the dragon. She quickly rebuked him for holding out his hands towards her hips.

"I can handle myself," she chided him.

The man stood back and watched her awkwardly get off the beast. She struggled enough before Retta arched her back so that she could slide down the side of her.

"Not all men are evil, ma'am," Mr. Milton told her with a somber look in his eye, almost as if he were sorry for her.

"And not all women are kind, sir," she responded.

"In my experience, most are kind until an evil man teaches them not to be." He sighed. "And that might be one of the saddest facts in a world that Mother Maker made out of kindness and love."

"Well, no mother that I've ever known can be said to have been kind."

"That's a tragedy."

Britt shrugged. "That's life. We all don't all grow up in manors on dragon-lands. Some of us dream of the dragons, while others dream with them."

She turned and walked away, running her hand over the dragon scales as she departed, humming a tune she had sung with Grace at the saloon.

Now that she was with the dragons, why would she ever leave them? Yes, they should probably go help the others, but what had the town done for her? She could go anywhere, and right now she wanted to be there at Titan's Creek in her little bit of peace.

Britt could live up here in the sky forever. She did not want to return to Grogtown. *Would the others let her stay while they returned and dealt with DB?* No, she would not even ask them. They would see this insane situation through to the end together. But she would make it back to Titan's Creek. She promised herself that much.

Twenty-Five

Tara

When Tara had said a couple of days, she had secretly wished she could be saying "forever." She did not want to return to Grogtown. That shitty latrine paled in comparison to her gorgeous refuge, her Titan's Creek. She would help the women round up some dragons to send back to the sick town with them. Maybe the Oath wouldn't come for her, since this act would still technically be helping them still technically. She had never heard of its taking anyone's life, anyway. Probably a bunch of dragonshit.

She wished Naz were there to run ideas by him. His desk chair did not send his logic and advice to her body through osmosis, sadly. Resting her temple in her hand and her elbow on the desk, she stared out at the map on the wall.

She missed Marjorie. She missed her family. She missed the joy that she knew before she had arrived in Shittown-er, Grogtown.

Self-assured steps approached behind her. Assuming it was Eve returning to gawk at the house more, Tara plastered a fake smile on her face and turned around. Seeing it was Sadie, she quickly removed the mask.

"You know," Sadie said, "it might not be as pretty as your house here, but that house is the best the three of us ever had. We were happy."

"You were sex workers," Tara retorted in her divided mentality.

Sadie nodded her head. "Proudly. I received more respect owning that brothel than I ever did from a caller out East. And I was more sure of myself in my own home that I built with my own hands than in the place that man purchased for himself. "

She entered, sitting herself on the sofa in front of the map at which Tara had been staring.

"You could be anything, why. Why that?"

"Because as much as man hates admitting it, he needs woman. Countless men entered my door looking for something: love, attention, release, quiet. Things his fellow man could not give him. That's where the true power lies, Tara."

"In what?"

"In resilience, still being able to provide for another when everything has been stolen away. A man who would enter Britt's room, sure, he might ask for a blowjob. But her power was that they never owned her, despite her getting on her knees. And sweet Eve? They would never get her heart."

"What about you?"

"Bastards would never get my respect." She waited a minute, watching as Tara internalized what she had said. Tara deliberated each woman.

Sadie quietly interjected her thoughts. "You must ask yourself, Tara. Where does your power come from?"

"Dragons," she replied automatically.

"No. Where does your identity and your power over subjugation and the toxic male come from?"

"I have no choice in this matter. The Oath—"

"So where is your power over the Oath?"

Tara thought for a bit. She had never been challenged in quite that way.

"I don't know."

Sadie stood up and brushed the wrinkles from her skirt. "You will when you need to." She walked out the door, leaving an emptiness that Tara knew was not easily replaced. "Is there a room that I can nap in before dinner? I seem to be quite exhausted from the day's activities."

Tara led Sadie back up the stairs to the one of the many guestrooms. With an ulterior motive in her mind, she pointed Sadie to the room next to hers, separated only by a bathroom.

Tara tossed and turned all night, debating leaving the dragonlands or staying and sending the dragons back. The Oath would begin tingling in her feet soon if she did not make a decision. If she made the wrong decision, the Oath would surely take over her body in consequence. While in training, her teachers instilled in their pupils that ignoring the Oath meant death, and not a pretty one. Depending on the nature of the calling being ignored, a healer would face a different ending. Tara had no desire to die in general, but to be frozen from the inside out, she was learning, was horrendous.

As Sadie had questioned her, she thought to herself, where did she get off being higher than any other person on this continent? Why did she deserve to live in peace when that's all the others had wished for, too? Instead, Dimin had interrupted their lives. And damn it, that was not fair. Part of her was angry with these women. *Why had they not stood up to the man?* They put her life in jeopardy because of their own mistakes. And yes, not standing up to him was a mistake.

Tara flung the blankets off her, pulling the dressing gown over her night-gown. Her blood boiled. Crossing through the bathroom, she threw open the door to Sadie's bedroom. Through the window, she caught sight of the leaves in the tall trees outside the window. Their once happy green rapidly changed to a crimson red, mirroring Tara's rage. Waking to the magic that roared within the room, birds flew out of their resting places.

"Your complacency led to this continent being in the clutches of evil. WHY DIDN'T YOU DO ANYTHING?" Tara's voice echoed despite the room's being well-furnished.

Sadie immediately sat up in bed and blinked twice. She must not have been completely asleep yet. "We tried to do what we could think of. Are you angry because you would have done things differently? You, with your current knowledge and life experiences, would have chosen a different route? You are not us, and you are not in our shoes, so you do not get to pass judgment upon our actions." Sadie's voice cracked like a whip through the room. Taking a deep breath, Sadie continued in a lethally calm tone.

"And if you knew that something was amiss, why didn't you do anything sooner?"

"Why did you wait to be obligated to help us, when it was too late for so many?" Sadie paused, anger radiating off her like steam from a boiling kettle. "So before you start throwing stones at us, I suggest that you," she pointed her finger at Tara, "check to ensure that your glass house is impenetrable." Sadie crossed her arms and stared at Tara.

"Nothing has happened to my house, as you can see," Tara quipped. "The same cannot be said for yours."

"Well, doesn't that make you the lucky one." Sadie's voice, soft yet heavy, carried truth.

She was lucky.

As an extra nail in the coffin, Sadie added, "We all fucked up. Which is why we all need to help each other fix this."

Tara turned and left the room before Sadie could see the hurt that the truth drew from her heart. Sadie was right. She could have acted to help when the papers had begun commenting on weird occurrences. But because she had not received a summons from the Association, she remained in her happy, cozy home.

Sadie had reminded Tara that she had the power to fix something bad in this world and was shirking from her responsibility as an inhabitant to do it. Feigned ignorance was dishonorable to her and the way that she had been raised in service to the dragons. Tara felt properly chastised and guilty. Her Oath was not calling her to fix this. Her conscience was.

Yesterday, others chose her for themselves. Today, she chose to live in service to herself and others.

She wondered how the other healers were getting on.

Curled up on the sofa, book open on her lap, Eve seemed peacefully unaware of Tara's inner turmoil as she entered the office and sat down at the desk. She quietly pulled a piece of paper and ink out of the drawer.

The filled fountain pen restored her confidence. This blank page needed only to be written on for her thoughts to be communicated far and wide.

"To the esteemed directors of the Association," she scrawled in her quick, scratchy handwriting. She paused, dripping a small blot onto the paper at the comma.

Stirrings from the sofa in her periphery caught her attention. Her eyes caught Eve's eyelashes fluttering open.

The woman, dressed in a long white nightgown of Tara's deceased sister-in-law, stretched her hands over her head. The book fell onto the floor, and Eve grimaced before picking it up.

Inspecting it, Eve commented, "I always worry that these books are going to wind up much more damaged when they fall."

"The most delicate objects oft hold the most strength with which to stand the test of time," Tara quoted from *Mother Maker's Manual*.

"Funny how men think we're the weak ones. It's almost as if they cannot afford themselves the moment to say 'I am weak.' If they would, they would find the moment passes quicker than perseverating on how to be a man through it. Whatever a man may be."

"I'm so tired of being the strong one, though, Eve."

"You don't have to be. You have us. Maker knows that Sadie is stronger than any man around, and Britt will end a man in conversation. You ever sit back and relax and let someone else play leading lady?"

Tara chuckled to herself. "No, it has always been me holding down the fort. Even when my brother's wife died."

"Well, you are one of us now. And we take turns holding each other up. When I was down, Britt lifted me up. That's what friends do. So we will help you, too."

That simple statement won the war within her. Tara crumpled up the piece of paper she had started to write upon and tossed it into the wastebasket. The next letter that she wrote to the Association would be an update on how many people had survived in Grogtown.

Twenty-Six

Sadie

Sadie had never met anyone like Tara. Beneath the logical veneer that she seemed to only show others, she saw a woman who cared very deeply for others. She wanted so much to know her vulnerabilities, to alert Tara that she was not alone in putting a hard shell around herself when dealing with the world.

"These men, Anaveh, they act like they can take and take and have no consequences. Or maybe they do have consequences, but the men don't care about them. Or the consequences are for someone else." Sadie audibly reasoned out the insanity of their current state. Shaking her head, she added, "I don't know." She felt a need to lead these women, yet could not even begin to start with whereto think where to start. She herself hadn't resolved herself with the proper outcome or the tactic.

Could the town be saved? Was it worth being saved?

Sure, there were many innocent lives there, but Tara was not wrong: they had not lifted a finger when Dimin came to town, bringing his rhetoric of bone-chilling hatred.

The day that Dimin arrived, he seemed possessed. Britt came home from a shift at the saloon, citing that Dimin would spout crazy rants that often ended with blaming everything on "her."

He was lethal with his common tongue, his polished look, as if he knew what he was doing, and he knew the way to do it. And his way was the only way. People would disappear if they dissented. Found seeming to have had heart attacks.

She recalled a time when Dimin flat-out froze someone's ears in the street, rendering the poor man deaf, simply because the man tried to offer an opposing view.

From "upstairs during Lounging Hour, she could hear a commotion. "There's no use in your listening to reason if you're not going to speak it," Dimin snapped at him, she could hear him say from upstairs during Lounging Hour. The man's screams instantly made everyone go soft that day.

They had known before Dimin arrived what had could happen. Grace had tried to warn them of his powers and the cold curse before she had left. The women had not expected the town to go under so quickly, though. At first, men continued to trickle into the house throughout the days and nights; business remained. But in no time at all, the air grew thinner. People grew gaunter. Streets grew bare, as those who didn't dissent succumbed to not making it out of their houses.

The saloon kept going. The brothel kept going. People needed warmth—whiskey and women.

It took Eve first. Eve with her impossibly delicate body and dreaming spirit.

Sadie had made coffee one morning, and Eve did not slink downstairs to grab it. In fact, she was still sleeping when Sadie went up to check on her after lunch. Putting her hand on her head, she did not notice a fever. In fact, if anything, the forehead sucked the heat out of the back of Sadie's hand as if starved for a meal. Eyelashes fluttered.

"Mama?" Eve's young voice piped up.

"No, it's Sadie."

"Oh, okay, can you bring Mama, please? Tell her I'm feeling quite indisposed for calling today."

Sadie shushed her, tucking the tendrils of her hair back behind her ears. The girl fell back to sleep. When she came down three hours later, she walked about as if nothing had happened. She had returned to her normal self. The absurdity of the cold sickness. The inhumanity that it wouldn't even let you know that you were failing. Wouldn't even give you a chance to say farewell to your present, as it yanked you back to somewhere else.

She had learned later that it was the past. At the time, she had thought it was a delusion. With the cold sickness, she lived through a new kind of hell: repetition of the worst times of her life.

For all of the horrors, she wondered why the street was as silent as fresh falling snow and not filled with shrieks and cries.

Perhaps everyone's Below the Staircase meant silent, uncomforted tears, and in this weather, not even the salt of those tears could keep the tears from freezing. Below was not hot. Below was cold and absent of love and hope.

Death became the neighbor greeting her on the street each morning. The grave-yard behind her house had more entrants than a summer carnival. A town meeting, if you would. The sickness claimed more souls than the cholera outbreak the previous June.

So, she would sit on her rocking chair, drinking coffee to warm her insides, wrapped in blankets to warm her outsides, and wonder which spot in that cemetery she would like to be hers. Whichever one had the best view of the dragons, if they ever returned.

Sadie followed the scent of coffee to the dining room the next morning. "You're right.," Tara said as she, Britt, and Eve sat at the big wooden table with cups of coffee in their hands. "And I apologize."

Words that men rarely uttered to Sadie without sarcasm or contempt in their voices.

"I don't know if I'm right, but I certainly have my views." Sadie shrugged.

"Then I'll say I agree and would like for us to help each other." Tara held out the carafe of coffee towards her. Eve offered her a cup. Taking each of them,

Sadie sat next to Tara, across from Britt and Eve. Neither of them sat at the head. The four of them would face this head-on together.

"This stay has been important. We had time to breathe and process, away from the trauma. But, we're going back to Grogtown, and we're going to free it of that stupid disease known as DB Egoman. I'm not living under the thumb of a man. I wouldn't let one dictate my life before, and I'm sure as hell not doing it now." Sadie promised the others.

"I have no skin in this game, except through the powers that I have inherited,. I am blessed with the ability to heal in a way that no one else can. The blight of the cold sickness needs to dissipate. I will heal," Tara said aloud.

"I have so much left to see in this world, but not if it's frozen. I'd like to learn how to fix other places that have had to deal with the insanity of one man." Eve piped up. "I want to thaw out our history and make it so we can make more."

"Well, I sure as hell am not going to let you all go into this alone," Britt said. "So it looks like we're all going back."

"I guess we need to round up some dragons." Tara smiled.

"Yee-haw!!" Britt yelled. "I'll get changed!"

As the two others prepared to go out into the meadow, Tara and Sadie waited for them outside. The warm afternoon sun had evaporated the morning's dew. A bright day was upon them. And not even the darkness of the future night would deter them.

"Dragon breath seemed to heal the sickness for Britt and Eve," Tara pondered aloud, feet in the dirt and boots in her hand.

"Not for me," Sadie reminded her.

"Oh, my sweet Sadie-girl," Tara patted her back. "Yes, it did. I am Tara Fuentes." Tara's back straightened, and Sadie imagined her commanding an army into battle. "I am descended from the dragons and carry their magic within me. And I breathed life back into you."

With that, she waved her work-loving hand over the land, and with a come-hither curl of her fingers, beckoned the land to her will. Up popped stalks, then leaves, then buds, and finally, poppy petals unfurled, redder than the sunrise. The blood red petals with the green that the land had begun to adopt, now released from its spell and saturated with the water of the melted ice.

A stunned Sadie took a step forward and plucked the healing flower from the earth. Those amber eyes of Tara's—were they aglow with the sun or the magic within her?

And in the magic of her eyes shone something deeper. A truth that had begun to take root and quickly blossom as this flower had done but moments ago.

Tara smiled and looked away, peeking back once. Sadie's eyes never left her.

Eve bolted out, "I feel like we're four wildflowers, blowing in the wind, wherever it may take us."

"I sure hope not, I for one will not be stomped underfoot," Britt wryly observed, bounding out the door behind her.

"When we came out here, I thought that we'd need more dragons so that we could box everyone in, like we did with Eve." Tara stared out towards the road. "But, I think there's a way that we can do the whole town at once. We could bring everyone back who is able to be healed." Tara proceeded to pace back and forth across the yard, toying with the frays on the ends of her long braid. "We wouldn't need to waste any more time while people slip away."

From her spot on the chair on the white front porch, Sadie twiddled her fingers. She had a funny feeling that interrupting Tara might not help the thought process. From all their experiences together, Sadie gathered that Tara was an internal thinker who needed to run through possibilities in order to make a decision that she could stand behind.

"And Maker knows that I can't stand to let anyone die that could possibly be saved."

Sadie picked a piece of lint from between her toes, marveling at the feel of the warm air rushing across the tops. She had no further thoughts on how to contribute to this situation. So, wait she would.

The curls of her own hair fell loose around her face, a welcome break from the tighter styles she was used to wearing at her home. It felt nice. Rocking back and forth in the chair, one strand fell across her eyes. Her finger twirled it around and around, like a whirling dust dervish.

So intent on twirling the piece, Sadie failed to realize that Tara had stopped pacing and was staring straight at her. Tara twirled her finger in the air slowly, mimicking Sadie's finger movements.

"That's it," Tara whispered. "We need something like a heat tornado. A vortex ..." She darted inside the house. Moments later, she ran out the door, holding a large book, flopping it with a thud onto the grass. Falling to her knees in front of it, her hands practiced a pattern of running back and forth down pages, and flipping them over, searching for what, Sadie knew not.

Tara's hands began pulling up the grass, then using her hands to make it rise and fall, and whip around in a circular pattern.

"A heat dome!" Tara's hands flew around, causing papers to whirl about. "We'll have the dragons fly around in a giant circle as they blow hot, magical air. It'll keep all the air in, much like we did with Eve, but for a defined area of the town. A dragon-created heat dome!"

Oh, the cleverness of this beautiful mind! Sadie's eyes took in everything about her. Tara opened her mouth, "So, um, in some pressure systems—"

Sadie held up her hand. "Don't waste time trying to teach me right now. It'll only exhaust precious time. I don't need to know the details. I only need to know what you need me to do."

Twenty-Seven

Eve

A ll four of the women were exhausted, three of them still working to fully regain their energy. One was exhausted from studying her books all day.

The warm air brought buzzing, swarming tiddly-nacks and their evening mating drones. Eve yawned and cracked her neck from side to side. She caught Britt's eyes next to her, trying to see the cards in her hand out of her periphery.

"I know your tricks, Britt," Eve told her dryly. "I've been living and working with you for years."

"You haven't seen all of them," Britt insinuated, blowing a kiss.

The sun's red-orange rays kissed the horizon line, letting its rainbow veil cover the sky. Dark dragon silhouettes moved across the scene like shadow puppets in front of a watercolor backdrop.

Next to Eve, Tara's feet jittered below the large wooden kitchen table as her hand hovered above each of her five cards before she chose one and threw it down. One of her brother's good bottles of bourbon sat half drunk in the middle of the table, next to the discard pile. Four glasses took turns out of order, clinking on the wood and making ice mix around them.

The silence in the room was replaced by the noise outside of it. Different colored eyes focused on the always reliable red and blacks.

Laying her hand down, Eve won a fourth round. Archibald had called her his lucky charm, but she had always considered it a term of endearment.

"I'm so exhausted, I can barely see the numbers anymore," she declared to the women. "Is any bedroom available to crash in?"

Without looking up from her cards, Tara replied, "Not mine or my niece's upstairs, but that one is pretty obvious with the dolls. And not Naz and Grace's down here."

At the mention of the name, Eve's head whipped around to Tara. Catching herself, she played it off nonchalantly. Surely other Graces existed. Oh, how she missed Grace and her wild, no holds no-holds-barred attitude.

"When will they be back?"

"Maker knows. Naz returned long enough to receive Marjorie and distribute any ranch instructions. Then, they set off to find Grace. I received a letter from him in the same post as my letter dispatching me out East."

"Do you like her?"

"It's hard not to. She has such a ride-or-die spirit and love of independence that quickly infects you with a sense of adventure."

Eve looked at Sadie, who at this point was staring intensely at Tara. "She sounds fun. Will they be marrying soon?"

"Nah, he told me that she made it very clear to him that she was not about to get trapped in a marriage, especially since she had just offed her fiancé who was chasing her across the country. Who can blame a girl, though, right? I wouldn't want to marry Dimin either."

Britt spat whiskey across the table, raining brown droplets down on Tara. "No SHIT," she said.

Twenty-Eight

Tara

Six eyes bored holes into Tara. "Tiddly-nacks are going to fly into your open mouths." She cut the silence. All three of them roared with simultaneous questions.

"The same Dimin who cast this cold sickness across the continent?" Eve asked.

"Does she have sandy-brown hair and jewel-like blue eyes?" Britt blurted.

"She's in love?" Sadie questioned.

Tara nodded at each of them, taken aback by the onslaught.

"How's Thalassa?"

"Do you have any letters from her?"

"How did she end up here?"

"Listen, I stayed out of her path for the most part. My brother worships the ground she walks on, though, and I'm pretty sure she'd go to Below the Staircase with him if she thought he'd ended up there. Which he wouldn't. Because he's Naz."

"But she's alive, yes. And well, yes. And still a thorn in the side of the world, while a rose to look at. Maker bless her." Tara threw back the rest of her whiskey. "I don't know about any Thalassa." Sadie swirled the ice around in her glass, not reaching for more, quiet in response.

"But how do you know Grace?" Tara asked.

"She used to work and live with us!" Eve said. "She's the one who told us that the cold sickness was coming. But we wouldn't leave. She's a delight and I miss her."

Britt sighed. "I miss drinking and whoring with her."

Tara laughed heartily. "Oh, Naz!" She shook her head at the ceiling as if he could hear her wherever he was. "You are certainly not bored now!"

"Nah, though he's probably quite tired!" Britt quipped back. Even Sadie smiled.

"Well, Tara, seems kismet that you found us. Maybe Mother Maker *does* have a plan." Eve beamed hope through her eyes.

"If she doesn't, here's to hoping one of the other two members of the Trinity do." Tara tipped her glass to the sky.

"And here's to Grace. May we all laugh with her again!" Britt toasted.

Three of them clinked their glasses and drank.

Feeling somewhat tired, Tara excused herself from the table momentarily. Stepping outside, the lush ground cradled her bare feet.

Tara stood, soaking the energy up from her soil, when Sadie approached her from behind. She knew that it was Sadie; she had come to appreciate the sureness of her steps when she had a problem or thought to work out.

"This moment, this is when I feel most alive. Firmly grounded where I stand, each individual blade of grass a cushion for my foot, sending energy to me. Surging through me, like I am invincible. And all I want to do is run out and use that energy for some good in this world. In that moment, between charging and deciding to move, that is the time I feel most alive with the potential that I can do. I haven't let anyone down with my limits."

"I've never felt that way anywhere else than at home," she whispered, "until I met you." Sadie reached out for her hand.

"When you touch me, it's as much a zap of energy as the ground I walk upon."

"What about when I do this?" Sadie reached her hand for Tara's cheek, bringing it to her own face. Tara had a moment to take a breath before Sadie's lips sucked in her own. Blood quickly left her brain, flocking to other areas of her body. She wanted more.

Feeling the quiver in Sadie's shoulders, she put her hands there and pulled back. They rested their foreheads together. Tara's face questioned Sadie. She didn't quite understand the quiver.

"If you hurt, I want to heal you, Sadie."

"I never hurt when I'm with you, Tara."

"May dragons curse me if you ever do."

Twenty-Nine

Eve

Wine and whiskey bottles in hand, the four women traipsed out toward the creek. The air was warm with a cool breeze, making ripples in the creek where they walked barefoot. The cotton dresses blew at their ankles, their hair whipping about. They looked like the most beautiful four-witch coven about to dance under the moonlight.

Eve looked about herself, realizing, though she seemed small in the greater scheme of things, this tiny moment in time was a great chapter in her book. Surefooted Sadie caught Tara under the elbow as the latter slipped while skipping across stones. Their faces glowed in laughter. Britt had her head tilted to the sky, gazing at the dragons that circled above them, keeping watch.

Eve drank from the wine bottle, relishing the rich taste on her tongue and breathing out. First cream tea, and now wine. She could die happily, now for sure.

When they reached what Tara deemed to be their destination, she told them all to "look for Newa. Newa is alpha of the group while she waits for her mate, Agrippa and daughter, Honor, to return home with Grace, Naz, and Marjorie."

"How the hell am I supposed to know what Newa looks like?" Sadie threw her hands in the air.

Tara shrugged. "Imagine what you'd look like as a dragon if you saw yourself in the mirror."

"Excuse me?" Sadie leaned back in indignation.

Tara giggled. Eve jumped in and said, "She means majestic."

"Or like she has a stick up her ass," Britt whispered.

"I own a brothel, Miss Britt Uriah. I have items that can find themselves lodged up your ass if you continue in this manner."

"I work at that brothel, Miss Sadie Hoffman. I will enjoy said items being lodged up my ass if I continue in this manner."

They all laughed. "All right, split up," Tara told them.

Eve took a breath. None of these dragons looked like the one that had failed her Archibald. They looked much more like that Slewja dragon that had brought Grace with him to their home. They had kind faces and, though so wild, a calmness about them. The one who had brought Archibald had needed to relax. It had looked stressed out of its mind. She wondered if Grace had been out here with the dragons. If she had found what she was looking for.

So the women tiptoed through the dragons, many of which were still awake despite the late hour.

"Newa."

"Newaaa."

"Newa."

"NEwa."

The tipsy voices acted like an echoing canyon across different parts of the meadow.

After about a minute, a large dragon stretched out its wings immediately in front of Eve.

"Newa?"

The dragon nodded its head in response, searching the woman for any clue as to why she had been awakened.

"Newa, we need your help." The dragon tilted its head. "There are towns that are frozen, there are women and children—"

With those words, the dragon's eyes grew bigger, and her head stood more alert. "Yes, whole towns that have come under evil. I don't understand much of the intricacies. I'm sure Tara could explain it. But we returned here with Camelia—"

At that name, Newa lifted her head and uttered a small sound as if she were signaling for another. Within a minute, Camelia had flapped her wings and landed next to Newa. The two dragons had a discussion through eyes, grunts, and head movements.

After a minute or two, Newa turned her attention back to Eve. Bracing herself for the response, she took a swig of wine. Tara had caught up to her at this point.

"What did she say?"

"I have no idea, but from what I gathered, there was a conversation."

"Hi Camelia, you filled her in?" Tara asked and received a nod in reply. "What do you think, Newa? Think you lovely souls might want to help some stupid humans?"

A smile cracked across her face. She took to the sky, crying out. Various dragon heads popped up at attention before joining her in the sky. They swooped low over the women's heads back toward the manor.

"They're going to help?" Eve asked, impressed.

"It seems that there will be a meeting and a discussion."

"Can you find the others?" Tara whispered to one dragon. A murmur set off like dominoes falling through the crowd. As Tara and Eve waited for Britt and Sadie to make their way over, they marveled at the dragons.

"As many times as I have been out here, which can be as often as three times a day, or even sleeping with them," Tara observed, "I am always in awe."

"You sleep with them?" Eve hadn't realized that was possible.

"I have! Sometimes I've stayed up all night to help with birthings or injuries or sickness."

"And they don't hurt you?"

"Not at all. They have a vested interest in keeping me alive since I can help heal. Besides, I'm basically like their cousin. We Fuentes are descended from the dragons."

Eve had never heard the extent. She had grown up hearing about Fuentes dragons and their breeding with awe. But she had assumed that they had bought a bunch of dragons and readied them for selling.

"So you actually are connected to them? Like a family?" Britt would be so jealous when she learned she could have been dragon-related in another life.

"Exactly. And when deals are struck for dragons, the dragons are just as involved in the negotiations and choosing to leave. The money stays with us to help pay to feed and care for the rest. Everything for the good of the thunder. And they see humans as a pack that they can help with, too."

"With that in mind, do you think they'll help us?"

"It's tricky. They have some idea of what went down here with Naz and Grace, so I don't think that many will want to dive into danger when it isn't at their doorstep. Most of them had to leave when Dimin came round. It took us the better part of a month to send word to all of them that the lands had been secured. They do have to ensure their own legacies after all." Tara sighed. "All we can do is explain the situation and ask if any would be willing to help."

Eve grew quiet, wondering what it would take to even spur these creatures to want to help another thunder. She was about to find out.

Thirty

Tara

It wasn't so long ago that the family had stood on the front steps of the house explaining how they would save the dragons to all the dragonhands. She felt a bit uneasy about now asking the creatures to go into certain danger. Sadie stood next to her. She hoped that she was doing the right thing and not alienating or scaring the herd away with the announcement that there was more danger. Granted, the danger was neither imminent nor approaching.

"If injustice was occurring in the world that I have been living in for hundreds of years, I would want to know. You may be a steward of the dragon, but they are stewards of the earth, Anaveh." Sadie pecked Tara's cheek. A thunder of dragons stood before them. Tara used her magic to pull soil together into a little hill. Stepping onto it elevated her slightly above the heads of the dragons when they stood on all fours.

"I'm sorry that I awakened you all." Tara's voice carried through the quiet, open meadow. The stillness of the moonlit night helped her voice to travel further back. "We women arrived here, not on a girl's trip, unfortunately, though it may seem that way, especially with our wine bottles." She held hers up in a cheersing motion to the animals. "We have seen things. I was sent to Grogtown to heal it from the nastiness that upset it by Greystock, may his soul twist in torment Below the Staircase."

"He froze towns. His evil created bubbles of unhealthy air that infected humans' lungs. He kicked the dragons out so they had no place to roam there. It was not safe." Tara paused, unsure for a moment whether it was even worth asking the dragons to help. Time would carry on, and they would still live; what did they care for the problems of man?

"But it can be again, if only you can help save it. My magic is not powerful enough. Camelia saw how much work it took to revive these three women from this terrible sickness. Women and children could be lying in their beds, not dead but living in a constant repeat of moments in their lives. No one deserves that fate because of the decisions of others, let alone men." Tara paused, letting the information sink in and considering her next communication.

"I'm not sure how difficult reviving the whole town will be. We have the baby bits of a plan, but we're waiting to see if we can count on the support of any of you to once again help some innocents out of a bad situation before we can create any more of the plan. We're leaving tomorrow. The flight takes a few days." She looked at the dragons that had encircled her. "I don't know what else to do. I know you take care of your own, and I'm asking a lot. The situation necessitates your life-giving magic. Would you help us?"

Camelia came forward toward Tara and bowed her head.

"Are you willing to go back? After everything that you saw?" Tara's hand stroked her friend's head. The dragon puffed warm air out, blowing the women's hair around before nodding her head.

"You are a true healer, my friend." In that moment, Tara had never been prouder to be a healer, descended from a dragon such as the selfless, ever-ready Camelia.

Three more dragons stepped forward and bowed their heads before looking at Camelia.

"We have four," Britt whispered in awe to her. "Four magnificent dragons."

The four grunted at the others, and three more stepped up. Newa stepped up last.

"Newa, are you sure?" A calm nod before Newa pressed her hand to her womb reassured Tara of her choice.

"How can you be sure?" Britt asked.

"Newa has a child who is safe. A child that fought against Dimin. She will do it for mothers and for the future," Tara replied. Newa bowed her head, showing her teeth, as if to say "we understand each other."

Three other dragons walked back to where they had been sleeping. "From what I can see right now, we have three healers, a wayfinder, and an alpha." Tara apprised the dragons, and her eyes filled with tears." But most notably, all eight of these dragons are women."

"You truly are the best of dragons," she said to the volunteers, "to answer the call of other females and their young."

"Settle up, ladies," Sadie said. "We return tomorrow!" The four women clinked their bottles together, toasting their accomplishment of the moment and their times to come.

Part Three

Thirty-One

Britt

The sign welcoming Britt home had said, "Grogtown, Population 238." Crossed off in red paint and edited to read "Egotown, Population 1."

No sooner had the four human-laden dragons touched down upon the ground than their riders quickly took to looking around for any sign of the single roaming inhabitant. DB would be sure to have things to say about their plans to rehabilitate the town that he had seemingly pronounced dead while they were gone. And Britt imagined the townsfolk would have some things to say about their time with the sickness and their previous treatment by the governing parties.

DB wasn't visible, but that didn't mean he hadn't seen their arrival. If she could just put a knife through one of his major arteries now, everything would be easier. No one was around to stop her. Maybe she would. She felt more daring after having spent time free with the dragons.

"It would be great if we had more people with us," Sadie lamented. She walked toward the front porch of the brothel, sitting on the wooden steps. She pulled her stockings off and pushed her feet into the dirt, muddy from the thawed snow.

"All it takes is one to start," Tara said, and Britt noticed Tara's hand gently resting on Sadie's shoulder. A twinge of excitement flitted through Britt's stomach. Oh, how she hoped that Sadie would let herself be happy with another person! And Tara's helpful nature would be sure to complement Sadie's need to put the world on her back.

With Sadie's lament, an orange dragon flew into sight, a dark silhouette on its back. The wind flipped some moist land into their faces, causing them to giggle as they brushed it off. Britt felt slightly irked that she had gone this long in her new cotton dress without getting it dirty. Who was this person to not care about her physical appearance? She brushed the muddy pieces off the ivory, unintentionally rubbing a bit into the bottom hem. Sighing at her lot in life, her attention returned to the perpetrators.

As the new arrivals entered the clearing, Camelia darted over to the new dragon, flapping her wings in excitement.

Standing up from the steps, Tara grabbed Sadie's arm. "Quick, say, 'It would be great if we had more champagne.'"

Sadie put her hand on Tara's. "I'm not wasting my wishes on champagne." How practical of Sadie!

"I would," Britt added as she walked past to join Sadie as part of the welcoming committee.

By this time, the dragons that had flown in with the women had taken up their resting places in the clearing. Britt followed her companion, weaving between the dragons' resting bodies. She was able to put both arms out on either side of her, rubbing her hands across their scales. Continually surprised by their smoothness, Britt sucked in strength as they did not flinch from her touch.

"Howdy, Sadie, who's the new girl?"

Britt knew that voice, that friendly, truth-telling voice with its tenor-like quality, but rich, not whiny.

A grinning man in motley pants and a dirty white linen shirt, not more than forty years to his life, greeted them as he stood next to the orange dragon. Bags were laden on every side of the animal in a hodgepodge mess. His two-day stubble only accentuated his smile. The green eyes, eternally observing the scene for his collection of stories that he would tell to anyone who would listen, reminded her of the green in the dragon meadows of Titan's Creek.

Britt's feet propelled her forward, her voice following her.

"VERDIS!" Britt slammed into the man, enveloping him in a tight squeeze and knocking him to the ground. His arm flew around her, and she felt his chest rumble with his chuckling.

This man had spent more time between her thighs than any other man she knew. She counted him as one of her best clients.

"Britt, I've missed every part of you!" He pinched her rear in playful affection.

"That touch'll cost you ten gold pieces," she told him.

"Ten! Price has gone up! Used to be five pinches for a coin."

"Supply and demand, honey." Britt motioned around her.

"No kidding." His voice became softer and more worried. "I thought you ladies would have been taken by the sickness for sure."

"We were, but Tara healed us!" Britt declared, full of pride for the woman that they had adopted into their tribe.

"You must be a mighty powerful woman."

Tara shrugged, brushing off Verdis's praise, as if she were used to having accolades thrown at her for her healing accomplishments.

Verdis, as Britt knew, did not praise just anyone, so Britt thought that Tara really should be pleased with herself. But when Tara showed no outward signs of being proud, Britt figured that she had her own reasons that she would press later in private. She wasn't about to go into it in public. Smiles painted her friends' faces. Happiness had arrived again. It would be like old times.

"Where's Evie?" He asked as he separated from Britt.

"I'm here!" Britt's best friend peered out from behind a dragon who blocked her way. Though Verdis had visited Britt on a number of occasions, he had spent much more time with Eve before leaving to help ward Dimin off Grace's scent.

"Come here and give me some sugar, mama!" He held his arms out to her, as a babe would for its ma, before he pulled Eve into him in a big embrace. Eve's joyous hug knocked all three of them to the ground in a heap of laughter, with Britt falling beneath him. Verdis pushed Britt aside onto the ground next to him with his left arm while his right clung to Eve. In no time, he had Britt and Eve each on one of his thighs, lounging about in the dirt. Britt could have sworn that his lips skimmed the top of Eve's head.

"Tara, meet Verdis, the wackiest little shit that I've ever met," she heard Sadie say through her own laughter.

"Pleasure, I'm sure," Tara said, as she put her hand out to pat the snout of the man's orange dragon companion. The creature closed its eyes and quickly nuzzled into her touch, before sitting and grabbing the woman in his arms.

"Yokel!" Tara remembered this creature from the times he had followed her around, head bobbing around in the goofy idiosyncratic manner that it had since he was born. "How is it possible?" she asked the dragon. A confused look crossed her face as she looked between the two creatures before asking, "Did you see my brother?"

"Your brother?" Verdis swatted at Eve, who was moving her hand away from his stubble while pinching something between her fingers. "I'm not following."

"Did you take him from the ranch?" Tara asked.

"Nah, this guy left with me not too long back when I hooked back up with a friend of mine. We've been looking after each other ever since." Verdis gave the dragon a look of fondness.

"But he wanted to go with you?" Tara was stuck on this situation.

"Yes, I tend to want my companions to want to be with me." He turned back to Sadie. "How are things going here?"

Sadie looked at him. "Oh, about as great as you can expect. Let's go inside before a certain asshole comes out here." Sadie escorted everyone inside with an open arm, directing them toward the door.

"Mmm, love a good asshole," Verdis remarked, helping Britt and Eve up from his legs. He stood and began pulling off the bags from Yokel's back.

"Yokel, you and Camelia and the others keep watch over each other. I don't know what sort of trouble that mayor-sheriff-politician-dumbass has been cooking up since he thought we left a week ago." Tara always seemed to be thinking ahead.

Britt grabbed a couple bags from Verdis and walked ahead to the brothel. Sadie held the door open for the travelers, demanding that they take their boots off in the front.

"We've never had to do this before, Madame Sadie," Verdis whined.

"I picked it up from another house. It kept things less dirty. Somehow dirt seems to travel like dust—you never see it, and then all of a sudden it coats everything and you need to clean for an entire week to get it off everything."

"I don't know if you noticed, Sadie, but this house has enough dust from the past few weeks; a bit of dirt won't hurt it." Britt had no idea where this behavior was coming from. Something must be bothering Sadie to have her feel a need to issue commands in the house again.

"Just take them off. Please." Everyone held onto the walls, fingerprinting the wallpaper in the front, as they kicked their boots off.

"The dragons need to rest, so that we can start the vortex and get people re-alived," Sadie started listing a to-do list as soon as they were all inside the house and sitting in the front room.

"I know that we need to get stuff done, but I want to make certain that man suffers, too," Tara said, appearing to zone out until Britt snapped her fingers in front of her face. "I'm so tired of him always shoving his nose and his rules into our faces. Maker knows he'll see the dragons flying around and start citing eminent domain for taking possession of them."

"You could always be the bigger person," the ever socially aware Eve offered.

"She will, when she holds him accountable," Britt supplied while cracking her fingers.

"Fuck that guy," Tara scoffed.

"He doesn't answer to anyone but himself and whatever weird values he holds," observed Sadie.

"Manliness," it dawned on Tara. "We're going to break his fragile masculinity like fine china on Terra Cotta." She tilted her head, making eye contact with Sadie.

Verdis wanted in. "I volunteer my services to this patriotic act." He saluted the four women.

"You do realize that you're a man, right?"

"Yes." Verdis looked her straight in the eye.

"Then forgive my confusion ..."

"Who better to help break a man than a man?"

"Well, I was figuring a woman, but sure ... if you think you know enough about this, then let's have it."

"It's not right. I don't aim to tell you what to do at all." His shitass grin spread across his face like wildfire. "I would simply like to continue standing in towns that are not threatened by people like him, who give a bad name to my sex. You're my friends, and I would like to help you."

As if kismet, a knock at the front door sounded. Everyone froze. "Hide him," Tara mouthed. Sadie hastily pulled the cushions off the couch, pushed Verdis onto it, and began piling the cushions on him to cover him. Eve plopped on top of him and pulled a blanket over her, covering the gaps.

"Can you breathe?" Eve whispered.

"Honey, this wouldn't be the first time you sat on my face." She gave him an extra bounce on his chest, and he chuckled.

"As I recall, you still paid me for the opportunity."

"And would again, thank you very much."

"Shutthefuckup," Britt hissed, trying to look busy with a book that was upside down, but it was too late to switch it to right side up, so she just rested it on her lap and pretended to look interested in whoever was at the door. Though there was only one other person alive and walking through the streets so the ruse was stupid.

Sadie opened the door, allowing DB to pass inside. He tipped his hat at her.

"Ma'am, how gracious of you to return to our town. I trust you had a safe journey, albeit a tiring one." He tipped his hat at Britt and Sadie, but paused to stare at Tara.

"How was your trip? I didn't expect to see you back here."

Eve had flung her arm over her face in mock sleep, partly to hide the fact that Verdis kept tickling her foot.

Sadie threw a hand over her hip indignantly. "Why in Good Granny's name would I not return to my home?"

"Well, as a proper businesswoman, I thought you would have gone out in search of a more fruitful place for your labors. Supply and demand and all that, as I'm sure you know."

"Oh, why I've always considered myself a small businesswoman who bolstered up her community by her trade. And my community does seem to need a bit of bolstering."

"She means you, DB," Britt chimed in. She quickly remonstrated herself. Sadie had told her many times that she needed to learn to bite her tongue on occasions that hinged upon a suave delivery. She needed to trust that Sadie had more experience in dealing with people so they would want to return to her. Britt knew this, but her instincts tended to run her mouth more than her reasoning. She tried to make up for her distracting interruption.

"Why, DB, we were just talking about how you needed bolstering, and you must be so tired of seeing all of us. We brought someone back with us on our trip, and we would all be delighted to entertain you tonight." His eyebrows lifted in curiosity.

"That is," Sadie chimed in, "unless you do not want any company. We sure could use some male company."

"I suppose so," he said warily. "What's the catch?"

"No catch," Tara replied. "We were all just talking, and we have nothing else to do, so we figured maybe we'd better extend the friendly olive branch to you since we all live on the same street. Well, they do anyways. I'm going to be headed out soon, I reckon."

"Did I see you brought more dragons with you?" His eyes betrayed greed as they grew wider. A bit of drool wet the left corner of his lips. Britt wanted to run out and throw herself in front of them. What did he intend with the dragons?

"We're just passing through until I can bring them further east, find some roaming lands now that towns are no longer functional and land is available," Tara adeptly lied. Britt felt a sense of camaraderie with Tara for the dragons' protection.

"Ah, I see you've had similar thoughts as me. I'd be happy to purchase those dragons and take them off your hands, for you. Be a shame if you had to fly all the way out east with them, just to find no buyers." DB wanted the dragons? Britt thought that he had just wanted the land that this town sat upon, unless he was hoping to start a dragon ranch.

She could sock him again. Over her dead body would he get the dragons.

"The dragons are never on the table," Tara told him. "They chose to help us, and they will choose when they will fly away and where to."

"Then, I really don't know why you returned, if those dragons weren't going to be used as bargaining chips for the rest of the town. My colleagues and I will be happy to show you the best exit out of here."

What did he mean by colleagues?

Sadie's face remained still, betraying zero thoughts. Britt did not know how to respond. Eve chose that moment to become dramatic, yawning and stretching her arms as if she had just woken up. Below the cushions, Verdis's green eyes glowed.

"Why, Mr. DB! Such a pleasure to see you! I'm so sorry that I so rudely slept through your calling, but if you come back tomorrow, I'd surely love to hear about what you've been getting your fine self into!"

Britt marveled. She knew society had molded these women differently than herself, but their ability to show themselves exactly as men expected really baffled her. Why did they need to do that? Why could they just not be straightforward and tell this guy off?

Remembering how she had just done damage control from her last outburst, she bit her tongue.

Thirty-Two

Eve

"Did you ever have to pretend to be someone you're not in order to get ahead?" Britt asked Eve of her time out east.

"Oh, it's not easy, running the double play. But you have to play into their hand in order to play their hand. You want to run the game, you make the runners into your puppets. And you do that by playing it sweet and dumb to their ways. Let them think they're clever."

"So are you saying that women are running this shitshow that we live in?" Britt waved her hand around. "Because you seem to be saying that women are the ones controlling men to be the way that they are. Everyone needs to be called out."

"If you call someone out, they become defensive, and then there's no working through or with them. Think about the right word, whispered in the right tone in the right ear. Think about how that word can cause a man's cock to grow, and then you can grip it easier. Smooth talk, Britt."

"I think I prefer just calling it as it is, Eve."

"And that's why I like you." She affectionately blew her a kiss. "I don't have to pretend or play stupid with you."

"Good thing you don't have a cock or I'd know the way to your heart," Britt joked.

"You'd just wrap your mouth around it and control me that way," Eve said with a raised eyebrow. "Wouldn't you?" She meant it in half-jest. Knowing what she knew about Britt's history, she knew that the woman held those men in the palm of her hand in her own way.

Tara and Sadie walked in. Sadie looked at Verdis with disbelief. "Verdis! Are your dirty feet on my ivory settee?!" Verdis opened his eyes from where he'd fallen asleep on top of the cushions and immediately put his feet onto the floor.

"No ma'am." She rolled her eyes at him. Eve stifled a giggle.

"We're going on an expedition," Tara declared. What had these two intelligent minds thought of? They were quite the pair, together, if only they would see it. Eve kept her mouth shut, though. Love needed to pave its own riverbed for it to run freely.

Verdis looked at the four women. "Never a dull moment around you all."

Eve asked, "So you're in?" She hoped he would be. He had a knack for filling the most mundane of moments with excitement.

Verdis's grin traveled up his face, raising his cheeks and creating crescents of his striking green eyes. "I love a bit of mischief."

Verdis walked up to the door, motley pants blowing in the breeze. The women hid in various locations around the house in their roles. Sadie would go through the back with the help of Tara; Eve, with the help of Britt, would go through the side of the house next to the well. The four women would sneak around as Verdis, skilled in the art of saying nothing in many words, maintained Egoman's attention as a distraction.

THUD. THUD. THUD.

Eve heard the assured knock on the door and waited for their mark to answer. A creaky hinge let her know that the target had answered.

"Good day, sir," Verdis said, with all the confidence of someone used to meeting new people and reeling them into his conversation. "I've been knocking on all the doors in the neighborhood, wondering if anyone was interested in buying a little liquid revitalizer?" Eve had no idea what he was selling, but she assumed that Verdis's packs on the dragon's back had hidden wares for sale. He used to have a peddler's wagon that he would bring around with him. He must have gotten rid of that somewhere. A story for later, to be sure.

Eve imagined that the silence from DB's end came from his surprise at Verdis's appearance. *Good, that man needed to be thrown off the scent.*

Britt dropped to her knees, and Eve climbed on top of her back, holding onto the window ledge for support. Eve took a moment and started bouncing with her feet, jostling Britt's back.

"Ooooof oof! Eve, fuck off! You're tiny, not weightless!"

Eve smiled at her joke before grabbing the windowsill and hoisting herself upwards.

She landed in an office with papers strewn about. If DB projected tidy fastidiousness, his office disproved that trait. Her mission was to see what he was up to. She could hear Verdis loudly at the front door.

"I swear, I never knew a better night's sleep than in the arms of this tiny jar."

She cracked a smile. That man could sell sand in a desert. Having paused too long, she reminded herself what she was there for: anything that could help them figure out a weakness or an angle.

Standing in one corner, she sifted through piles of newspapers. "Egoman" had been underlined on the top issue. Holding the paper in one hand, she moved the other papers below. Scanning her eyes across the page, again, "Egoman," had been underlined. A continual perusal of the stack informed her that it was a curated stack of all the times he had been mentioned in the newspaper. What a narcissist!

Footprints outside the door made her put the papers down. She glanced around the room, looking for a spot to hide. A small upholstered chair had been placed diagonally across a corner of the room, directly across from the door. With swift feet, she launched herself onto the cushion, then into the space between the back of the chair and the wall. Squashed in like a preserve in a jar for the winter, Eve stilled her breath.

The door opened. Footsteps quickly entered before it closed again. Someone was inside the room with her. Verdis's voice still carried into the house, so DB was occupied. Who could it be? No one else was around in the town.

Eve deduced she knew whoever it was in that room with her. And if she was wrong, she would be very much surprised. Peeking out, she recognized the curly black hair pinned atop a head, bent over the stack of newspapers that Eve had recently examined.

"I already looked there," Eve whispered to her.

Sadie flinched, throwing her hand to her chest in surprise. Looking up at Eve, she shook her head.

"I went through four rooms already. What's taking you so long?" Upon scanning the room again, Sadie said, "Oh, this is the treasure chest right here," she said as she saw all the papers.

Eve tried climbing out from behind the chair. Eventually, she needed to move it, which she did as quietly as possible. Thankfully, it did not make any noise across the wood floors.

"Don't sign up for the circus," Sadie snorted. Eve gave her a half smile and said, "Where do you want to look?"

"I don't want any of your quack treatments!" DB yelled at the front of the house. The slam told them time was up.

"Just grab a bunch of the important-looking stuff," Sadie directed.

"He'll know someone was in here if we steal his papers!" Eve whispered back quickly.

"Yeah, but we'll maybe have an idea of what he's up to by that point, so we'll have something to one-up him with." Sadie and Eve both grabbed up a handful of papers. Eve rushed over to the window, putting her bottom on it and swinging her legs out. She expected Britt to still be on all fours as she dropped down way farther than she had expected.

"Oh!" she softly exclaimed as she fell forward onto her knees.

"Move, Eve!" Sadie sat with her bottom on the sill and her legs dangling toward the ground over Eve's rear. Eve half rolled, half stumbled away from the window, near the well. Rearranging the papers in her arms, a name grabbed her attention. She moved the paper with "Man, Man, and Man" printed at the top. The company seemed to be from another life. She stared at the paper, searching her memory.

"What are you waiting for Eve, let's go!"

"Holy fucking Maker," Eve whispered in disbelief as her brain found the memory.

RothMAN. EgoMAN. She wasn't sure of the last one, but Archie had been traveling out here to deal with DB. She would have been on the other side of this situation had the dragon not let them down.

"Archie was working with DB!" Eve demonstrated the papers to Sadie, pointing at the name. Sadie's mouth dropped before she shook her head.

"And my ex, Justin! That's his last name of Hoffman. I've seen this company before!" She shook her head, helping to right the papers. "We gotta go. We'll read that back at the house." Sadie moved toward the street, holding the papers to the side of her, away from DB's house. If he had looked outside, she would have appeared to be going about errands in a hurry with Eve tagging along behind her.

Verdis caught up with them halfway down the street, out of view from their surveillance target.

"Why do you look like you've seen a ghost?" he asked.

"Because I just saw the name of my dead husband in a place that he never lived," she said. She shoved the papers at his chest, too much in shock to be able to make sense of it. When they made it to the steps of the brothel, Tara and Britt greeted them.

Eve watched Verdis as he read. "This isn't great. It's less than great. DB has no intent of healing anyone here. He wants the land, all of it. This trio is setting out to make a dragon ranch. A *huge* one."

"Let me see." Tara held out her hand. Perusing the paper, she shook her head, denying the world this situation. "No wonder DB wants us out of his hair. No one will be left to contest the claim to this land if everyone here is dead."

Thirty-Three

Sadie

T he dragons should have warned Tara, warned her of his presence. Instead, that familiar deep, gravelly voice growled, "There you are, I've been looking for you."

The tiny hairs on the back of her neck bristled with the familiarity of the growl.

"Mothermucker," she muttered to herself. "Of course you were." She tented her hands over her face, cresting them at her brow. Breathing in, she closed her eyes. *Please tell me this asshole isn't here, and I fell asleep on the dragon.*

A pat from Tara's steady hand on her back reminded Sadie of herself, the person that she had grown to be without him. In spite of him. Because of him. Because of herself.

She needed to respond to whoever she feared that voice belonged to, because she was Sadie. She had thrown men out for failing to name her as "Madame Sadie." She had built a damn house with her bare hands. And with every nail that she had hammered into that house, she had promised herself that she would neither owe nary a cent nor an explanation to another.

Glancing first at Tara's naturally wide eyes, but forever full of steady support, she took a breath in. Bringing her hands in front of her in her best attempt at a neutral body stance, she hoped she communicated nothing but strength as she turned around.

Inside, the wounds in her heart had started to weep into her lungs and stomach. Her breath was forced. She wished she had sucked on a peppermint to calm her stomach before she had turned around. Exhale and turn.

Justin. With that idiot, DB, in tow. *Fuck that guy.*

Oh, but that beautiful man was smiling at her. Years ago, she would have dreamed that he would do so once again. Now, she was faced with her dream and left to debate if the dreams of her youth were the same as the ones of her middle age.

And for the first time in a long time, she was shaken with no idea what to say. Only her fingers betrayed her as her right forefinger tried to figure out the smoothness of the left and how her emery board had performed upon its recent use.

She looked him over. He still stood straight and tall from his torso down to his feet. Looking at his legs, she remembered the last time that she had seen him. His once confident form, stumbling in through the threshold of the door, requiring a servant to carry him upstairs, having drunk himself into a stupor over his own pathetic "values."

In her times of anger, she would practice what she would say to him should she ever see him again. *Fuck off; eat shit and die; asshole; opportunist; handsome mothermucker; heartbreaker.* Every word she had wanted to call him for more than a decade melted into her mouth as saliva. Working it around in her mouth, she spat upon his shoes.

"Get the fuck off my land, you poor excuse for a human." And then she pushed him away from her straight into DB. With distance between them, Sadie extended her arm next to her and unhooked Tara's gun from its holster. Holding it up to between his eyes, she stared him down. It was she and Justin. She had the power now.

"Ma'am, if I were you, I'd take your gun away from an enforcer of the law," DB's smarmy voice chimed in.

Her eyes rested on the burnished star on Justin's chest, standing as a stalwart for everything she had walked away from. Sadie had forgotten that anyone else was around at this point.

"So far, the only person in violation of the law is you, sir. I own this plot, rightfully. You had best back away slowly, or who knows, the dust might fly up into my eyes and distract me from reflexively pulling the trigger."

In his silence, she searched every minor proof that his brain controlled his body, looking for minute movements that would challenge her resolve. *Challenge away.* By staring straight at him, she had full knowledge any time part of his muscles flickered. She wished they would. But they did not.

"One of my clients defaulted on a loan payment, so I had the ability to invest in a rather lucrative business venture out this way. I've been looking for you since the day that you left, Sade." He stepped forward til his forehead touched the barrel. The gun's cocking made a lovely click at his forehead.

"Round these parts, it's Madame Sadie to you. But you're new here, so you naturally wouldn't have known that."

The pressure of Tara's hand on her forearm pulled her back to the ground from the swirling eddy of emotions within her.

"I'd heard you might be out this far when you'd sold all the furniture and ran," Justin said.

"I don't run from my problems. I solve them and then I move on. If you're still hung up on me, that's your problem, and I suggest you stuff that problem into your back pocket and leave."

"Funny thing is, we never divorced."

"You should have assumed me dead. Common-law death after ten years."

Tara extracted the gun from Sadie's hand, lowering it toward her holster.

"Not only is Justin an upright lawman, but he's one of my investors." The cocky voice of DB piped up from behind them.

"You've gotta be fucking kidding me," Britt muttered so only the three women could hear. With that, Tara placed the gun at DB's eye sight.

"Lots of flinging that gun around, little lady. Didn't your mommy ever teach you that guns are a man's tool?"

"My daddy taught me that a man's tool was in his pants, and a woman's was in her head, and it was up to her to make sure his stayed there because he sure as fire wouldn't."

"Your Oath prohibits you from shooting him," Justin said with zero authority in his voice.

"Why any healer would carry a gun has me stumped. It's like a woman having vocal cords. Dead nuisance, really," DB added.

Britt bumped between Tara and Sadie, taking the gun but keeping it level at DB's head.

"Funny thing is, I have no such oath," Britt quipped.

Justin jumped back into the situation, trying to take control with his toy star on his chest. "If you shoot that man, I'll have to arrest you and hang you."

"Not if we shoot you too. No one would know. Nothing goes in or out of here."

"Unfortunately for you, there has been communication between myself and the outside world when I left." He swatted the gun away, but Britt quickly returned it to the position. "In fact, many people hadn't heard from this man in quite some time, so we figured we would come out here and ensure our investment was still sound. If we don't hop on a dragon and ride back in a week, others will follow. There will be consequences for you all."

"We're going to cure this whole town, and then you will be held accountable for your actions."

"The town is dead. Do yourselves a favor: leave while you can," Justin replied. "We own it all, now, anyway, without anyone around to claim otherwise. I as good as own that plot of land that you call your home, Sade."

Sadie's arms crossed her chest in disgust. "Oh no, you did not just try to throw me out of my house again."

Justin was about to respond when a shot rang out close to their heads.

"Shit!" Tara shouted next to her.

They all looked around for where the gunshot came from. On the balcony of the brothel, Verdis smiled, holding a shotgun.

"You're gonna wanna stop messing with these women," Verdis yelled down. Verdis's antics provided a distraction for everyone. DB grabbed the pistol from Britt, disarming her, and shot at the balcony of the brothel. Without waiting to watch Verdis fall, he turned back to the women, waving it back and forth at them.

"Verdis!" Eve exclaimed, running toward the brothel.

"Eve, stop!" Sadie reached her hand out to stop her, but she was halfway up the steps already.

DB aimed at Eve.

A knife hit his hand, dropping the pistol to the dirt. DB's jaw dropped with shock as blood oozed out of his right hand. A sly smile stretched across Britt's face.

"I don't think they've been hearing what I've been saying." DB smiled at Justin before yelling at the women, "I AM THE LAW." He held his arms out to his sides in a T, as if to taunt them by saying, "What are you going to do about it?" Droplets of blood hit the dirt.

At that moment, Camelia shoved her head between the men and the women. She kicked the pistol back to Tara, who stooped down to pick it up and rehouse it in its holster.

"You are the worst," Britt snipped back from around the dragon.

"You can't hide behind the dragons. You will need to come out, and the pure matter is that we have you out powered on every level—physical, political, spiritual," DB said. "In fact, if you leave the dragons and go, no one will know that you couldn't revive the town. Your Oath will be fine."

Sadie wasn't sure that this was true.

"Fine," Tara said with a flat voice. "You win. We'll leave. Just let us get packed up."

"Tara!" Sadie seethed through her teeth. Tara put her hand on Sadie's back and turned her around, pushing her toward the brothel. Sadie turned her head to make sure that Britt was joining them.

"You knifed him," Justin said in amazement. "You're a woman, you shouldn't have those skills."

Britt retorted, "My cunt only determines if I'm standing when I'm peeing on your suede shoes."

Sadie watched as she walked toward the brothel behind her and Tara. Passing DB, she stared him dead in the eyes and yanked her knife from his hand.

Lemme know if you want to visit my cunt while you're healing. I'll give you a discount if you don't bleed all over my sheets. Maker knows I don't."

The men were left behind in wonderment.

Thirty-Four

Eve

T he stairs had never seemed as treacherous as when she stumbled up them while failing to remember to hoist her skirts.

"Hold on, Verdis!" She ran out onto the balcony. Blood spatters decorated the posts in a macabre polka dot pattern. In the corner, back against the house and away from the railing, Verdis clutched his bleeding shoulder. The viscous red liquid covered his thighs and hands.

"You need to apply pressure," Eve said to him, her nerves flying to her chest as she ripped a piece of her skirt. "Why did you do that?" She knelt down and her hands gently replaced his on the wound.

He shrugged. "Didn't like the way he was talking to my friends. Figured a warning shot might scare him off."

She took the shotgun out of his hand and carefully leaned it against the side of the house. With the movement of his arm, he grimaced slightly.

"Nothing seems to scare him off. He remained as the cold sickness invaded the town and never got sick, as far as I know."

"Some people simply were immune." His eyelids grew droopy.

"Like you?" Eve asked casually.

"I dodged it enough and made my way west. If I am immune, it's probably because I'm already cursed—"

"You are?" *Why had he never told her this information before?* He did not seem to have any curse markings on him.

"With not seeing your eyes every morning that I wake up," he completed his flirtation. That shitass grin popped across his face, despite his eyelids shutting.

"Even losing blood, you keep charming," Eve shook her head.

The door slammed below, stealing her attention, protective of the wounded. Through the balustrade, Eve could see the men leaving. Footsteps at the top of the stairs preceded Tara's calm but hasty entrance.

"Don't know why you've been putting up with this asshole. Our beloved Grace would have shot him already," Verdis told Tara as she peeled away the cotton from his shoulder.

"It's not that easy. Out of the four of us, three of us possess that ability. And who knows how terrible the consequences would be, especially with the investors returning." Holding her hand over his clothing, Tara magicked away all of the blood.

"I've seen our healer do that sometimes," Eve said in awe. "How do you do that?"

"I have a store of energy and I just pull the blood off like a blanket and then push the molecules of it so far apart that they are microscopic and part of the air."

"So there's blood particles just floating around in the air?" Eve was disgusted.

"And urine and skin and cum and ..."

Eve held up her hand to stop Tara. "I get the picture."

"Ha, it's like you've given infinite blowjobs just by breathing," Verdis said weakly through his still closed eyes.

"Gross," Tara said with disgust. She was about to motion for Verdis to lie flat, but in his weakened state, Eve caught him as he slumped over to the side. She carefully laid his head on top of her lap.

Britt entered the balcony area where Eve cradled Verdis's head as Tara worked on him. Taking command of the situation, Tara instructed Britt to pick up the rifle and stand lookout lest the offending men make a return in their moment of vulnerability.

"I can't use this thing," Britt objected.

"They don't know that," Tara replied to her, picking it up and shoving it at her. Turning to Eve, she said, "He'll make it, but I want to make sure that this experience did not scar him. He does not deserve the hate of a man any more than a woman does. Any more than anyone else does, really. Hatred should rot Below where it was born."

Tara continued to place her hands on various parts of Verdis's body.

"I'm going to start by staunching the internal bleeding. Then I'll need to pull the bullet out of his shoulder." She rubbed her fingers together and placed her forefinger straight inside the wound in his shoulder. In a moment, she withdrew her finger, some metal pieces sticking to it.

"Metals are in the ground," Tara informed them both. "I can control them when I want. As for the pieces, I'm going to have to get in closer. One piece has migrated."

Tara's entire finger went into the hole, blood seeping out in response. Eve closed her eyes, trying not to imagine the pain that Verdis was in as Tara worked.

"Got some juices on that one!" Tara quickly fit the pieces of the bullet together like a puzzle.

"We hardly have time for that," Britt said from above them. Eve agreed, but trusted Tara too much in this arena to say anything. After all, Tara had brought them back from near death.

"No sense in my pulling out the pieces and healing him back up just to find out that there was one bit left in him, and then he gets blood poisoning." Finding the pieces fit, Tara placed her hands over the wound and pushed.

"If you have land magic, how are you able to heal?" Eve asked.

"The Trinity put us together from dirt and all the good things of the land, so I can manipulate parts of us." When she removed her hands, the wound had closed. With that, she placed her hands on his head. "If he bumped his head, and he has a concussion, which seems to be the case from his sleepiness—-but that could also be blood loss—-" Tara explained, "I'll ease any sign of that."

As she worked, Eve brushed his hair back from his face and kept whispering, "You're going to be brand new, soon."

"You must really care about him," Tara remarked to Eve, trying to make conversation more than anything to keep the girl from fretting too much.

"I do. We all do," she conceded. "He holds a special place in this house."

"I'll bet he's glad to know he has a home here," Tara said as she ran her hands over all of Verdis's body, checking to make sure all internal injuries were covered.

"He seems peaceful ... he isn't ..." Eve's voice choked. She could not bear the idea of losing another person in her life.

"Nononono," Tara reassured her. "The magic overtook him and is doing its work. I left some residual magic in his body when I ran my hands over him. That magic will travel through his bloodstream and cleanse him. He'll have the biggest piss of his life when he comes to in a day or two. We should get him off the floor and away from the balcony window."

For the first time in a few minutes, Eve remembered that they were on the balcony.

"Let's bring him into my room," Eve suggested. "It's the closest." Eve played lead in the situation, talking them both through hoisting him up. Carefully, she hooked her hands under his armpits, lifting the front part of his torso. Tara nodded and picked up his legs so his body drooped like a swaying bridge. Last to leave the balcony, Britt backed up as she kept her view on the street.

When the women reached Eve's bedroom, they, as gently as feasible, placed him on the ground and debated how to get him onto the bed.

"Go get two long towels or sheets or blankets," Tara told the others. She laid each one perpendicular to his body below him. "Now, we get on either side of him and hoist him up by pulling up on the sheets tightly."

After much maneuvering and swearing and multiple fails during which Tara reassured everyone that she'd re-mend anything that they might break on him, Verdis was positioned in the bed.

"Think we should watch him?"

"Stop fretting, Eve," Britt told her. "He can handle it, he's a big boy." They walked down the hallway to Sadie's room.

Sadie sat on the bed, opening a bottle of champagne. "I believe you wanted me to make champagne reappear." She poured it into glasses that were on the bedside table.

"Maker, Sadie," Eve rubbed her hand over her eyes. "Verdis is in there half-dead."

"He's fine, Eve," Tara said. "He was shot, and not in great condition, but I like to think that I know how to heal someone. He'll be better than new in a day or two," Tara finished as she reached out for some cold champagne.

"How'd you get this bottle so cold, Sadie? Was it in some cold sickness victim's arms for the past month?"

"Ew. Morbid, Britt."

Britt merely smiled and held up her glass. "Here's to our last night."

Eve's eyes grew wide with fear. "We can't just sit up and leave Verdis to face these evil men on his own!" The man had returned to check on them; they could not very well abandon him now.

Sadie calmly put her hand on Eve's shoulder. "We're not leaving him." Eve immediately exhaled in relief. "We're not leaving the dragons, either."

"I can't leave the town in this state. As far as I can assume, everyone in this town is alive until the cure has been administered, enacted, delivered, whatever you want to call it. I refuse to believe that DB massacred an entire city, or I'll stay up all night with the nightmares." Tara shuddered. "Hopefully, he is recovering and figuring out the next steps if he is going to try to kick us out when we don't leave tomorrow."

"I think we bought ourselves one night of peace," Sadie agreed. "One night of being left alone. So let's take it. We can figure it out tomorrow. We never promised what time we'd leave. And we never promised not to cause chaos when we did."

How patient Tara must be to dwell on one side of life, battling death at any given moment. Eve knew she had nothing to worry about with Verdis, but telling someone not to worry does not make the anxiety disappear instantaneously. She heard the clinking of glasses after she had left the room; nothing within her wanted to celebrate.

Eve had heard and seen true evil. Banged on the door and tried to cast it out. The moments frightened her that such a creature could exist in this world. They needed the town to wake, and soon.

Four dragons circled the town, while four more waited on the sidelines, resting. Yokel and Camelia waited for any further orders from the gang. She hoped that the vortex was working, though she did not seem to be feeling much warmer.

Climbing into bed beside him, Eve placed her hand on the forehead of the self-sacrificing victim. He had no fever yet. She should have grabbed a book and kept vigil. Instead, her head rested upon his, and she slipped her arm behind his neck, the other going in front of his shoulders to clasp hands. She had him secure, and she had a reason not to worry about what was occurring outside those four walls.

Thirty-Five

Sadie

Justin had resurfaced in her life. *Was there no peace or justice in this world?* She thought that she would detest him the moment she saw him, but all she could see were the smiles and laughter they had shared in the good times.

Time had not made him ugly, sadly. *They would still make a handsome couple.* She shook her head, clearing it of these thoughts.

She remembered the pain. She poured it into the construction. Every nail that she had hit building this building, she'd imagined it was going into his dick. Every saw stroke that she had made, she considered ripping out his testicles. Every time she hammered, she pictured it tearing into his handsome face. Poor Nicholas Charles had been a revenge screw that she imagined going through Justin's heart.

Maybe, now that they were older, he would be okay with not having children.

But what if he had remarried? She had basically left him long enough that he could say she was dead. He could have divorced her without her knowing, or even without her signing the papers. Then he could have remarried and had that passel of brats that he needed to get him onto the staircase.

She prayed that Mother Maker and Granny Good would vindicate her in the afterlife for his terrible rejection. And here she thought they had been in love. She tossed the empty champagne bottle into the cemetery.

Now that Tara was here healing up the town, she would be able to import them soon. She had complete faith in Tara. That woman's mind was damn sexy. The machinations formed quicker than any man's plans. DB might think that he had her beat, but she knew that Tara would find a way around him. Sadie was an excellent judge of character. Well, usually, except for that sonofabastard Justin. Tara had already proven that she had a plan for resurrecting the town. And Sadie could not wait to be there when everyone came round to shower her with her well-earned praise.

She walked back inside the house. Tara sat on the settee in Sadie's bedroom, staring out the window, biting her lip in thought. Her gaze remained, eyes narrowed, despite Sadie's entrance.

How different Tara was from Justin! Whereas he was a douchebag, she was a kindhearted, socially aware creature. Whereas he was dashingly handsome, she was earthily beautiful. He was a social climber; Tara stood at the top of the social ladder. Justin stomped on her heart; Tara could hold it in her hands. Justin had lorded over her past; Tara was in her present.

The big, dragon-amber eyes followed Sadie as she sat down. A resolute energy fizzed throughout the room.

"I've made up my mind," Tara said.

"I have, too," Sadie replied.

It wasn't a question of man or woman. It was a question of her heart and what she wanted for her future.

Thirty-Six

Britt

D read woke her, clasping its talons around her heart. Her wide eyes searched for light to pick up within their purview. With none to be found, she needed to wait for them to adjust to the dark. Terror possessed the silence with its own breed of turmoil, seeping into her joints, as she lay frozen on her bed, wondering what had awoken her.

Unfamiliar creaks crept up the stairs.

She heard nothing except the slight weight changes across the planks of the floors. She was used to hearing them; different foot placements caused creaks. She knew their magic treasure map trail toward the back. She had been caught unaware with someone's partner too often in her early days. A good paid girl could tell her client how to get out, so she could get the money again in two nights' time as they recollected the high from almost getting caught.

Where were these creaks headed?

The first person's room to be accessed and violated would be Eve's. No screams came from the room. Nothing.

She waited for the creaking sounds to pass her in the hallway before she lightly jumped out of her bed. Her steps echoed the times she would check on her pa, who would sneak in and fall asleep outside her ma's door. She grabbed a heavy whiskey bottle in her right hand, ready to hit the intruder over the head with it.

Her opposite hand cracked the well-oiled hinges of the door open. Looking left and right, she noticed that Eve had also stuck her head out.

"Are you okay?" Britt mouthed at Eve, who nodded in response. "What do they want?" Britt mouthed again.

Eve shrugged silently in return as if to say, "I don't know." Britt spotted a heavy tome in Eve's hand. Eve's head motioned for Britt to look to her right.

Three men in triangular formation stalked the hallway.

As she peeked out from her doorway, wondering what grounds she had lost in the minute she had taken in making her decision, a booming voice beat her to it.

"Leave this place!"

A force threw the men backward, slamming Britt's door with only the vestiges of a force beneath the door eking through.

Footsteps down the hallway caught Britt's breath in her throat.

The scrambling of feet headed out the door before it slammed behind them.

Two moments seemed like two hours later before a single shot pierced through the anxious silence.

The breath caught in her diaphragm; Britt lay with her bottom against the door, trembling, too afraid to lift herself up to find a blanket. Her hand over her mouth and nose left space for the minimal amount of air to sustain her while the other clutched a tricep to remind her that she was in reality.

Man had come for its reckoning, and woman had answered.

Thirty-Seven

Sadie

S adie and Tara sat in Sadie's room finishing the champagne remnants in
their glasses.

"Never once have you made me feel old," Sadie commented.

"Age is for insurance agents and gravestones, Sadie-girl. Your life defies numbers."

"Yet you were born well after me, Anaveh."

"Ten years isn't much. You needed to see life without me to see how great it is
with me." Tara smirked. That smirk stirred in Sadie's lower regions. She would
kiss that smirk right off Tara's face if it didn't decorate that face so well. That
playful confidence backed by a clever mind and humble soul.

Sadie thought back to when DB and Dimin were taking over.

The second in command of a tyrannous regime is the one to fear, for he is
not necessarily the psychotic one; the second has chosen to subscribe to these
views of his own accord. And he seeks to propagate them at an exponential rate
beyond that which the first in command had ever imagined.

But DB would soon be under control, if he had not left already, the town
would soon be waking. By Daughter Dreamer's hand, she prayed that enough
folks would volunteer to stand up to him so they could regrow their community.
As they had failed spectacularly to do last time, to the detriment of their town.

The heat dome created by the dragon vortex would work. Clever Tara was certain of it. The science scienced. Which was quite an odd phrase when it came to magic. Sadie didn't have much experience with magic, other than knowing people from her society days who had had it. Justin had always seemed enamored by the idea of the godliness associated with it; he revered those with powers, wherever they may come from.

She wondered if he had run into DB or Dimin in any of his dealings. She did not expect that he would have done much to stop them; in fact, he probably funded their campaigns with whatever little money remained in his possession from her escapade.

Tara coughed, "The bubbles never fail to tickle my throat."

"Supposed to make you laugh lightly like you're a lady in silk dresses with no problems," Sadie told her.

Tara swirled the coupe glass with the champagne. "Even ladies with silk dresses have problems," Tara drolly stated, watching the bubbles rise in vertical lines. "Speaking of beautiful ladies, I noticed a certain problem arose for you today."

"My ex-husband. I don't know where he got all of the money, but there he is, speculating with the King of Below. Why do you think they want the dragons?"

"I can only assume. We have wards outside our lands to protect the dragons. I have heard of them being mistreated in various parts of Cosimo. Humans disregard the dragons' respect as weakness and seek to control them."

Sadie worried her lip. "Didn't he say something about wanting the land?"

"Maybe he thinks he can use the land for the dragons?"

A creak outside the door stopped them mid-sentence. Tara's hand flew to her holster, unhooking her pistol and giving it to Sadie.

"You do it," she mouthed at Sadie. Sadie nodded in response, recognizing that not only could Tara not kill without forfeiting her own life, but this was Sadie's loose end. Her hand hovered over the gun. "Trespassing," Tara mouthed. The reminder that he, for whoever was approaching was certainly a he, was violating her space sparked the anger within her. She was a legend around these parts, not the bedfellow of a whimpering fool who had no idea of the trials of life. Picking up the cold pistol and muffling the barrel, Sadie nodded at Tara.

Another creak on the floorboards, and the doorknob twisted. Sadie knew the women's foot sounds. She also knew the steps that the rapscallion Verdis made. These were neither.

The soft glow of the lamp highlighted the cracks on Justin's face, confirming Sadie's memory of his footsteps.

"Leave this place!" Sadie's voice boomed. Beside her, Tara pushed her hands out, throwing the men who stood behind Justin backwards.

As Tara dealt with the two henchmen, Sadie aimed at Justin and pulled the trigger. "There's your divorce."

Britt and Eve tumbled with the men in the hallway. They did not take much time in whacking the men repeatedly before the henchmen rolled down the stairs, stumbling out the door.

Thirty-Eight

Tara

From outside the room, Tara heard sounds of women and men tousling. Britt and Eve bounded into the hallway

The body lay still, warm blood pooling out of it. Hotter still was the tension between Sadie and Tara. They stared at each other. Tara had never been so turned on in her life. This woman in front of her had conquered her demons without whining or wavering.

Silently, Sadie set down the gun on the table. She pushed Tara back onto the bed, walking between her legs. Tara could feel her eyesight glazing over. *Could it be possible that she wanted Tara, too?*

"I might be the madame of this house, but tonight, you're *my* whore," Sadie told her.

Tara was used to being the one always in power, the family member that the female dragonhand did not deny. Not that she had ever even considered forcing herself on anyone, but she had never quite felt like they were in it for more than a roll in the hay. Some past partners even thought to try to blackmail her family about her trysts, running to her parents or her brother with her sexuality.

Naz surprised the hands every time with his nonplussed reaction. He knew. The whole family knew. And it wasn't a scourge to them. "All dragons fly different routes," the saying had been drilled into her young. Each person in her family embraced the other for their gifts and presence.

Sometimes she had wondered whether Naz was really straight, especially when he married that turf turd, Esperanza. But then she saw him with Grace, and she knew that he had undeniably found his own path.

So when Sadie took control, Tara started dripping. Sadie slid her soft hand up the inside of Tara's thigh, almost to her apex, and then pulled back.

"I haven't fucked in ages," Sadie started.

Tara quickly interrupted, taken aback. "So I'm just fresh meat?" She sat up. Sadie pushed her back down.

"Because I haven't found anyone desirable. Then you walked in and fucked with my head."

"How did I do that?"

Sadie breathed on her neck, upward to her ear. "You made me remember what it was like to be hanging on someone's every word, dripping for more."

Tara shut her eyes, breathing Sadie's floral scent in deeply. Goosebumps rippled up the back of her neck.

"I wonder what pretty things your body has to tell me." Sadie's hand cupped her breast, and out of reflex, she put her hands back up on Sadie's chest in response. Her nipple hardened as Sadie rolled it between her thumb and forefinger, pinching it gently with her nails. Tara bit her lip in echo of the glorious pain.

"I've been wondering what you like. I've caught you looking at my ass." Sadie knelt with one leg between Tara's thighs and her right thigh on the other side of her leg. She picked up Tara's hands and placed them on her ass.

Tara was dumbstruck. *This woman had noticed?* She felt the roundness and wondered how it would feel to move in time with this being, to bring her ass near it.

As she gazed upon Sadie, those rich brown eyes became to her as clay before pottery. A beautiful realm of potential and forever molding.

Sadie reached down and pulled Tara up so she could pull her out of the dress.

"Are you okay with this still?"

"Maker, yes, go on. I'm yours," Tara panted, almost drooling at the mouth as she helped Sadie unclip out of her bodice. At the sight of her round bosoms, Tara was overcome with lust, her eyes blurry. She needed touch, and only Sadie's would do.

Sadie slipped her legs between Tara's, raising their knees as they were in a seated position.

"Now, I want you to get off on me." Sadie pulled Tara in for a kiss, and Tara met her, exposing her sensitive bud. She began grinding her hips, relishing the sweet softness of Sadie's folds. As she swiveled her hips in one motion, Sadie let out a gasp. Tara pushed her hair back from her eyes, catching the gasp on her lips.

Moving her hips in a curving motion, Tara found the perfect angle. She knew she would be done for in a moment, so she reached down between them and inserted two fingers into Sadie's wetness and curved them in a stroking motion, pulling another gasp from Sadie's lips. She could feel the throbbing that seemed to keep the same beat as Sadie's breathing, which gradually increased. Her chest heaved, and Tara wanted her hands to be everywhere at once—inside Sadie, around her breasts, under her ass, and moving her closer. She wanted all of her.

With Tara's fingers in her, Sadie seemed to slip from wanting to tell Tara what to do and switched to taking her pleasure from Tara.

Tara peppered Sadie's neck with kisses, her short nose trailing a line of goosebumps down her skin. Her slender lips claimed Sadie's full ones, and Sadie's hands caressed Tara's smooth back. And as Sadie moved closer and closer, her hips moved faster, chasing her orgasm. Sadie's moans cued Tara to pull out her fingers. Staring into Sadie's face, she licked them, tasting the ice cream of the gods.

"Fuck," Tara moaned. The sensations were building to a frenzy as they both worked their over-sensitive spots.

"Don't worry about me," Sadie moaned as she held on tightly to Tara.

"The fuck I won't," Tara said around Sadie's breast as she licked circles around the hardened peak. "But I'm not going to hold out much longer."

They grabbed onto each other's hips, helping each other move faster until Sadie brushed a thumb over Tara's hard nipple, and Tara cried out, throwing her head back. Sadie kept moving through the wetness, chasing her own orgasm, which followed quickly, while she bit down on Tara's shoulder, causing Tara to scream in delight and dig her fingernails into Sadie's hips.

As the two came down from their moment, they stared at each other. Neither wanted to break the silence of the moment with a dumb comment that would end whatever they had. In that moment, they finally breathed, clinging to one another behind foggy windows, the only sign of their existence to the outside world.

Thirty-Nine

Tara

The dragons' cries woke her from where she and Sadie had fallen asleep. The dead man's body still acted as an entry rug into the room.

"Sadie," she nudged her shoulder. "Sadie, wake up." Long eyelashes fluttered, and the head that had been resting on her dislodged from her armpit.

Another cry from the rooftop, and Evie bolted in wearing her silk pink nightdress.

"FIRE ... TORNADO!" She screamed, red-faced.

Tara bolted out of bed with Sadie not far behind her. They both ran to the window. To the left, they saw an entire building in orange. It wasn't quite a fire tornado, but flames seemed to swirl around from rooftops.

"NO!" Tara screamed. This wasn't supposed to happen. She had worked too hard to develop the plan. It was in action. It was going. She was going to help the town.

She grabbed a blanket, wrapped it around her, and bolted down the stairs, stepping on the fringe and pulling herself down as she went. She stumbled getting back up, and Sadie pulled her up by the arm. Britt and Eve clamored about, the sound of cupboards opening and closing.

She needed to get out. The dragons. The people.

The cool ground on her bare feet jarred her more awake when she pitched herself out into the night.

"We need water, Tara. The whole town will go down." Sadie started to head back inside, but was met by Eve and Britt rushing out the door toward the well, buckets and bowls hanging from every part of their bodies. The wind blew them back and forth, and they stumbled to keep the buckets upright. They handed her some, and she joined them in their paths.

Fires were not unheard of, but they needed to be quickly tended to, or they would swallow a town whole. They were a town affair, and this town was about to become a cremated town.

The smoke billowed up to the sky, the dragons flying in and out of the blackened tendrils. Their cries carried around, hoping to wake the undead.

Tara stared at the scene, wondering where to start. All these people would die. Yet, how had the fire started? Though the dragons' path overhead during the day had already sucked much of the moisture out of the town, leaving the wood structures dry and flammable. However, their warm breath would not have ignited such an inferno.

The girls ran back and forth from the well at the end of the street to the next building over from the fire, hoping to douse it, soak it so it would not pick up any embers.

Yet the strain of saving their home by running down the street to the well and back to the brothel with heavy buckets tired the girls. And that was when Tara spotted DB lighting a cigar and slowly puffing it until the end flared orange. He pulled another out of his inner pocket and used the lit cigar to light what must have been a cut end already. He then tossed one into the lower window of the very house that Britt and Eve were working to soak. The second flew in a higher arc.

Tara watched, mouth ajar and wide eyes following the path of the second cigar onto the roof where the embers quickly became flames.

"What are you doing!?" She yelled at him, running forward. She could feel her magic surging in her hands. "There are people alive in there!"

"Now now, I'm pretty sure if they haven't awoken yet, they're not going to. Just need to cremate this whole town. Perhaps you could help me say a few words to Mother Maker, while I ready the next starter?" He reached into his pocket again.

"You're out of your damn mind! You need to stop!" Tara moved toward him.

"Or what? You'll heal me?" He sniggered at her and struck a match, holding it up to the end of the cigar.

"You're going to burn this whole town down!"

"It's not much of a town if there aren't people. Or a worship house. Or a post office. Or a brothel." He puffed in. "Besides, what do you care? You'll be able to return to your hoity-toity living on your dragon ranch."

He was right that her Oath would be fulfilled if he were to burn the city. But she could never live with wondering about the futures of everyone in the town and what they could have been, especially as she knew how to heal them. Tara tried a different tactic with the man.

"You won't be in charge of anything if you do this."

"That's what you think." She really needed to stop this guy from throwing that cigar. She felt the pull to help the others start dousing the flames, but if he continued lighting fires, they would never win. She needed to stop the fires at the source.

The heat was making her sweat. As she wiped the sweat from her brow, he flicked the cigar toward the other side of the street. All the mercantile goods, whatever remained in their storage, *PHWOOP*, up in flames.

"You'll have nothing but a dead town. In fact, it won't even be recognized as a town anymore. Then what'll it be?" Then the thought hit her: it'll just be free land for the taking. Justin had spoken about an investment.

"I have to thank you for bringing the dragons out to me. And with a Fuentes girl here to help me out, I'll have complete legitimacy to my venture."

Her chin could have scratched the ground. "WHAT!? I don't condone ANY of this!"

DB's face glowed with pride at his own intelligence. "Of course you do. You need to. You brought all of these dragons here on your own. No one asked you to. For all intents and purposes, this business dealing occurred."

She hated him. He needed to be removed from here. Picked up by the dragons and dropped in a mountain to live out his days as a beggar.

To the left behind her, Sadie directed the other two women to start dousing the saloon in water. "If we get the wood soaked here, then it should stop the fire from spreading to the house. Maker help us if it doesn't work and the alcohol goes up in flames." *Good thinking, Sadie-girl.*

In Tara's periphery, Sadie ran down the side of the street to douse blankets in water at the well as well as to grab more water. DB caught her movement and laughed.

"I can't believe you four are of the mind that you'll be able to stop these buildings from burning. You'd be better off stopping a forest fire. I could watch you do this all day. Toss some corn into the heat, and have some popcorn made for a light snack while viewing the entertainment."

She had no time to work out the science in her head. In her frenzy to soak the saloon, Sadie must have forgotten about her surroundings. She was on a mission to save her home. DB grabbed a plank from the mercantile store and stalked toward Sadie as she was dousing the building with water.

"No!" Tara yelled. Passing her hands over the earth and flipping them over in her come-hither motion, she motioned to the ground. Rocks, specks, crumbles, and pieces of dirt of every shape and size began quaking below DB. As Tara commanded them forward, the force propelled DB to move backward away from Sadie.

"So the rumors are true," DB said. His big eyes took in her glowing hands. "You Fuentes do have dragon magic." The display only acted as a momentary distraction. "Imagine the way we could build up this land for the dragons."

"You're out of your Makermucking mind." And in that moment, she had no thought but to protect her thunder, these women around her, as well as the thunder of dragons around her. Heaving a breath, she pulled the energy upward.

Exhaling, she flung it with all the force she could muster at him, hoping to use it to push him back and to the side of the road.

But DB was not stupid. He dodged the force, and it spun past him, curving to the side, in the pathway that Tara had intended for him to take.

At that exact moment, Sadie ran down the side of the road, back toward the well. But Sadie was too in her own world to know.

"Sadie!" Tara alerted Sadie too late. As Sadie turned her head, the force hit her in her right thigh. A crack rang out through the street, and Sadie collapsed onto the boarded walkway.

Tara needed to get to her. She needed to heal Sadie. A tingling sensation overtook her toes.

Oh, no. The Oath. Running toward Sadie, she threw up a dust wall between them and DB. Yet, as Tara ran, the tingling spread, and the dust wall weakened. Two feet from Sadie, Tara's right leg gave out under her.

Quickly, she mustered up all of her remaining strength and army-crawled over to Sadie. Tara needed to get her away from the burning that continued to spread down the street.

The barrier between them fell, revealing that DB had already moved away, content to light more buildings on fire now that he had managed the distraction.

Tara whipped off her shoes. She was able to move her left leg toward the curb, but she needed to lift up her right leg and position it to a spot where her sole could touch the land. She hoped that she could soak in whatever magic she could from the ground, that some had made it from the dragons above. Closing her eyes, she focused on connecting with the energy in the land.

"Let it go, Tara. I suppose it's time that I go with this town. I'm old."

"Shut up your stupid spewings." Tara focused on the ground, leaning over to put her hands on the dirt next to her feet.

"It's not working," Tara murmured to herself. How could that be?

"Save your remaining energy to deal with that bastard," Sadie insisted.

Tara shook her head. "I don't have any left, and I can't seem to pull any from around me." Her mind raced through her past.

When had something like this ever happened to her before?

She could not think of a time.

Had she ever heard of this happening to someone in her family?

The only times that someone lost their magic had to do with a curse or breaking an oath.

The Oath. She had hurt Sadie. Oh, her sweet Sadie-girl.

Sadie's calm voice cut through her mental spinning. "Listen to me, Tara. You need to find a way for the dragons to deal with this crazed mess. They are our only hope." Their hands found each other and held on tightly.

"I promised you that if you ever got hurt with me, Sadie, that I'd let the dragons curse me. They don't even have to because the guilt right now is enough to eat me alive."

Sadie unclasped her hands and grasped Tara's cheeks. She pulled her into a kiss.

Shadows born of dancing flames and evil ways moved toward them, catching their eyes. DB had picked up the large plank and was stomping toward them, as if he were hunting. The women had nowhere to go.

"Hey, rabbitshit! You're not done with us!" A female voice called out from the other end of the street. Britt appeared out of the saloon with a sawed-off shotgun in both of her hands, prowling down the middle of the street. DB turned away from his intended victims. He walked toward the middle of the street, across from where she stood in a standoff position. Adeptly, she loaded some bullets as she walked straight down the street, stalking her prey with her aim on the man.

DB laughed. "You impetuous fool."

She quickly fired off two shots, both of which missed him by more than a foot. DB merely stood there unflinching. Swearing under her breath, Britt cracked the shotgun and reloaded it with bullets from the satchel on her hip. Moving closer, she shot again. This time, the bullets hit a bit closer. DB looked only slightly concerned by Britt's demonstration.

Tara did not want to distract Britt from the immediate threat that she had placed herself under.

"You and Sadie get out of here," Britt directed Tara as she reloaded quickly, muttering something unintelligible under her breath.

DB laughed, reaching his hand slowly into the holster at his side for his pistol.

Tara and Sadie held onto one another tightly, neither able to move her right leg or to take her eyes off of Britt.

Forty

Britt

Her hands shook. She had never been this close to death before, where a man wasn't there to cover her ass. Yes, she knew how to get out of various scrapes. She could kick a man's ass in general.

But she had never been the shooter; she was always the loader when Rusty went hunting. She could work a knife great, skin a rabbit clean out of its skin in under a minute. But shooting had never been her job.

Before leaving the brothel, she had hastily dressed in some fishnets and an old blue showgirl costume, worn last by someone with much more courage than she had. She inhaled, trying to channel her best Grace.

"You and Sadie get out of here," she commanded Tara. They both needed to get themselves as far away from the wrath of this man as possible. As she reloaded, she found herself muttering, "I only know how to load! He never let me shoot!"

She tried to remember every lesson that Rusty had given her, every tip for shooting straight. Push the butt into her shoulder. Pull the barrel back. Look with both eyes.

Staring this man down as he raised his hand with his gun at her, she shook. At this distance, she had one shot to protect her herd. *Mother Maker and all her dragons, please help me protect my family.* And exhaling, she pulled the trigger.

DB crumpled to the ground an instant after the gunshot cracked at him. The pride of victory over a moment overtook her. She had done it! She raised her gun in the air and turned to her left to look at her friends with a jump and whooping yell.

They yelled with her ...

But they were not yells of triumph. They were the yells of caution, for Britt had never learned about the kill shot.

The burning hit her on the side of her back, near her liver, and she grabbed it, twisting as she fell to the ground. DB's boot stomps came closer, kicking dust into her eyes. The burning added to the discomfort of her injury and her shallow breathing.

DB knew about the kill shot. And he had her shotgun in his right hand, his left hand hanging limply at his side.

He pointed it directly at her chest. Maker knew she could use a miracle at that moment. Looking up, she saw the dragons circling overhead. In her lightheadedness, she could have sworn that she called out to them, but she could not tell. The ground moved around her, as if she had the spins from drinking a full bottle of whiskey on an empty stomach.

BANG!

Instantly, light overtook her vision as her soul drifted upward toward the dragons that circled overhead, leading her home.

Forty-One

Eve

"**N**o!!!!" Eve shrieked from down the street behind Britt, where she had been working to keep the brothel from taking Verdis up in flames with it. A dragon stepped in front of her, between her and the shotgun. She could no longer see the man who had taken one of her best friends.

"I should have just offed you when you three came back around. Damn, I should've offed that dragon lady when she came in with sights on healing this town, whatever that means."

His voice became clearer and less distant. Eve tried to look around the dragon, but it gave her a sneer with a puff of smoke that meant to stay out of sight.

Torn between finding a gun and firing it rapidly at this demon and throwing her sobbing body across Britt's, Eve stood paralyzed. Another person that she loved had been yanked cruelly from this world. Was she forever cursed to lose people that she loved? To be abandoned like a mystery novel that was read only once?

As the man grew closer, the dragon growled. He looked like a man possessed: hair disheveled, blood streaming down his arm, sweat drenching his shirt.

The dragon opened its mouth, for what purpose Eve did not know. But she heard a *THWACK* and the sound of ten books thumping simultaneously to the ground. The dragon nudged her out from her spot behind it. Sadie, propped up by Tara, had used the large plank to knock DB out and onto the ground.

"He didn't even realize that we were behind him." Sadie kicked him in the ribs. Tara moved her away.

"I thought you could do no harm," Eve cited to Tara, as Sadie hobbled past her toward where Britt lay.

"I didn't harm him. Sadie did. But I sure as hell ain't about to save him from justice." She picked up the rifle from next to DB and used it as a golf club, swinging it at the man's head, intentionally missing it by a hair. "Oh, though how I wish that I could dole it out myself!"

Eve spied Sadie with Britt's head in her lap, tears streaming down her cheeks. Sadness clenched her heart, wringing its pain out through her eyes as tears. Surely her friend would stand up soon and brush it off with laughter. The life had been zapped from Britt's limbs, though. Slowly, Eve moved as if trapped in a vat of viscous fluid from which she could not escape.

Where she once had stood behind a dragon, Tara now roped that bastard's hands together behind his back.

Forty-Two

Sadie

U sing whatever strength she had left, Sadie pulled herself to the middle of
the street where Tara held their prisoner. "I'm not waiting for some man
to come and dish out justice. Tara, get the dragons."

"They wouldn't burn him then; they're not going to burn him now," Tara
replied.

"That's right, they won't burn him. What happened when Icarus flew too
close to the sun?"

"Sadie, you cannot ask them to kill. That goes against everything that they are
in their purest souls."

"I'm asking them to dole out justice."

"Then you need to ask them, not command them. They will lead the way."

Newa brought up a rope and laid it over DB. Sadie quickly tied the rope
around DB's neck, tightly.

"I want to see justice done," she implored. With the three women and DB on
her back, Newa flew to the brothel, where Sadie told her to stop. The dragon
hoisted them up to the balcony, where Sadie fed the rope through the balustrade,
tying it in a strong knot that she had learned back in her sewing days. The
balcony would hold. She had ensured that every part of her home would be as
strong as her resolve.

She stood the man up on Newa's back, then motioned for the women to slide back down. Looking up at their work, Sadie noticed DB's eyes starting to blink.

She turned around, walking slowly away. "Let's go, girls." The other two walked with her. Neither of them looked back as Eve whispered to Newa, "Hee-ya!" Newa followed the thunder.

The cracking of DB's neck echoed throughout the town.

The legend of Sadie would live on in the hearts of these four females.

"Neither of you killed him," Sadie mentioned. "I tied the rope."

"I said the words," replied Eve. "And if I were struck down with the cold sickness again, reliving this night, I would find a bit of peace in knowing that I said them."

Sadie looked at Tara. "You'll be fine. No Oaths were broken. Trust me," she said, slipping her hand around Tara's waist.

"I do," Tara said simply in return, putting her head on Sadie's shoulder.

"He didn't stop these people from dying." Eve's fists were balled up, and tears streamed down her face. "He didn't help them. And then he *killed* one of the people who decided to try to help her community."

Sadie's heart melted into her stomach. Death kept breaking Eve's heart, and through bravery alone, she remained to glue it back together herself, every time. She chose to endure the pain of losing—a sacrifice for the pleasure of loving. Now, she had something to say about it.

"He's dead, Eve. Justice has been served," Tara assured her.

"By the Maker, yes, but not yet by me," she seethed. The woman stood, flames painting her face with a raging red glow. Her voice, no longer gentle and wistful, now commanded sharply. "Use some of the extra wood and the tools that you grabbed from the Charles' place. Tie him to it. I'll return." Eve assigned the women the duty. Sadie wondered what Eve would do; she seemed so resolute in her actions.

Tara used her gun to shoot through the rope, bringing the body down into a slump like a rag doll that Sadie played with as a little girl. With all their might, they hoisted the man to a standing position and tied him to the post near the dragon clearing. Tara picked up the remainder of the rope from his neck and wound it around his body and to the large spike. His head dropped. Tara ran inside the house and returned with a broom. She used it to prop his head up and arrange his body, making sure to tuck his hands inside his pants in a lewd gesture.

"The people who enter this town will see him and know that he was more concerned with his manhood than mankind," Sadie commented.

Eve returned from the house with a stack of papers. Eve took a string and tied it around the man's shoulder, under the armpit. With a bandaged hand, she stretched the pieces of paper across it as if she were draping a banner across the mantel for a birthday celebration. Written in red paint, one letter on each sheet, she had spelled out "POISON."

Sadie couldn't place where she got the paint until she put two and two together with the bandage that Eve had used her own blood to write the letters. She stepped up to assist with tying the other one under his other arm, for Eve had a bit of trouble with her bandaged hand.

The man's staring creeped out Sadie. She didn't want to see those callous eyes anymore. She moved to close the eyelids, but Eve put a hand out on her arm.

"Let the crows feast on his eyes, for he saw and did nothing." Fiery rage glowed through sweet Eve's eyes. Sadie knew that though they all were forever changed by this pandemic of hate, the dreamy Eve had been smacked across the face with the two-by-four of harsh reality. And Eve was about to burn that wood that smacked her with all of her suppressed wrath.

Forty-Three

Tara

"I'm surprised the heat hasn't warmed people up enough."

"It's just fire, not dragon fire or dragon magic. Otherwise, I would've lit this town up the second that I arrived. But we do need to put it out, since it's burning everyone inside."

Though blessed with different powers, her brother and she could both control the environment. She reached out with her hands. Closing her eyes, she reached into the ground with her toes. Relief poured through her at the confirmation that only her healing powers had been affected by The Oath's curse. The power surged through her fingertips. It wound outside of her body and attached itself to the melted snow that rushed over the dry ground, unable to absorb so much water in such a quick time. She could feel the droplets levitating, waiting for her direction. With a wave of her fingers, she pushed the droplets toward the tongues of fire, smothering them in their wake.

She heard the gasps of Eve and Sadie as she did it.

"You could have done that to begin with!" Eve yelled at Tara. "Britt would still be here!"

"If she could have done it, she would have," Sadie said softly, holding Eve back from charging at Tara.

"It takes too much concentration. There was too much going on at the time with DB threatening the ground where we stood. I can only now do it."

Eve dropped to the ground in grief next to their friend.

Forty-Four

Eve

Camelia nuzzled Tara to get her attention, then scraped her foot on the ground, shaking her head. Lifting her snout to the sky, she let out a small stream of fire, flapped her wings, and made a noise.

Fire from dragons was next to unheard of. Eve had been watching the whole thing with interest.

Tara clarified to her, "They want to honor her as one of their own." The faucets in Eve's eyes opened, and tears streamed down like waterfalls.

"Can they get her upstairs so we can get her body ready?"

The dragons gingerly held the limp body in their claws. Eve painstakingly wrapped her friend with a sturdy fabric that she had found that Britt had once contributed to the lounging room. A woven blanket of unknown origin. Maybe it was her baby blanket. Maybe it was a blanket that her ma had knit for her. Maybe it was just a store-bought item because she needed to cover herself up one day. She would never know. Eve's eyes started to water. Never again would she be able to answer her friend's call in the middle of the night or splay out on her bed with a bottle of whiskey between them.

The image of Britt's face, once so perfectly pouty, now just decimated to a bloody crater, haunted her. Never again to smile.

Standing with Sadie and Tara, she looked at their clasped hands. She wished that she, too, could have some human contact. Britt would have known that Eve needed some grounding.

Never again to clasp her in her arms and be reminded of their female camaraderie.

She looked away as the icy-blue dragon carried the wrapped body in its forelegs towards them, slowing for a landing. Her eyes caught on the back of the saloon.

Never again to sing a bawdy drinking song in the wee hours of the morning.

The body rested atop the pile of dull greens that had been gathered and dried by the dragons. Eve squeezed her arms across her chest, hugging herself.

Never again would her friend give her hope that all would be alright.

She glanced sideways at Tara, who nodded at Camelia. A steady stream of fire burst out of the dragon's throat, aimed at the pile of shrubbery. Yokel and the others followed likewise, igniting the pile into a pyre. Their fire-breathing halted when flames engulfed the body and greens.

As they all watched, the dragons made slow, low noises.

"They are singing for her," Tara whispered, just barely audible. Eve could not make out a tune, but took Tara's word. "They only sing for their fallen brethren, and each song is unique."

Hearing this detail, Eve's heart cried out more than the night her husband had fallen, and that cry escaped her mouth as she crashed to the ground in a heap. Her cheeks oversaturated with wetness from whatever small amount of hydration remained in her body. Her precious Britt had followed the dragons away from the place of misery to a place of promises. Her burning rewarded her venture.

Never again would her friend, Britt, exist, for forevermore her spirit would fly with the dragons.

The tears eventually evaporated due to the flames in front of her. She had never felt this warmth inside her before. This hatred for the fellow humans that she had once served. She stood up and quietly walked to the back door of the brothel.

To the others, she could only suppose that she appeared in a catatonic state. *Whatever.*

Only she knew that everyone involved in this mess would pay. Docile Eve had been abandoned for the last time. Relentless Eve remained.

A knock on the door interrupted her mental planning.

"What?" She whirled around in impatience at the distraction.

Verdis stood at the door, leaning on the jamb.

"Where the fuck have you been?" she swore, which she rarely did. She knew that he noticed by the momentary widening of his eyes. And she didn't care. She returned her attention to packing the bag.

"I'm pretty sure I was knocked out in your bed."

"Well, you missed quite a bit. There was a fire tornado, DB shot Britt, Sadie's hurt, Tara raised water from the ice melt, the dragons are back circling, getting ready for another go. DB's in the middle of the street. Britt's burning out back."

Verdis stood awestruck before looking between the exit and Eve.

"He's not going anywhere. He's breakfast for the bugs. And the dragons will keep vigil until the morning. What are you looking so confused about?"

"I am trying to figure out where to help first."

"Afraid we took care of it all," she replied curtly.

"Are you mad at me for having been knocked unconscious?"

"I'm mad at every man in this town that Britt had to sacrifice her life for when they would do nothing to help her in a pinch. We three, then four, then three were all we had because no one else would lift a finger to help us if we were bleeding out in the middle of the street. All we were was an hour and a price."

He had no reply to her. She had never heard Verdis this quiet before. Good, she had shut him up. She couldn't stand to hear another man speak.

She had a secret stash of money hidden in a knot in the wood behind her headboard. She had carved it out slightly and then shoved a robe over it. So many robes all over her room decorated the space. Strewn across the chair. Hanging from a hook on the bookshelf. Over a window. Anyone would figure that she hid things in the bookshelf, never that the robes were strategically placed, not haphazardly thrown.

She pulled the gold out of its hiding spot and shoved the coins in various locations on her person.

He made his way toward her. She pulled the satchel over her shoulder, ignoring his steps.

"Evie. Evie ... EVE."

She whirled back to him. "What?" She knew that if she stayed much longer, her eyes would betray her grief and cloak her thoughts.

His eyes seemed softer. "Eve, where are you going?"

"I'm asking a dragon to go, and I'm leaving. And I'm going to make every single one of those goons pay for what they have decided to do here."

"I thought that you chose to be alive."

"I feel dead inside," she whispered. Another person was gone from her. No more laughter with Britt. No more late nights gossiping. No more doubles for double coin. No more washing and drying dishes together. No more sweet good nights to each other at four in the morning.

"The pain will go away," Verdis said in failed reassurance.

"I feel nothing, which angers me. Because for a time, I thought I'd be okay, and I'm now back to square one," Eve continued.

"I'm coming with you," Verdis told her.

Shaking her head, Eve refused. "I won't lose another person."

"You can't lose me if you never had me."

"I had you a few times, if you weren't too drunk to remember."

"We'll be fine." Verdis could not tell a lie, so she accepted this response.

"Fine, but we're leaving now," Eve relented.

She heaved a sigh. He was going to be a bigger burden than she wanted, but seeing the earnestness in his eyes compelled her to uphold her agreement. After he changed, they walked outside. Verdis insisted upon carrying her satchel.

As they traveled outside, they didn't see Sadie and Tara. Did not stop to say goodbye. She would not. She could not. It was her turn to leave others for once, rather than them leaving her. It was her turn to abandon some and abolish others.

In her silence, Verdis guaranteed that his orange dragon friend would transport them to wherever she needed to go to fully rid Cosimo of man's evil blight upon it. As predicted, the friendly creature left the pyre and lolled over to where they stopped and waited in the clearing. Verdis climbed up and pulled her up in front of him.

"I hope you have panties on; otherwise your lips are going to be stuck to that saddle, like a suction cup, as we ride. Especially once the sweat starts."

Eve scrunched her nose as if she had smelled something terrible. "That's disgusting."

"And physics. Where to?" Verdis held onto her hips with familiarity. As utterly unbalanced as she felt, his hands were steadying and grounding.

"East. To abandon and abolish." With a pull on the reins, they lifted into the sky, leaving Grogtown behind.

Forty-Five

Sadie

A s the dragons circled the few remaining buildings, they blew into the epi-
center. Warm, magical air swirled about Sadie and Tara like an embrace.
Sweat dripped down them like they were in a sauna.

In one way, they were. In all the buildings that were structurally safe to enter,
as Sadie had learned to evaluate through her construction of the brothel, the
two women entered and assessed for signs of life. Those that were frozen and
pulseless received a ride on a sheet to the dragon clearing.

Those who began stirring were tended to. Camelia and the two other healing
dragons helped transport the living to the saloon, where the swinging doors
were knocked off the hinges thanks to the Charles' hammer.

No one spoke more than to say, "alive" or "no pulse."

After all the humans that could be safely reached were divided, Sadie and Tara
went and counted the victims in the saloon.

"Ten," Tara lamented. "Only ten."

Sadie grabbed her chin. "Look at me. Not only ten. Ten. We saved ten. That's
ten more than we had yesterday."

"I thought I would save so many more. I couldn't."

"Now now, no use in crying," Sadie said. "You're exhausted. I'm going to
keep watch here over them while the dragons fly."

"What happens if they wake?"

"Suppose they'll have to deal with the town whore taking care of them." She gave a soft smile.

"The woman nursing them," Tara corrected with a soft smile returned. She kissed Sadie's cheek, and she walked out the door.

"Sadie, we need to stop and get some water," Tara reminded them both. Refreshing themselves at the well, Tara down the street in the direction of the brothel. "I hope Eve is okay."

"She's not," Sadie said matter-of-factly. "When she arrived, she had just lost her husband. Britt brought her in. Her face was caked with dirt and blood from where she had later told me that she had dragged her cheeks in the dirt in her agony. Belongings were scattered everywhere, blowing about the street. Books surrounded her, some open with their pages blowing in the breeze. Some were on their sides. A few of the dragons had caught some of her more personal items as they fell from the sky. They stood around snatching things as they blew away."

"But those are only material possessions. They could not bring back Eve's husband, whom she loved very much. Or that was to the extent that she could put her feelings into words. For being such a well-read woman, her ability to communicate her actual feelings about the ordeal was quite stunted."

Sadie started walking back toward the saloon.

"No, she won't be alright," she reiterated. "I don't even know how she pulled herself together after her husband's passing, but somehow she weathered the storm. Britt's death," Sadie's eyes began to tear." Britt's death hits us straight in the heart of our home."

The home no longer felt the same once she stepped inside of it. She knew that Britt would never walk the stairs anymore, but somehow her brain dismissed it as if she were simply working next door at the saloon.

"Eve?" Sadie called from the bottom of the stairs. No answer or footsteps. Wary of what she would find in Eve's room, Sadie walked slowly up the stairs.

"Eve?" she asked, as she opened the door to an empty room. Bedding was bunched on the floor. Books were strewn about. A storm had passed through these walls, and that storm's name was Eve. Who knew where that storm would go next, but it was not up to Sadie to track it in that moment.

How could she when sadness overtook her heart at the realization that the only family she had known had left her.

Forty-Six

Tara

Nary a cloud threatened to enter the land. The heat of the morning sun kissed their skin. Tara willed a small breeze to come through so that they would not bake completely. So many had been deprived of Vitamin D that they could all use it.

The scene was set for a happy community picnic. Instead, the twelve people stood around the pyres of bodies in the clearing. As if some virus had swept through the town, the bodies would be burnt. Dragon fire, a hardly seen spectacle, would burn the bodies, sending their spirits directly to Mother Maker.

The dragons stood around the piles of bodies that they had made. Tara's hands twitched, ready to pull water out of the ground and the atmosphere should the fire start spreading uncontrollably.

One of the townspeople had brought a scripture text with her. A text about the staircases and the merits of man spewed from her lips.

What good had man done for them?

Four women had saved the town. They would not be remembered. They would not be appreciated. She should have just let the fire sweep the town away. She had not heard one mutter of, "Thank you," from any of the survivors. *The ungrateful turds.*

She did not do it for the praise. It was her Oath and her duty to help those. And the dragons could not have healed those remaining had DB been around. But would these people have even known if DB had razed the town to the ground? *Would it have been a blessing?*

She thought back to Eve, who had thanked Tara for giving her a choice. These people had no say, and she gave them their voices back. If they wanted to dig themselves into a hole again, that was their issue. The Association could send a new healer out here next time.

"The rest, we bury. I'll have the dragons start digging the graves."

"Grave," Sadie corrected her. "Just throw them all into one hole. I'm so done with all of this."

Forty-Seven
Sadie

I cannot stay here, Tara. These people." She shook her head. "We were all warned. Something in me felt a need to stay and to bond with my towns-people. I thought we would all band together and be able to withstand the curse and Dimin. But they did not care. I can count on one hand the number of people that helped care for the sick."

Sadie felt angry, nauseated at the memory. "They gave him and DB the town. Just handed it over. There were a few dissenters, but they were hot-heads. If we had worked together, we could have kept him out."

"Probably," affirmed Tara.

"How am I supposed to just go back to running my business as if none of this happened?"

"That's your call, Sadie-girl. It's your home."

"I thought it was, but the more I consider it, no one ever greeted me here. When I was growing up out east, I would walk through my house and feel peace. I knew everyone who worked for us. I could say hello and ask the servants about their lives, and they would happily converse with me. I had respect and love."

She remembered the simple trips to the post office when the townspeople of Grogtown would move out of their way if they saw her coming, sometimes go-ing as far as to walk across the street to avoid her. On grocery trips that required extra bartering, mothers would shoo their children around Sadie, teaching them to ignore her. Men who would regularly visit her establishment pretended that they hadn't spent an hour or two debating the best bookkeeping methods or the merits of a town bank.

She had not dwelt upon the moments, preferring to focus on how she was ruined goods by any man's standard and was happy to just be alive and walking around.

However, the more that she considered this turning point at which she found herself, the more she realized that she could define the next part of her life.

She did not need to have secret relationships with people. *What would it be like to have the support of people and not be constantly warring to maintain a piece of her own? Not to fight to prove that she was worthy?*

She had worth, and her worth wasn't the money that she made. It wasn't the respect that she commanded within the community.

Her life had intrinsic value, and she refused to be treated as dirt. She meant something in this world, more than just as a female playing the game. She didn't want her life to be a game anymore.

Tara had never seen her that way. Tara looked at her like she was the freshly baked cinnamon roll on the breakfast table.

Sadie nudged Tara's shoulder with her own. "Where are you headed next?"

"I figured I'd go home." Tara gnawed at her lip, in the way Sadie had learned she did when she was nervous. "I need a vacation and you look like you could use one, too."

Sadie laughed. "Dreamer knows, I don't even remember the last time I took a vacation."

Tara rubbed her face, which glistened with sweat from the hot air. "Titan's Creek has an empty room or two, prime chef service, in a quaint pastoral setting," she started.

"*Pfft.* I would not call the dragonlands quaint," Sadie replied.

"No," Tara agreed wistfully. "They are beautiful."

Sadie wished that she would extend the invite. She did not want to encroach on Tara's personal space if she did not want to. Yet she did not want to be separated from Tara after their ordeal together. Both from a trauma response and a budding appreciation for her presence.

No, not appreciation. A caring for her presence, strong feelings.

"I've loved being near you," she blurted, then immediately blushed.

"I've loved being near you, too, Sadie-girl." After a moment, Tara said, "You know, you don't have to stop being near me."

Sadie smiled. "Good, because I'm not ready to do that yet."

"But I need to go home."

"I need a new home," she asked more than stated.

Tara captured her hand in her own. "I'm glad we're in agreement, then. We leave in the morning."

On the back of the dragon, Sadie clung to Tara.

"You asked me once when I felt alive."

"I assume you feel alive now that we've kicked that man out of your life, my feral female." Tara's memory knew no match.

"Well, yeah, but I feel alive with the new possibilities that are open to me. I'm surging with the energy of what's next."

"You tell me, Sadie-girl."

Though the nickname felt like a kiss on her cheek, she couldn't help but respond. "I'm ten years older than you, Anaveh."

"Yeah, but the way your eyes are lit up right now as you look forward to dreaming, you look ageless." Tara's eyes searched Sadie's. "Would you ever consider making a home with me?"

"What if your home becomes our home? You need it to survive. And I need stability, which Titan's Creek seems to have, because it has you."

"You don't want to rebuild your brothel?" Tara asked.

"Only the gods can bring life from ashes. We are but women."

"Ah, but we bring life in our own way, so in that way, are we not the gods that men should be worshipping?" Tara asked.

"I could happily live out my days worshipping you," Sadie flirted with her.

"All I'm asking for is tomorrow, Sadie-girl. We'll figure out the next day as it comes."

Epilogue

C amelia sped up. Tara felt the surging energy of the wards as well. She patted Camelia on her head.

"We're almost there, girl." Tara held her hands up to the wards, meeting the rhythm of her family's magic, letting them know that she and Camelia were home.

Sadie's strong arms encircled her hips. Two fewer people rode the dragon than the last time they had traveled this route. This place that had stood for generations would be their home. She could run a house again if needed. She was ready. Her situation was not defined by having what was hers and due to her. The only thing due to her was her future, and she foresaw happiness.

As soon as they landed in the field, Camelia gave a loving nuzzle to each of the women, nipping Tara in her behind before she ran off.

"Oh, that female deserves some good attention." Sadie put her arm around Tara as they walked inside.

Tara threw her shoes off and immediately felt the surge of the power through her. She wondered if her Oath had been fulfilled. *Would she ever need to be called to heal again, especially without her powers?*

As if in answer, Sadie remarked, "Either I gained some of your powers or this place truly is magical. My leg doesn't bother me anymore."

Tara noted that her leg, too, had stopped aching. She knew in her heart that her Oath had been fulfilled and all was right in her world.

The familiar scent of home greeted her as the two women crossed the threshold. Tara led Sadie straight up the stairs to her bedroom, eager to give Sadie some attention of her own.

A loud thump in the direction of the front door put them both on alert. Two firm thuds, followed by more jaunty thuds, and a pitter-patter of two more echoed throughout the house.

Tara's eyes brightened, and a smile took over her face from her chin to her eyes. "Oh!" She grabbed Sadie's hand and dragged her behind her out of the room and to the stairway.

"Aunt Tara!" a little voice piped up from in front of Tara, who immediately crouched down at the bottom of the step.

Sadie laughed heartily at the loving welcome. Movement caught Tara's eye as Sadie continued past her halfway down the steps. Tara looked up and saw her brother, who scratched at his scruffy beard and began to introduce himself to her companion. "Hi, I'm ..."

"SADIE!" A familiar playful voice yelled from behind him. Naz lurched forward as a force pushed him out of the way and flew around the two females on the ground.

The sandy-brown haired woman flew up the stairs and flung her arms around Sadie's neck. The weight pulled them both to a sitting position on the stairs where they both began to cry in each other's arms.

"You survived," Grace gasped out between sobs.

"It's going to take a lot more than some petty men throwing temper tantrums to rid the world of the indomitable strength of us women. After all, we're descended from the gods. These mere mortals of men need to be reminded who truly holds the power every once in a while. We allow them to enter into this world, and we sure as hell aren't going to let them burn it down."

The four women looked at each other, smiling with the prevailing power of the dragons.

Acknowledgements

No one warned me about how hard writing my second book would be. I have not triumphed over its challenges by myself.

Robert, thank you for loving me through this messy writing. I'd much rather whisper all my thanks to you in your ear for only you to hear. I love you.

Daphne, yes, I've FINALLY finished writing this book. I know it took awhile, but we females are complex creatures. Always remember that strong women like us can handle difficult problems, even if searching for the solution requires a bit of time.

Bruce, you've been by my side every day and every night. I owe you an extra walk a day, my good boy.

Laura. You listened to every part of the process but never read the book until the end when I placed it in your hands to bring all together. You keep my real world together so I can write worlds from my imagination. You kept me sane when I almost freaked out. You are an incredible and indispensable companion on this adventure.

Joe and Kristen, thanks for alpha'ing this book and finding enough sense in it to prod me along in one good direction rather than twenty that I wanted to take all at once.

Ana, this cover is incredible. You have once again outdone yourself. I'm so thankful for your talent and patience.

My beautiful betas: Victoria, Renna, Sara, and Millie. You found the heart in this story and gave me words of encouragement that I lived on for months.

My editors, Jessica and Allyson, you asked all the important questions that forced me to grapple with the grit of this story.

To my street team, thank you so much for jumping on board with this concept even when I told you that it would be different from Grace of Dragons.

Every single one of my friends, yes, I have some free time now. Thanks for not quitting me when I stopped returning calls and started only answering texts internally.

To everyone who excitedly signed up for ARCs, thank you for your support!!!

I'm sure I forgot people here. But I'd originally made a list and then I lost it. Typical me. Just know I appreciate you for reading this book and taking a chance on a new genre.

Thank you!

About the author

Maggie grew up with a strong love of reading. As an avid beta reader, others have inspired and encouraged her in her dream of writing. She is co-founder of the Indie Romantasy Reads Book of the Month Club. She lives in Chicago with her husband, daughter, and Duck Tolling Retriever who lovingly support her in her endeavors.

You can follow her reading and writing antics on Instagram (@maggiehoopis.author) and her website (maggiehoopis.com).

Also by Maggie Hoopis

The Thunder of Cosimo Series (interconnected standalones)

Grace of Dragons (Book #1)

Best of Dragons (Book #2)